Praise for novels by Nicola Marsh

"Full of twists and turns, tension and suspense, I've no doubt that [The Scandal] will get your heart beating just that little bit faster!"
—Stardust Book Reviews

"A nice story, with plenty of tension, and a hard-won happy ending." —The Good, the Bad and the Unread

"Marsh takes the reader on a thrilling journey in her latest as one woman unravels a family's lies, deceptions, and hidden secrets. . . . What makes this novel engaging is Marsh's ability to instill her story with a horde of twists, as well as a healthy dose of suspense. The book will appeal to fans of light domestic thrillers."
—The Prairies Book Review

"Stripped by Nicola Marsh is a sexy and enjoyable workplace romance. . . . An entertaining island-set romance!"
—Harlequin Junkie

"I couldn't put this one down! What a delicious read, filled with secrets and suspicion. . . . A twisty, tense family noir. Dysfunction at its best!" —Jan's Book Buzz

"Nicola has crafted a well-organized, page-turning plot that is full of lies, secrets, and deceit. . . . The Last Wife is one hell of a read. It is wickedly twisted, highly addictive, utterly deceptive."
—Once Upon a Time Book Blog

"If you are looking for a book that has a lot of salacious story lines like infidelity, secrets, murder, mystery, and lies, then this is the book for you!" —Monn's Book Reviews

the
BOY
TOY

NICOLA MARSH

JOVE

New York

A JOVE BOOK
Published by Berkley
An imprint of Penguin Random House LLC
penguinrandomhouse.com

Library of Congress Cataloging-in-Publication Data

Names: Marsh, Nicola, author.
Title: The boy toy / Nicola Marsh.
Description: First Edition. | New York: Jove, 2020.
Identifiers: LCCN 2020025761 (print) | LCCN 2020025762 (ebook) |
ISBN 9780593198629 (trade paperback) | ISBN 9780593198636 (ebook)
Subjects: GSAFD: Love stories.
Classification: LCC PS3613.A76986 B69 2020 (print) |
LCC PS3613.A76986 (ebook) | DDC 813/.6—dc23
LC record available at https://lccn.loc.gov/2020025761
LC ebook record available at https://lccn.loc.gov/2020025762

First Edition: November 2020

Printed in the United States of America
1   3   5   7   9   10   8   6   4   2

Cover art and design by Vi-An Nguyen
Book design by Elke Sigal

For Martin.
Heads-up, babe: being six weeks younger than me
does *not* make you a boy toy, no matter
how much you think you are.

One

Samira jiggled her key in the lock the same way she'd done over twenty years ago, when she came home from school. It felt strange to let herself into her childhood home in Dandenong, the heart of Melbourne's southeast ethnic hub, especially after having lived in California for so long, but her mom never heard when anybody knocked. Kushi would be in the kitchen with the stove exhaust fan on full blast to absorb the cooking smells while watching Hindi news on high volume or listening to jangling bhangra music.

The ancient lock finally clicked, and she turned the key and knob simultaneously, bracing for the inevitable. Her mother may not have seen her for five years, but Kushi would pretend like nothing had happened, and the first order of business would be finding her another husband candidate—despite being partially responsible for Samira fleeing her home city a decade ago after her mom's first choice turned out to be a lying, cheating sleaze.

During their frequent phone calls, she didn't have the heart to tell Kushi to leave her alone. The few times she'd been firm with her mom over the years resulted in crying jags that went on forever or guilt trips insisting Kushi would be dead before she held a grand-child.

Samira had no intention of getting married now or anytime in the near future and certainly not to a guy of Kushi's choosing, some Indian doctor or lawyer straight off the plane from Chennai or Kolkata or Delhi who'd insist she be proficient in cooking him *aloo gobi* and parathas and *rava dosa* but could barely turn on a stove himself. Been there, done that, had the divorce decree to prove it.

Dad had been her buffer, and she missed him every day. Ronald Broderick, the quiet academic who'd traveled to India on a gap year and fallen in love with Kushi Singh, a progressive student of archi-tecture in Mumbai but originally from Melbourne, ensured Samira had grown up a hybrid of two cultures: with her dad's laid-back American spirit and her mom's traditional Indian values.

She'd always managed to tread a fine line between both, never telling her folks about being bullied at school for being a "half-and-half" or a "mongrel." Born in Melbourne, she was Aussie through and through. She loved Australian rules football and Vegemite and couldn't let a week pass without a Tim Tam Slam, but she felt just as comfortable eating with her hands and attending Indian dances at the local town halls. The best of both worlds. Now with her dad gone, she felt increasingly stifled by her mom's maneuverings de-spite the Pacific Ocean separating them.

The fragrant aroma was the first thing she noticed as she pushed the door open. The comforting familiarity of onion, garlic, and ginger being sautéed in ghee, along with ground cumin, cori-ander, turmeric, fenugreek, and garam masala, filled the house. The smell permeated everything, from the curtains to the blinds, and had for the last forty years since her parents moved in. Growing up, her mom had whipped up Indian feasts for people living on their street, and their house had been filled with Sudanese, Sri Lankan, and Lebanese neighbors. Since her husband's death, Kushi rarely mentioned them. All she could talk about was the disgrace of divorce and her only child being three years off forty without procreating.

"Hey, Mom, it's me," she called out as she slipped off her sandals at the door and padded up the hallway to the kitchen. Her fingers trailed along the ancient wallpaper, gold-embossed elephants on a cream background, the instinctive reaction the same as when she'd been a child cavorting up this hallway after school.

Back then, she'd been eager to get to the kitchen, knowing her mom would have plenty of snacks laid out on the tiny wooden table tucked into a corner. Mango lassi, the sweetness of the fruit combining perfectly with the tart homemade yogurt, carrot *halwa*, and almond *barfi*, the Indian sweets made predominantly from milk and sugar she could never resist.

Today, her footsteps slowed as she neared the kitchen. Guilt tightened her chest. She'd stayed away too long. She blamed her mother for too much. She felt like a failure despite kicking ass with a booming physical therapy practice in Los Angeles.

She'd felt the same sense of inadequacy five years ago when she'd last set foot in here, and it looked like nothing had changed.

When would she get past this?

Rubbing her chest, she took a few calming breaths and invoked patience. Her mom would never change. She had to deal with it.

With three strides, she entered the kitchen and spied Kushi by the stove as expected. While Kushi tidied the spice rack she would've raided to create her culinary masterpieces, it gave Samira time to study her. A few extra pounds graced her mom's five-foot-two frame, smoothing out the scant wrinkles that creased her face, lending her an ageless quality Samira hoped she would inherit. A new shade of gray streaked her glossy black hair, which was woven into a thick plait that hung halfway down her back. And her signature gold bangles adorned both wrists, jangled as she hummed a vaguely familiar Bollywood hit.

Samira loved the musical clinking of those bangles. It signified warmth and peace and calm: Kushi all over. Except when she was meddling in her love life.

"Hi, Mom."

Kushi glanced up from the stove, her face easing into a beaming smile that made Samira's eyes sting and her throat tighten.

"Just in time, *betee*. I've made your favorites." She bustled toward Samira, her voluminous sari billowing like a giant blue shade sail before enveloping her in a hug.

Samira wrapped her arms around her mom and lowered her head to kiss the top of hers, fragrant with coconut oil, a smell that never failed to invoke comfort, a smell of home.

Samira knew her mom begged for blessings from Shiva, Lakshmi, Vishnu, Durga, and whatever other Hindu deities would listen to her to keep her safe and happy, because Kushi told her during phone calls that went on forever. Though she'd never admit it, those phone calls kept her grounded. If only Kushi could lose the obsessive focus on her unwed state, their relationship would have a better chance of repairing.

She missed her mom. Missed the closeness they'd shared in her childhood. Back then, her mom had been her champion, her best friend. Then Kushi had pushed her toward Avi, and everything had imploded.

Hating how thoughts of her ex-husband infiltrated every inter-action with her mom, she lowered her arms.

"Hope you're hungry, *betee*." Kushi released her and waddled back to the stove, where she removed pot lids with a flourish. "*Rasam*, spinach with paneer, and okra curry."

Samira's stomach rumbled, and saliva pooled in her mouth. No meal came close to her mom's home cooking. "Let me help."

She ladled rice onto two plates, then dished the delicious food over it and poured the *rasam* into a cup. She had loved drinking the fragrant Indian broth flavored with tamarind and spices this way ever since she'd been a kid.

However, they'd barely sat at the table and Samira had taken a sip before Kushi said, "I want you to meet someone."

Samira's appetite vanished, and she put the cup down. "Mom, I haven't seen you for five years. Can we please leave the matrimo-nial machinations until dessert at least?"

Kushi snorted, the battle gleam in her narrowed eyes alerting Samira to the fact her mom had been softening her up with her fa-vorite dishes. Single at thirty-seven did not make for a happy In-dian mother. "No one is pushing you into marriage, *betee*. I'm merely making introductions in the hope you will find happiness."

Kushi had called her "daughter" three times since she'd arrived, something she always did when she had some romantic scheme in mind. This latest "introduction" must be a real prince—not. But Samira knew all the arguing in the world wouldn't stop her mother in matchmaking mode.

"I promise you, this one is the opposite of that good-for-nothing ex of yours." Kushi pressed a hand to her heart and lowered her eyes. "He fooled us all, and I made a very poor judgment call in facili-tating your romance with that slime."

Samira gaped. Not once in all their conversations since her divorce had her mom admitted she'd played a part in the resultant mess of introducing her to Avi. It gave her hope for the two of them.

"You never mention Avi—"

"That's because he's a *kutha*." Kushi made an awful hawking noise in the back of her throat. "Pure scum."

Samira agreed her ex was a bastard, but there was more behind her mom's uncharacteristic vitriolic outburst. Kushi couldn't meet her eyes, and she stabbed at a piece of paneer with particular force.

"What's going on, Mom?"

The Indian community in Dandenong was close, and it wouldn't surprise Samira if her mom heard regular updates about her ex.

After jabbing at the paneer another few times, Kushi raised her gaze slowly. "Avi's wife is expecting another child," she said, her voice soft and tremulous, her expression stricken.

Samira's heart skipped a beat, but she feigned indifference and shrugged. "Who cares? Can we please eat? I'm starving."

But Samira did care, the slash of pain in her chest testament to the overwhelming inadequacy that arose every time she thought of her ex procreating with that woman.

In their short-lived, barren marriage, Avi had never failed to degrade her, to make her feel worthless for not bearing him the child he so desperately wanted. He'd known about her infrequent periods—oligomenorrhea, the docs she'd consulted had labeled it—before they married and the challenges they may face having a child, so impregnating another woman had been the ultimate betrayal.

Acid burned the back of her throat, but she swallowed it down and chased it with several gulps of lassi. She couldn't show her mom that Avi held the power to affect her after all these years. She'd moved on. Time to start acting like it.

"The sooner you find a nice Indian boy to rid you of the memories of that nightmare of a man, the happier you'll be," Kushi announced, with an emphatic nod.

Hearing her mom trot out the old "nice Indian boy" adage she'd heard countless times before sparked a glimmer of an idea. If Samira suffered through the indignity of meeting another one of her mother's prospective matches for her and likened him to the blacklisted Avi, would Kushi finally back off once and for all?

The idea had merit, and she'd mull it further, but for now, this was her first night back in her childhood home, and she intended on filling her belly with the delicious food and laying foundations for repairing the fractured relationship with her mother.

She'd managed to spoon the tangy okra into her mouth before Kushi said, "Why aren't you staying here?"

Samira sighed and put down her spoon. They'd had this conversation many times over the last two months, when her cousin Pia first approached her to consult on her new allied health practice.

Samira had given Kushi valid excuses—the Southbank apartment she'd rented would be closer to Pia, she needed to be near the new center, she'd be coming and going at all hours because of her work schedule—but her mom wasn't a fool. She knew those reasons were vague and nebulous and the real reason stemmed from this: the last time she'd lived in this house had been pre-wedding, and she couldn't go back.

"You know I would've loved to, Mom, but as the primary consultant on Pia's new practice, I have to be nearby, so living in Southbank is easier right now."

"Southbank?" Her nose crinkled as she pressed her knuckles to her temples in disgust. "The city is filled with crime these days. You don't know because you haven't lived here in a long time. Stabbings every night in Melbourne. Gangs of thugs roaming, looking for trouble. Muggings. Worse!" Her hands rose and fell in the way they always did when she spoke. "Why do you persist in being so independent?"

Samira reached out and laid a hand over her mom's, when it finally came to rest on the table. "Because I'm thirty-seven and have lived on my own in LA for over a decade."

Kushi's expression softened. "You know I worry because you can get hurt—"

"Life's full of risks, Mom, and even when we don't take any, bad stuff happens."

Understanding lit Kushi's eyes, and they immediately filled with tears. "You need to be careful, *jaanu*."

Being called "darling" brought an unexpected lump to her throat. "I am." She leaned over and draped an arm over her mother's shoulders, pulling her in for a swift hug. "I love you, *Matha*."

"Mother" was one of the few Hindi words she knew, and Kushi loved when she used it.

"You're a good daughter," she said, patting her cheek. "Now eat."

Samira managed to eat several mouthfuls of delicious paneer, the soft cheese flavored with mustard and cumin seeds in a rich spinach gravy, and the amazing okra fried with chili and curry leaves, before Kushi said, "Go live in Southbank, do a good job as consultant for Pia's fancy-schmancy new practice, but don't think I'll forget about introducing you to a nice Indian boy."

Samira groaned and shot her a filthy look, resulting in a soft chuckle that couldn't help but warm her heart. According to Pia, Kushi didn't smile much these days, let alone laugh.

"You will find love again, *betee*, mark my words."

Kushi waggled a finger in front of her face, and Samira swatted it away.

She'd let her mom indulge in fanciful daydreams about fixing her up, but Samira knew better.

Love was for schmucks.

Two

Dinner with her mom had gone better than expected, but Samira needed a drink when she got back to her apartment, a nightcap to help reset her body clock. Her excuse; she was sticking to it. Her hankering for bourbon on the rocks had nothing whatsoever to do with her mom's nagging as she walked her to the door that she must meet "the man who'll be perfect for you" next week. Yeah, right. The perfect man ranked alongside unicorns and flying swine.

She'd rented an apartment for the next six months in Melbourne's tallest residential building, Eureka Tower, for one reason: when she'd lived in Melbourne, she hadn't visited it with Avi. It had the added bonus of being near the one woman guaranteed to join her in a drink and make her laugh enough to forget her mother's meddling matchmaking.

Pia strode into the bar, and heads turned. At five ten, with a rocking body and cascades of black hair falling to her waist, she looked like an Indian supermodel. The elegant emerald *salwar kameez* added to her air of mystery. Samira had shunned her mom's choice of Indian clothing from childhood, and Pia had done the same, but once she'd married Dev, an Indian engineer from Bengaluru, she'd chosen to revert to tradition. It made her stand out in all the right ways.

"Hey, babe, do you come here often?" Pia opened her arms when she reached the bar, and Samira stepped into them, hugging her cousin and best friend tight.

"Lame," she said, gently shoving her away. "Now sit your gorgeous ass down and let's order a drink."

"Perfect." Pia wrinkled her nose and pointed at Samira's glass. "Is that bourbon?"

"Don't judge. I needed it." She downed the rest of her bourbon and gestured at the bartender. "Vodkatini okay?"

"Better than okay." Pia unwound the silk scarf from around her neck and slid onto the barstool next to her. "I take it dinner with your mom was a bit of a trial?"

"It was fine," she said, her gaze darting toward the bottles lining the back of the bar, unable to sustain contact with Pia's astute stare.

"Let me guess; it went something like this: *Samira, my girl, I have a nice Indian boy for you to meet. He's a doctor. Tall. Handsome. Fair and all.*"

Her mimicry of Samira's mother was so accurate she couldn't help but laugh. "It's not funny. Even after the Avi disaster, she wants to poke her nose into my love life."

"She's getting old. She's alone. And she's Indian." Pia shrugged. "What else is she going to do?"

"She could butt the hell out," Samira said, but her chest tightened. Her mom was aging; Kushi would be seventy this year. She'd been widowed five years ago, and that had been the last time Samira visited Melbourne, for her dad's funeral. Kushi had no family in

Melbourne except her sister, Sindhu, Pia's mother, and during their intermittent phone calls, she never failed to make Samira feel guilty for abandoning her and moving to "that horrible, godforsaken place."

"It's tough being back here," she said, hating the defensive edge in her voice. "I need time."

The bitterness of her divorce should've faded twelve years later. But the moment her plane had touched down on the tarmac at Tullamarine Airport, she'd been swamped with an unwanted blend of regret and anger and sadness, tinged with the faintest hope. Hope that she could move past this and mend the breach with her mom once and for all.

"She cares about you." Pia patted her cheek in the same way her mom had done to Samira many times growing up. "We all do."

"I know." Blinking back tears, Samira nodded her thanks when the bartender placed two vodkatinis in front of them.

"Moving on to more important matters." Pia leaned in close, her exaggerated whisper conspiratorial. "Did you pack condoms?"

Samira elbowed her away. "I'm here on business, not a Samira-does-Down-Under jaunt."

"You're here for six months, right?"

"Right."

"And you've seen the kind of guys Australia produces? Chris Hemsworth. Hugh Jackman. Sam Worthington. Eric Bana. *Hello?*"

Personally, Samira was a Shahid Kapoor kind of gal. She may only be half Indian, but her love affair with Bollywood couldn't be denied.

"And you're single after a dead-end relationship I warned you about?" Pia smirked and nudged her.

"Hamlyn was a nice guy."

Pia snorted. "Nice is pink tutus and octogenarians and a white Christmas. Nice should *not* be used to describe the man of your dreams."

Samira ran a finger around the rim of her glass, a small part of her agreeing but not willing to acknowledge it. "Hamlyn *was* a nice guy. He treated me well, he didn't leave the toilet seat up, and he always recapped the toothpaste."

"That's awfully *nice* of him, but did he rock your world?"

Heat seeped into Samira's cheeks as she silently cursed the girls' night out they'd had when Pia last visited LA three months ago, when she'd consumed too many margaritas and blurted the sorry tale of her lackluster sex life.

She loved her cousin, and despite living on different continents, they were closer than ever. They Skyped and emailed several times a week, and Pia made an annual pilgrimage to LA. Yet another thing Samira felt guilty about: not reciprocating.

"Whatever." Samira shrugged. "Besides, Hamlyn is history."

She'd made sure of it when he suggested they move in together after only dating four months. He'd been her longest relationship post-divorce, but familiarity bred comfort, and to her that meant one thing: trouble.

"Uh-oh." Pia's eyes widened before she shook her head. "You're not still pining for Avi?"

"Hell no." Bitterness clogged her throat. "I got over that prick a long time ago."

She hadn't loved Avi, not at the start. That had come later, after she'd allowed herself to be swept into the Bollywood fantasy she'd always craved. Avi was handsome, suave, and charming, and she'd been sucked in, marrying him within nine months. Over a year later, she'd discovered he'd had an affair, got some nineteen-year-old *kuthi* pregnant, and was leaving her because that bitch could give him something she couldn't: a baby.

Since then, she'd vowed to find love her way. Twelve years later, she was still looking.

Pia's smile waned, and something soft and warm flickered in her coal black eyes. Samira loved that about her. As hard as Pia pushed her, she always knew when to back down. "Fine. You're over Avi, the Hamster's history, and you've got a smorgasbord of hot Aussie guys waiting for you."

"I don't need a fling."

Samira gestured to the barman for another round of drinks and reached for a strand of hair to twirl around her finger, a lifelong habit, and came up empty. Maybe getting a layered bob the day after she'd dumped Hamlyn hadn't been such a great idea.

"You're in denial." Pia's plucked eyebrows shot high. "We both know Wham-Bam-Ham was a three-minute wonder. He was a fuddy-duddy stuck in his ways and boring as bat shit." She snapped her fingers. "You know what you need? A boy toy. Some hot younger guy to give you a damn good screwing to get rid of the cobwebs."

Samira wished she could duck behind the polished chrome bar as the barman placed their second round of vodkatinis in front of them, his deadpan expression and barely perceptible twitching mouth signaling he'd heard every word her mega-mouth cousin had said.

Samira reached for her drink and gave her cousin some serious side-eye. "Don't you have a husband to go home to and annoy?"

"Dev knows where I am. Besides, he's had his quota of annoyance for one day. It's your turn."

"Lucky me," she said, rolling her eyes.

Pia studied her with an astute gaze. "You'll have a ball while you're here. You'll meet guys, you'll flirt, you'll have a fling, and you'll feel fabulous."

"Well, when you put it like that." She clinked glasses with Pia.

"Here's to Samira Broderick doing the entire eastern seaboard of Australia." Pia raised her glass before downing her drink in one long chug without spilling a drop.

"I'd settle for one not-so-nice, sex-mad, no-strings-attached type of guy."

She imitated Pia's effort, tossing it back quickly, hoping the vodka would help her residual insomnia from crossing the international date line and result in blissful slumber. Considering it was her third drink in twenty minutes and she had a buzz going, goal achieved: she'd probably pass out the minute she hit the bed.

When Pia continued to study her, the scrutiny too intense, Samira changed the subject. "So how are things coming along at the health center?"

Thankfully, Pia bought her diversion. Her cousin's eyes lit up as she waxed lyrical for the next fifteen minutes about her pride and joy. Samira interjected when needed, but she was content to sit back and listen to Pia. Her cousin's excitement was infectious, and she looked forward to the challenge of helping her launch the center as a primary allied health venue in Melbourne.

Pia eventually ran out of glowing reports and poked her in the arm. "You should've told me to shut up. You know I can talk all night about the center."

"I like seeing you this enthusiastic." Samira smiled. "We still on for lunch tomorrow?"

"Yeah. Meet me at Dosa Villas at midday, and we can discuss more of the nitty-gritty details about the practice."

"Sounds good."

She needed to focus on work, not the odd disassociated feeling plaguing her since she'd come home. She'd built a reputation as one of LA's best physical therapists specializing in unusual therapies, from clinical Pilates to dialect coaching, but consulting on a new, first-of-its-kind, innovative health center in her home city had filled her with a trepidation she didn't usually associate with her job.

It was all about being back in Melbourne and the overwhelming guilt she felt returning home. Guilt for not being woman enough to keep her husband. Guilt for not producing the babies he wanted. Guilt for intrinsically blaming her mother for it all and driving a wedge between them because of it.

Samira could feel her emotions starting to spiral, so she faked a yawn.

Pia immediately stood. "I should go and let you get some rest."

Samira raised her half-full glass. "I'll just finish this. That way I'll be fully comatose to fight off the pitfalls of jet lag."

"Go for it." Pia rewound her scarf before dropping a peck on her cheek. "It's good to have you home, Cuz."

Samira knew if she responded with "it's good to be home," it would sound like a hollow lie, so she settled for, "We're going to have a blast hanging out, both in and out of work."

Pia hesitated and glanced around. "Are you sure you want to stay here? You're always welcome at our place—"

"With you and Dev trying to make a baby?" She grimaced. "No, thanks."

The moment the retort popped out of her mouth, Samira wished she could take it back. Her cousin had been trying to have a baby for the last two years, and while Pia joked about it herself, Samira knew firsthand the pain of not being the baby-maker expected of a good Indian wife, though in Pia's case their fertility problems stemmed from Dev.

Thankfully, Pia appeared unfazed by her blunder. "Well, if you get tired of apartment life, you know you're always welcome."

"Thanks, you're the best." Samira stood and hauled Pia in for a hug.

"You're only saying that because I'm your new boss."

Samira bumped her with her hip. "And I'm your world-renowned consultant, so you'd better treat me nice or I'll head back to LA where I know I'm appreciated."

Pia rolled her eyes and blew her a kiss as she strolled away, elegant and stunning in a way Samira never could be. Pia owned her heritage. While they both had Indian mothers and Caucasian fathers, everyone recognized Pia as being Indian, while Samira, with her streaked light brown hair, hazel eyes, and lightly tanned olive skin, was consistently mistaken for other nationalities, from Greek to Spanish to Maori to Hispanic.

It served to accentuate her inherent feelings of not belonging, of being lost. Lost to her heritage, lost in relationships, lost in the divide between countries and culture.

She downed the remainder of her vodkatini in two gulps, only to find a replacement appear before her like magic.

"You look like you could use another?" The hipster, barely out of his teens, stroked his beard as he studied her with blatant speculation. His brown eyes glittered with intent behind black-rimmed glasses.

Jet lag, a bellyful of Indian food, and the alcohol had lowered her resistance. She didn't want to appear rude, so she picked up the glass and said, "Thanks."

"Your accent is hot." He slid onto the barstool Pia had just vacated, and Samira guzzled her drink to refrain from responding.

"Can I get you another?"

"This is fine for now." She raised the almost-empty glass in a silent cheer, and he shrugged, obviously nonplussed she didn't want to flirt.

"Care to share my cab sav?" He picked up his wineglass and waved it under her nose like a sommelier. "Then we can share anything else you want."

He leaned on the bar, making his biceps bulge beneath a black T, continuing to swirl his wine like he wanted to hypnotize her.

He winked, and Samira stiffened, dread making her skin prickle. Avi used to wink at her all the time, and she hated that such an innocuous gesture could awaken her old insecurities.

If her mom knew about Avi's impending fatherhood, the entire Indian community would. Their overt pity would stifle her as much as their sly glances, their effusiveness as bad as their gossip. Her twelve-year-old divorce would mean nothing in the face of momentous news like Avi's second child. And the fact she was still single and childless would only add to their rumormongering.

The less time she spent at home in Dandenong over the next six months, the better.

"Hey, was it something I said?" Hipster Dude touched her hand, and she flinched.

"I'm old enough to be your mother. Go hit on someone your own age."

His eyes narrowed, but not before she glimpsed a mean glint. "Not sure if you know, but when a guy buys you a drink, you act a little nicer."

Before she could tell him to take a hike, his arm shot out and grabbed her arm, his fingers digging in too tight.

"Hey." Outrage warred with shock, but before she could react, a shadow fell over them.

"Sorry I'm late, honey."

Samira's head spun a little—four drinks in less than an hour had been a bad idea—but she registered a surprisingly deep voice. A Chris Hemsworth voice, low and resonant, the kind of voice that sounded sexier with an Australian accent. Confused, she glanced at the owner of the seductive voice, and he looked nothing like what she'd imagined. From its bass timbre, she'd expected a Connery-Clooney clone, an older guy, suave and mature. Instead, he had a surfer thing going on, with ruffled hair the color of her favorite caramel latte, vivid blue eyes bordering on aquamarine, and the kind of jaw and cheekbones that channeled Chris. She really needed to stop watching *Thor* on repeat.

He was incredibly handsome. And *young*, mid to late twenties, max. Way too young to have a voice like that, and she wished Pia hadn't put the thought into her head about boy toys and damn good screwings.

"I'd appreciate you taking your hands off my girlfriend," he said, eyeballing the hipster, as she gawked like an ingenue.

"Whatever," Hipster Dude muttered, releasing her, his mouth downturned in a sulk as he raised his glass in a mock cheers. "Old chicks have too many hang-ups anyway."

Samira had no idea what happened next. Maybe she pushed away from the bar too hard, maybe Sexy Voice deliberately bumped the hipster, or maybe Hipster Dude was a vindictive jerk, but in a split second his wineglass had upended all over the front of her *boyfriend's* white T-shirt.

"Fuck," he muttered, as Hipster Dude smirked before sauntering away and Samira stared at the burgundy stain spreading across his T.

"I'm so sorry," she said, ineffectually swiping at the stain with napkins she snatched off the bar.

He smiled, his eyes crinkling in the corners as he watched her pat down his chest, and Samira held her breath. He had a killer smile, one of those smiles that could make a woman swoon or rip off her clothes or both, the type of smile that transformed his face from cute to drop-dead gorgeous.

"That guy was a douche."

"Yeah, thanks for saving me." She placed the sodden napkins on the bar and eyed the stain with horror. "That's my fault."

"Don't sweat it."

"I've got something in my apartment that could get the stain out . . ." She trailed off, heat scorching her cheeks. She'd offered in a genuine attempt to fix his T-shirt, but it sounded like a ploy to get him upstairs.

If he noticed her discomfort, he didn't show it. Instead, he fixed those bright blue eyes on her, his stare unwavering so she detected ridiculous things like green flecks around the irises.

"Th-thanks, that'd be great."

Stumbling over his words made him cuter, if that were possible. Did her invitation make him nervous? He didn't have to be. She was jittery enough for the both of them.

He thrust his hands into pockets, and she noticed his body for the first time. If the smile and face hadn't been enough, he had some rig. Broad chest, stand-out pecs, great arms, all wrapped up in a plain white T. Impressive.

"It shouldn't take long." Were the green flecks in his eyes actually glowing, or did jet lag lead to fanciful observations? "It's the least I can do."

The knowing glint in his eyes made her flush, a rush of heat from her face to her feet and some choice places in between.

"Great. I'm Rory."

"Samira." She held out her hand. "Pleased to meet you."

The minute his fingers closed around hers in a firm, warm handshake and unexpected lust arrowed through her, she wondered if she should renege on her offer. What if he got the wrong idea? She should bolt for the safety of her apartment fifty floors above and let him do his own damn laundry.

When she continued to dither, he pointed at his stained T-shirt. "Once this dries, it'll be hard to get out."

"Yeah, you're right."

Flustered and hot and more than a tad drunk, Samira slid off the barstool and teetered for a moment, before lifting her chin. "Follow me."

Three

When Rory's casting agent had called him earlier for an urgent meeting, he never would've guessed it would land him in an elevator going up to a stunning woman's apartment two hours later.

In fact, Rory usually kept his expectations low when Chris called. "Urgent" could mean anything from filling in for a soap opera stuntman who'd broken his leg to signing on with a low-budget movie.

But thirty minutes ago, Chris had stridden up to the bar and slapped him on the back before sliding onto the stool next to him. "Rory, thanks for meeting me on such short notice. Beer?"

"No." Rory took a deep breath and let it out slowly, determined not to stumble over the "th" sound. "Thanks."

He'd learned to manage his stutter most of the time, but the last thing he needed was his casting agent figuring out why he eschewed speaking roles in favor of the physical demands of a stuntman.

"I'll get straight to the point." Chris placed his laptop on the bar, lifted the screen, and tapped at a few keys. "There's a role coming up I think you'll be perfect for."

An outback snapshot with a big, bold RENEGADES across the middle filled the screen. "This is going to be the next big thing in reality shows. Huge."

Chris bristled with excitement as he jabbed at the screen. Rory had never seen him this enthused. "They need a down-to-earth, rugged host who looks like he wrestles crocs in his spare time."

Chris radiated smugness as he stared at him. "You fit the requirements perfectly."

A dull roar filled Rory's ears as he focused on one word: "host."

A TV host fronted the entire thing. He spoke. A lot.

Mistaking his silence for surprise, Chris continued. "I know you're not big on speaking roles, but don't worry. I'm hiring you a dialect coach. They'll work closely with you in the lead-up to the audition so you'll kick ass."

"Right," Rory managed, at a loss for words and not because he couldn't articulate them clearly.

The thought of having to read lines made his gut churn. His palms grew clammy, and he surreptitiously swiped them down the sides of his jeans. He may have learned to mask his stutter from countless speech therapy sessions over the years, but that meant jack when he got riled up or overly excited. Then no amount of pausing, mentally rehearsing, and breathing could stop the Ts, the Ds, the Gs, and all of the other problematic letters from running into one another as they spilled from his lips.

He'd never forget the embarrassment of kids at school discovering he couldn't speak clearly and the resultant teasing. Worse, enduring countless classes where sadistic teachers who knew of his condition called his name repeatedly to answer questions out loud.

So why the hell would he deliberately set himself up for a fall by speaking in front of the cameras?

"You're overwhelmed. I get it." Chris grinned, his glance flicking between the screen and him. "But this is it. Your big break." He rubbed his thumb and forefinger together. "Not to mention the money."

Rory managed to nod, desperate to come up with a reason as to why he couldn't do this but coming up blank. In a way, his awful childhood had ensured he put in the hours with speech therapy as a teen, determined to master control of his wayward mouth. It had helped, and these days only those closest to him knew he stuttered, but he'd be damned if he slipped up and let the world know.

He may need money desperately, but at what cost?

Oblivious to his discomfort, Chris brought up his calendar. "The audition is in four weeks, so I'll tee up a dialect coach ASAP and forward the details to you."

Again, all Rory could muster was a lame "Right," but if Chris registered his monosyllabic responses, he didn't show it.

"Ever had a dialect coach before?"

"No."

But he'd had a shitload of speech therapists hired by his father to "rid his son of his affliction." While his father had never come out and said it, Rory knew he embarrassed the great Garth Radcliffe.

For as long as he could remember, his father had finished his sentences or supplied words when Rory got stuck. He hated it. Or worse, his dad would get this look in his eye if Rory struggled, part embarrassment, part cringing, like he didn't understand how such a smart kid couldn't string a sentence together.

Turning his back on his economics degree and entering the entertainment business had initially been about flaunting his freedom.

That, and the fact the best speech therapist he'd ever had, Amelia, had guided him toward drama classes to improve his confidence as a kid and to practice techniques learned to control his stammer. He'd been hooked since.

Hosting a reality show would prove to his father he wasn't a loser and, even better, that other people wanted to hear what he had to say even if Garth didn't. It would show him how far he'd come. That nobody finished his sentences for him these days. That he could be successful despite his stutter.

"Because you've never done any speaking roles, the dialect coach will train you in vocal delivery of lines, help improve diction, get a good balance between tone and articulation, that kind of thing." Chris closed his laptop and stood. "It's all about getting the speech of your character right in the context of on-camera work, so don't stress. You'll be fine."

Easy for him to say. Would a dialect coach pick up on his stutter? Reading lines off a monitor shouldn't be a problem, as he'd had to read out loud for years as instructed by a therapist, but ad-libbing could trip him up.

"Any questions?"

When he didn't respond immediately, Chris's eyebrow rose, and Rory quickly shook his head.

"Great, then I'll set everything up and text you the details." Chris stood and held out his hand. "You deserve this, mate."

Rory smiled and shook his agent's hand. "Thanks for the opportunity." It took more effort than usual to articulate the sentence clearly while he was a jumble of nerves.

His own TV reality show. It defied belief.

Becoming a stuntman seemed the perfect choice once his

acting course had finished. Since then, driving behind the wheel in a car chase or jumping from a burning building gave him the adrenaline rush he craved.

The thought of standing in front of a camera, reading off a script, learning lines, left him cold. Not that he hadn't done it before. That acting course had been a major step forward in managing his stutter. No, he knew his funk stemmed from something deeper.

A fear of being called out as a fraud.

Being up front and center on a show would entail interviews and promotions and a plethora of speaking opportunities that had the potential to undo him. Rehearsing lines that could be edited post-production was a far cry from answering questions on the spot by curious interviewers.

He'd never come out of it unscathed.

Six whiskey shots later, his nerves blurred. He didn't give a shit anymore. Another few drinks and he could forget everything, at least for tonight.

He'd ordered a boutique beer chaser when the couple a few feet down the bar caught his attention. The exotic woman snagged his gaze first: shaggy brunette bob, figure-hugging black dress, manicured purple toes peeking from sparkly sandals, petite, curves in all the right places. Big hazel eyes, high cheekbones, and a lush mouth that had him imagining all sorts of fun ways he could forget about the dramas of this upcoming audition.

A wannabe hipster was coming on to her. Sidling up with a drink first, then putting the moves on her. Smarmy prick. Then he saw the guy grab her and her expression morph from disinterest to fear. It had him off his barstool in a second. Considering the whiskeys he'd consumed, he didn't hesitate in posing as her boyfriend.

Those acting classes came in mighty handy at times. The part where the dickhead deliberately tipped his wine down his shirt hadn't been in the plan, but it got rid of the douche, and that's all that mattered.

Having the stunner invite him up to her room was a bonus.

Now, as they rode the elevator in uncomfortable silence, Rory mentally cursed his inability to make small talk. One of the speech therapists he'd seen in his teens had admonished him for being afraid to speak. They'd encouraged him to practice the techniques he'd learned rather than clam up. Easy for them to say. They'd never experienced the gut-deep fear of embarrassment, the mortification that came with people's overt pity when he couldn't formulate a full sentence.

He could control it most of the time, but in moments like this, with a gorgeous woman inviting him up to her room, he hoped he wouldn't turn into a stumbling mess. He'd already had a brief lapse at the bar he hoped she'd missed.

"I'm renting here for six months," she said, as the elevator dinged on the fiftieth floor and the doors slid open.

"You're here on business?"

She nodded as he fell into step beside her. "My cousin's opening a practice in South Wharf not far from here, and I'm acting as a consultant."

He hadn't pegged her for a doc. "You're a medico?"

"Physical therapist." They stopped outside 5050, and she slid the key card through the slot and opened the door. "And no wisecracks about groin pain or magic hands, okay?"

He laughed. "Wouldn't dream of it," he said, immediately imagining her hands on his groin.

They hadn't remotely flirted, but he'd seen the way she'd looked at him downstairs. He knew the signs. He wasn't vain, but stunt work meant long hours at the gym, and he knew women appreciated the result.

He'd craved a distraction tonight. If the alcohol didn't cut it, maybe the lovely Samira could.

Placing a hand at the small of her back, he guided her inside. Her swift intake of breath confirmed he hadn't misread the signs.

"I'll get the stain remover pen I always carry when I travel," she said, sounding breathy, leaving him standing inside a smallish, modern apartment with killer views of Melbourne from the floor-to-ceiling glass windows. She returned quickly, brandishing the stain remover.

"You'll have to take off your T-shirt," she murmured, her cheeks crimson as she stared at his chest, the tip of her tongue darting out to moisten her bottom lip. "There's a bathroom next to the kitchenette."

He didn't move, and when she continued eyeing him like she wanted to lick the stain off, he made a lightning-quick decision fueled by one too many whiskey shots and a desire to obliterate the next ten minutes of dancing around their attraction.

"Okay," he said, grabbing the hem of his T-shirt, peeling it off, and bunching it in his fist.

He blamed the alcohol, having the balls to blatantly throw down the challenge. If she felt the attraction, she'd do something about it. If not, he'd grab the stain remover from her and take his dirty T-shirt into the bathroom.

"Wow," she murmured, gnawing on her bottom lip as he saw indecision cloud her eyes, her coy reticence surprising him. She had to be a few years older than him, and women over thirty were usually more confident.

When she continued to stare at his chest with wide eyes and not make a move, he held out his hand.

"If you give me that, I'll take care of this?" He gestured at the balled-up T-shirt in his hand.

"I'm hopeless," she muttered, as she took a step toward him. However, she didn't give him the stain remover. Instead, she took the T-shirt out of his hand and laid it on a nearby coffee table, along with the pen.

"And I'm drunk," she said, shaking out her arms like she wanted to take a swing at him. "And I'm too old for one-night stands—"

"Hey, it's okay." He ran his thumb down her burning cheek, from her temple to her jaw, savoring the soft skin, eager to explore her skin all over. "You're stunning. And I'm drunk too."

She laughed as he'd hoped, her lopsided smile making him want to bundle her into his arms, the surge of protectiveness at odds with his intention to fuck all night.

She took another step closer and placed her palm on his chest, the heat from her skin branding him. She smelled amazing, like a bouquet of flowers, predominantly jasmine. Heady. Fragrant. Intoxicating.

As her palm skated over his chest, exploring every contour, he gritted his teeth against the urge to sweep her into his arms and back her up against the nearest wall. Instead, he raised her free hand to his mouth, turned it over, and bit the soft pad of flesh beneath her thumb. She jolted and let out a soft moan that made his cock throb. He did it again, harder this time, and she swayed toward him.

With a deliberate swipe of his tongue, he licked the redness away, giving her a taste of what he'd love to be doing between her legs right now.

"You feel amazing," she murmured, her hand sliding from his breastbone to his waist, dipping into the curve of his hip, before stroking along his waistband. Toying with him. Teasing him. Driving him wild.

He ducked his head to nip her earlobe. "I want you."

She made a cute whimpering sound that had him smiling as he dropped to his knees. He started at her ankles, exploring the dips and ridges with his fingertips, teasing her with the lightest of touches, before moving at a snail's pace up her toned calves, lingering in the backs of her knees.

As his palms slid up her thighs, the slight callouses on his fingers rasped against the softness of her skin. She made a soft mewling sound when he stopped short of nirvana and pried her legs apart.

"Hike your dress up for me." His command came out a growl because being this close he could smell her muskiness and had to taste her, now.

She obeyed, bunching the silk in one hand, revealing black lace panties with a sheer front panel. Beyond sexy. He didn't hesitate to rip them off. She chuckled, a wanton, joyous response that shot straight to his cock.

He pressed his thumbs to her, and she slumped against the nearest wall with a moan. Prying apart her slick folds, he slid his thumbs from front to back, over and over, savoring the soft noises she made.

When her hips arched toward him, he leaned forward and swiped her with his tongue.

"Oh . . ." Her head fell back with a thunk as he did it again, lapping at her with the tip of his tongue, teasing her, tasting her.

He slid a finger inside her, then another, setting up a slow rhythm designed to drive her wild. It worked, because her hip thrusts became uncoordinated, which was when he sucked her clit, hard.

She cried out as he picked up the tempo with his fingers and his tongue simultaneously, licking and sucking, sliding in and out, drenched with how turned on she was.

He felt her clamp around him a second before she came on a drawn-out moan that was the sexiest thing he'd ever heard.

Her eyes were closed, her head still lolling against the wall, a small, smug smile playing about her lips. She didn't move, so he stood and made quick work of getting a condom on.

She opened her eyes and reached for him, resting her hands on his shoulders as she hooked a leg around his waist.

"You're incredibly sexy. You know that, right?" He nudged her, and she locked her leg tighter.

"Right back at you," she said, gasping as he slid inside, inch by inch, gritting his teeth against the urge to pound into her the way he wanted to.

"Perfect," he said, claiming her lips as he started to move, her tongue tangling with his, wild and sinuous, challenging and giving.

She deepened the kiss like she wanted to devour him, her hands clawing at his shoulders as he thrust into her, over and over, the friction driving him wild.

His balls tightened, the pleasure too much too soon, but he wouldn't hold back. If he had his way, they'd do slow and sensual later.

As she started to writhe against him, he slipped a hand between them and zeroed in on her clit. Circling it with his thumb, maintaining the pressure, he let go as she moaned into his mouth, pounding into her as his muscles spasmed and his mind blanked, hurtling headlong into welcome oblivion.

Rory had no idea how long they stood there, bodies entwined, sweat-slicked skin growing cool, but when they finally drew apart and Samira met his eyes with surprising shyness, he knew without a doubt this was what he'd needed tonight.

No words. No mulling. No second-guessing about auditions or coaches or opportunities.

Time enough for that tomorrow.

Four

Samira enjoyed sex. Sex was fun, relieved tension, helped promote sleep, and given the right partner, could be a fantastic aerobic workout.

Sex with Rory exceeded every preconception she'd ever had.

"Wow." She fell back on the plump pillow for the second time in half an hour, totally and utterly blown away. Literally.

"That good?" He lay next to her and propped on an elbow, a self-satisfied smile playing about those heavenly lips. Correction: Lips that had sent her to heaven. Lips that could kiss and suck and coax the most amazing orgasms out of her, the type of orgasms she'd only ever dreamed about.

"Are you being cocky?"

"Hell yeah," he said, broaching the short distance between them to place a long, lingering kiss on her lips. "You ready for more?"

"Oh. My. God."

She squeezed her eyes shut, wondering if she'd be able to walk in the morning and not particularly caring. Rory had stamina and then some.

"How old are you anyway?"

"Twenty-seven," he said, his slow, sexy smile hedonistic. "I'm legal, so do your worst."

Twenty-seven. Thirty-seven. She didn't have to do the math. Ten years. A freaking decade. For tonight, it didn't matter. Boy toy indeed.

"Do you know how old I am?"

He squinted slightly, studying her. "Early thirties? Is it important?"

Either the guy was seriously charming or seriously drunk or in need of a serious eye checkup. Whatever, she realized he was right. It wasn't important. Thirty-seven was a number. She didn't feel her age, and it wasn't like she was applying for a marriage license. Never again.

"I guess not," she said, gasping as his thumb grazed her nipple deliberately.

Around and around in slow, languorous circles, sending heat streaking through her body and pooling between her legs.

This was crazy. Totally, over-the-top cray-cray. She'd never been so easily turned on before and could count her number of one-night stands on one hand, drunk or otherwise. After Avi and before Hamlyn, she'd dated infrequently, guys who were staid and sensible, like her. Guys older than athletic, eager-to-please, quick-recovering Rory, guys who didn't give her half the buzz.

Emboldened by how much he wanted her, she tugged the sheet lower, revealing exactly why that decade between them made all the difference. He was ready to go, again.

"You sure you're up for my worst?"

His lips curved in a smug smile before he dropped the lightest of kisses on her mouth.

"I'm up for anything."

She didn't second-guess her response as mind-numbing lust pulsed through her.

"Show me."

*L*ater, she breathed out a sigh, her eyes closing with what felt like twenty-ton weights on the lids as she slid off him like a limp rag doll and crashed onto the pillow.

"You're incredible," he whispered into the comfortable silence, and she struggled to open her eyes.

The ease between them surprised her. She thought she'd feel tacky, ashamed, or an awkward combination of the two, hooking up with a stranger on her first night back home. Instead, lying next to Rory after they'd explored each other's bodies intimately felt strangely comfortable.

Words weren't needed. They seemed to fit. Corny? Maybe. But she wasn't going to question it. Maybe she should get drunk and let cute guys rescue her from jerks more often.

"Sweet-talker." She opened her eyes with difficulty and rolled toward him, unable to control the thump of her heart as she saw moonlight bathing his bare chest in incandescent shadows, caressing the hard planes, accentuating his beauty.

He was gorgeous, breathtakingly so, and for the tiniest, infinitesimal second, she fantasized what it would be like to have this sort of perfection beyond a night. She reached out and laid her hand on his chest, feeling the strong, rhythmic pounding of his heart beneath her palm, enjoying the closeness she hadn't anticipated when she'd initially lost her head and brought him to her apartment.

"You can stay if you like?"

She hoped she didn't sound needy, but the thought of a rousing bout of morning-after sex before they parted ways seemed like a good idea.

He smiled and placed his hand over hers, an intimate gesture that went beyond anything they'd shared in the throes of passion.

"You've worn me out, so I better stay."

She quirked an eyebrow and glanced at his impressive package, still semi-erect. "Doesn't look like you're worn-out to me."

"You're insatiable."

"I don't hear you complaining."

He laughed at her boldness, and she slid her hand out from under his, skating her palm across the expanse of lovely bronzed skin across his chest and lower. Caressing the ridges of abs, savoring the definition.

"I'm not usually like this," she said, toying with the sheet covering his bottom half. "It's probably jet lag."

"In that case, every time you fly across the international date line, you better look me up." He winked and swooped in for a kiss. "Promise?"

Samira wasn't in the habit of making promises she couldn't keep, especially to a guy she wouldn't see after tonight no matter how much they surprisingly connected.

So she settled for yanking the sheet away and covering his mouth with hers in a slow, sensual kiss as her hand slid lower . . .

Five

To keep his body in peak physical condition, Rory rarely drank. So the fact he'd consumed six whiskey shots on an empty stomach last night ensured he had one mother of a headache as he let himself into his place.

Considering those shots had provided the impetus in saving Samira from that hipster creep, and the resultant night of scorching sex, a hangover was a small price to pay.

The sexy brunette had been insatiable, and he'd been all too eager to please. How many times had they done it? Four? Five? It had been a long time since he'd met a woman so into it, and the memory of her beguiling mix of shyness and sex kitten made him grin.

He'd wanted to stick around this morning, to see her coy smile when she woke and discovered him up for it. But no matter how great their night, he knew how the morning after panned out. Awkward and stilted at the best of times, he hated struggling for words while trying to extricate himself. Much easier leaving her a brief note.

The temptation to jot down his number had come from left field. They'd both been drunk and seeking a night away from the norm. He, to obliterate the terror of the upcoming audition for his own TV show; she, he had no idea. Feeling homesick and seeking comfort wherever she could? Just out for a good time?

Whatever her motivations, he hadn't scribbled his number on that note for the simple fact they were worlds apart. What would a physical therapist here for only a few months want with a stuntman? Beyond the obvious, that is. Besides, one-night stands rarely turned into anything more, and in this case, it wouldn't. He had too much going on right now, and a relationship would be a giant complication he didn't need, so he'd slunk out of her apartment and headed home.

Home. What a crock. He could never call this one-bedroom studio apartment on the ground floor of a grungy block of flats in Middle Park home. With its peeling mauve paint, cracked mock-wood linoleum, and damp patches on the ceiling corners, it could never be anything more than a stopgap. But he couldn't afford to move. Not with every cent he earned being directed toward a cause close to his heart.

With his mouth as dry as the Simpson Desert, he padded into the kitchen and filled a glass with water. He'd drained half of it when the blinking light on his answering machine snagged his attention. Nobody rang his home number. Everybody called his cell, which he'd switched to "do not disturb" mode while at Samira's last night.

Hoping Chris hadn't been trying to reach him, he stabbed at the button on the machine and braced against the small island bench.

"Rory, it's me. I hate to bother you at home, but we've hit a snag with some of the recent donors. Is there any chance we could meet to discuss possible solutions?" Amelia's nervous laughter made him clutch the glass tighter, as the implications of what she was saying sank in. "I hate asking for help when you've been more than generous with your time, but maybe if both of us contributed money, it could work? We really need the funds if I'm to help those kids. So please call me."

She hung up, and as the dial tone hummed, he slumped into the nearest chair, downed the rest of his water, and placed the glass on an overturned crate he used for a coffee table before he was tempted to fling it at the wall in frustration.

If he could, he'd fund Amelia's entire program. She'd been the only speech therapist to truly get him, and he credited her with the fact he could string more than a few words together these days without stuttering. She'd changed his life, and he owed her.

It had been a no-brainer helping her establish a small start-up program with housing commission kids. He'd been one of the lucky ones, having a rich father to pay for endless therapy sessions. But other kids, mostly migrants and refugees, weren't as fortunate, and not being able to speak fluently would affect their entire lives.

But it sounded like the program wouldn't get off the ground if she didn't have more money, and she'd asked him to contribute, which he'd be more than happy to do . . . if he had any to give.

No way in hell he'd approach his father for the cash, so that meant he'd have to nail this upcoming audition no matter how much he balked at the thought of it.

"Fuck," he muttered, as his cell buzzed in his back pocket.

Sliding it out of his jeans, he glanced at the text from Chris, sending him details on the dialect coach. An appointment scheduled for tomorrow afternoon at four. Great.

With his bank account hovering in the low triple figures, and

Amelia's plea for a donation, he needed to suck it up. The money from fronting a show like *Renegades* would enable him to help Amelia launch her program and give back, repaying her faith in him a decade ago.

So he'd face his fears and meet with this bloody dialect coach tomorrow.

What was the worst that could happen?

Six

Samira spied Pia at a small back table as she entered Dosa Villas, her favorite South Indian restaurant in Dandenong. She'd been coming here since she was a kid, and the aromas of sautéed curry leaves, cumin, and mustard seeds catapulted her straight back to her life as a twelve-year-old, when the hardest decision she had to face was what costume to wear for Book Week. Considering she'd always had her nose buried in novels, she'd been torn between which favorite character to channel and which outfit to wear to school, yet Anne of Green Gables always won out.

If only life were so simple now.

Pia waved her over, and she wound her way through the tiny, no-frills restaurant sporting ten tables, a chipped counter for ordering, and a fridge stacked to the top with lassi.

"I already ordered you a *masala dosa* because I couldn't wait," Pia said, patting her flat stomach. "I'm starving."

"Thanks." Samira slid onto the seat opposite her cousin, sending a pointed look at Pia's belly. "Is there something you're not telling me?"

Pia gave a quick shake of her head, the spark in her eyes diminishing. "Our latest IVF attempt failed."

"I'm sorry, sweetie." Samira reached across the table and squeezed her hand. She should know better than to ask about Pia's attempts to get pregnant, but they hadn't talked about it in a while.

She knew firsthand the ongoing disappointment of discovering a single blue line on a little white stick rather than two. And while she'd tolerated Avi's constant badgering after they'd started trying, only to throw countless pregnancy tests into the trash under his judgmental, disappointed glare, she wished she'd had someone back then to hold her hand through it all. She could be that person for Pia.

"I know what you're going through, and I'm here for you." She squeezed Pia's hand again, but her cousin withdrew it on the pretext of reaching for her water glass.

"It sucks being thirty-five and surrounded by friends who procreate just by looking at their husbands." Pia blinked rapidly, but not before Samira glimpsed the sheen of telltale tears. "And it's harder being so in control of my professional life while . . . failing at this."

Samira's heart broke. She knew exactly how Pia felt. "You're not failing. You're freaking amazing, giving this your all, just like you do in your marriage and your career."

She should know. She'd done the same, juggling a burgeoning career as a newly graduated physical therapist with marriage. Thankfully, compassionate, devoted Dev was nothing like demanding, egotistical Avi. "You've only tried twice and—"

"It costs a fortune, and I'm over it." Pia grimaced, her gaze steely. "The injections, the invasiveness of the procedures, everything."

"How's Dev coping?"

"He seems okay, but the stress of it all is taking its toll on both of us." The corners of Pia's mouth pinched, causing tiny lines to fan out. "He's putting on a brave face, but I know he blames himself, and sometimes I think . . ."

"What?"

"That he's only doing this to please me, and the fact we have to use donor sperm to conceive is killing him."

"Oh, sweetie." Samira reached across the table and squeezed Pia's hand. "He's a good guy, and you two have a great marriage. He'd tell you if he was feeling that way."

Pia shrugged, doubt in her eyes. "He thinks we should wait awhile before trying again because of the health center opening and all the extra work that will entail."

"He's probably right."

"I guess." Pia shrugged, her uncharacteristic moroseness making Samira wish she could take away her cousin's pain.

While Avi having an affair and getting his girlfriend pregnant had gutted her at the time, maybe in some warped way he'd done her a favor. She couldn't imagine going through the rigors of IVF with an impatient man like him, and he'd betrayed her before they could go down that route.

Pia and Dev adored each other and would be great parents. Their ongoing trials in having a baby must be devastating.

Determined to change the subject, Samira said, "Speaking of the center, I checked the schedule, and I've got six clients booked in for tomorrow."

Pia gave a sheepish shrug. "Seeing as you're touring the facility later today, I thought you'd want to hit the ground running to-morrow."

"What if I'm jet-lagged?"

Though the strange fuzziness in her head had nothing to do

with a mucked-up biological clock and everything to do with a lousy night's sleep. Or lack of. She'd managed a grand total of three hours between the erotic escapades with Rory.

"That's not jet lag I see," Pia said, her eyebrows arching as she pointed at her cheeks. "You're blushing. What's that about?"

Samira felt the heat in her cheeks intensify, and Pia let out an excited whoop. "Did you hook up after I left the bar last night?"

Samira couldn't keep the goofy grin off her face. "Maybe."

"Good for you." Pia reached across and slugged her on the arm. "Let me guess. You chatted for a while, flirted, then bolted for the safety of your apartment."

"Not quite." Samira's grin widened along with Pia's eyes.

"You didn't."

Samira nodded, smug in the knowledge she'd done something completely out of character and felt fantastic because of it. "I did."

Pia leaned across the table to murmur, "You actually had S-E-X?"

Samira mimicked her and responded with an exaggerated whisper, "Y-E-S."

"No way!" Pia squealed and clapped her hands. "Didn't think you had it in you, Cuz."

"Well, I did." She winked. "Several times."

Thankfully, their order arrived at that moment, while Pia continued to gape at her in blatant admiration. Samira salivated as the *dosa*, a crispy, paper-thin, rolled-up rice pancake filled with spicy potato and as big as the table, was placed in front of her.

LA had some great Indian restaurants, but not one compared to this small, simple café in her home suburb of Dandenong.

She pointed at Pia's plate. "Eat your *vada* before it gets cold."

However, not even Pia's favorite spicy lentil donuts could distract her.

"Not until you tell me what happened last night." Pia smirked. "And don't leave out a single detail."

Samira rolled her eyes. "Anyone ever tell you you're an insatiable gossip?"

"I'm a speech therapist. It helps hone my ear to hear people talk, so technically, listening to your weird hybrid Aussie-American accent is work and beneficial to my professional development—"

"Enough with the BS." Samira laughed and held up her hand. "I'll give you the quick version because I'm starving and I don't want to drool all over my *dosa*."

Pia grinned and absentmindedly dunked her *vada* in coconut chutney as she focused all her attention. "Go on."

The hollow sensation in Samira's stomach had nothing to do with hunger and everything to do with remembering how she met Rory and what had ensued.

She filled Pia in on the basics, leaving out the juicy details. The memory of Rory's mouth and hands all over her made her flush enough without going into specifics.

"Wow, I'm proud of you." Pia's eyes glowed with admiration. "I'm glad my pep talk worked so quickly." She wiggled her eyebrows suggestively. "So, are you going to see your *boy toy* again?"

Samira ignored the instant disappointment that hollowed her stomach. She'd experienced the same gut-drop when she'd woken this morning to find Rory's note, thanking her for a great night. She hadn't expected anything beyond a steamy night together, but it irked just the same that her first night back in Melbourne encapsulated her life: an unexpected high followed by a resounding low.

"It's called a one-night stand for a reason," Samira said, her tone clipped. "Now let's hurry up and eat so you can give me the grand tour of the practice."

She expected Pia to push for details, and when she didn't, Samira sighed in relief. Rory had been a spontaneous, fleeting interlude. Something wonderful to sustain her for the months ahead when she'd be swamped with work and fending off Kushi's matrimonial machinations.

Last night had been amazing, but Samira had to ground herself in reality.

Starting now.

Seven

Rory's nose twitched as he strode down the main corridor of the dilapidated basement in one of the housing commission blocks of flats in Carlton. Pungent disinfectant warred with cloying lavender freshener, like the cleaners had tried to smother the mustiness. The corridor opened into a large rec hall, where Amelia sat behind a makeshift desk, frowning at a calculator.

The fifty-something woman had a pencil stuck behind one ear and her silver bob pushed back by sunglasses perched on top of her head, her deep frown alerting him that whatever numbers she crunched, they weren't good.

"Hey," he said, moving toward her, his footsteps kicking up tiny whirls of dust. "Your office said you'd be here, so I thought I'd swing by."

She glanced up and her frown cleared. "You're a gem."

"I t-try."

He hated slipping up around Amelia, not when she'd put in countless hours to get him to the point where he could speak almost fluently, but nerves made him stumble.

He'd come here to tell her in person he couldn't pledge a financial contribution for now. No way he'd get her hopes up about the
audition and the show, not until he had something concrete to tell
her. It wouldn't be fair. He'd contemplated asking her to be his dialect coach until he realized that was exactly what would happen:
she'd pin her hopes on him landing the role to secure funds for the
program, and if he failed, the guilt would be unbearable. He didn't
want to let her down, and if worst came to worst, he'd end up approaching his father for the money.

As for getting a major bump in salary courtesy of *Renegades,*
he'd wait until he saw the dialect coach and practiced the required
techniques before making a judgment call on whether he had a
chance of nailing the audition or not.

Thankfully, she didn't mention his slight stumble. "So you got
my message?"

She never wasted time making small talk. He liked that about
her. Direct and concise, she'd managed to convey techniques clearly
while exhibiting enormous patience. He'd thrived in her sessions.

"Yeah, sorry for not getting back to you yesterday."

She stood and moved around the desk toward him, her expression hopeful, and he inwardly cursed that he'd have to dash her
hopes.

"You mentioned some of the donors pulled out?"

Disappointment pinched her mouth as she nodded. "Apparently, this speech therapy program isn't glamorous enough for
them." The frown returned, slashing her brows in a V. "They won't
get much recognition, so they won't contribute."

"Charming," he muttered, tension creeping across the back of
his neck. For the first time since he'd turned his back on a career in
economics, he regretted it. He could live on his wage from part-time

stuntman gigs, but it didn't leave a hell of a lot left over to give to others.

Amelia hesitated, as if weighing her words carefully. "I hate to ask you for money, particularly with the amount of time you've already spent helping me get this off the ground and lodging the relevant applications to get started here." She swept her arm wide to encompass the rec hall.

"But without more money, I won't be able to man the program. Staff are only willing to volunteer for so many hours . . ." She trailed off, before giving a brisk shake of her head. "Anyway, the logistics are my problem, not yours."

But not being able to help fund this was his problem, and right now, he couldn't do a damn thing about it.

"I'll be honest: I can't promise any money now." He held out his hands like he had nothing to hide. "But I'm working on something big, and if that comes through, I'll be able to help out."

Hope reignited in her eyes. She assumed he'd ask his father. As if. That would be a last resort.

"You're a good guy, Rory. I'm lucky to have you on board."

Uncomfortable with her praise, he managed a terse nod. Taking a deep breath so he wouldn't stumble over his words, he pointed at the calculator. "How much do you need exactly?"

"Too much," she said, with a self-deprecating laugh. "But another ten thousand should ensure I can get the program up and running, and provide the local kids with services for six months."

Ten grand.

Fuck.

He had to nail the audition for *Renegades*, no matter how much he squirmed inside with fear of screwing up in front of a massive audience because of his stutter.

Maybe the dialect coach Chris had teed up could help with the rampant nerves making his throat tighten at the mere thought of landing a role that big?

"I know it's a lot to ask—"

"I'll be in touch," he said, forcing a tight smile before swiveling on his heel and walking away.

When she called out, "See you soon," he raised a hand in farewell. He couldn't speak, not when he'd blurt the truth: that the chances of his earning ten grand in a short space of time ranked up there with addressing the country alongside the prime minister on New Year's Day.

Landing the *Renegades* hosting gig had just become imperative.

An hour later, he entered a sleek glass-fronted practice overlooking the Yarra River and Melbourne's Central Business District beyond. The glamorous foyer, boasting black marble floors and a chrome reception desk, looked more like a hotel than a health facility. A list of practitioners in bold gold letters took center stage behind the desk, but the spaces next to the titles of Occupational Therapist, Podiatrist, Psychologist, Exercise Physiologist, and Physical Therapist were blank.

The latter brought an instant image of Samira to his mind, naked and sated, spread-eagled on her bed. Damn, she'd been hot, but now wasn't the time to rehash that one sensational night in his rather bleak week. He needed to find the dude who would coach him for the next four weeks in the art of delivering lines so he could nail the audition and take steps toward providing Amelia the funds to help those kids who needed them.

With no one manning the desk, he slipped his cell from his pocket to check the details. Yeah, four o'clock today, at this address.

"Can I help you?"

Rory glanced up to see a gorgeous Indian woman wearing a white coat walking toward him.

"Yes, thanks. Rory Radcliffe. I have an appointment at four with the dialect coach?"

An eyebrow rose slightly as she stared at him with blatant speculation, before nodding and pointing to the corridor on his right. "Head down there. Last door on your left."

"Thanks."

Confused by the strange gleam in her eyes, he strode down the corridor, determinedly ignoring the nerves making him sweat.

He could do this.

He had to do this.

When he reached the end of the corridor, the last door on the left opened into a luxurious office filled with exercise equipment of all shapes and sizes: a Pilates machine, free weights, resistance bands in bright colors, and several plinths.

He knocked and entered, hoping this dialect coach could give him the guidance to secure the role, and the paycheck, he desperately needed.

He stepped into the office and caught sight of a woman behind a stack of exercise balls. "Hi, I'm looking for Sam Broderick, the d-dialect coach."

Damn his bloody nerves for making him stutter at a time like this.

But that wasn't the worst of it, because as the woman stepped out from behind the balls and said, "I'm Sam," he locked gazes with an equally startled Samira, the woman who had rocked his world.

Eight

Samira gaped at Rory for a good five seconds before pulling herself together. She pasted a smile on her face and moved toward him, her hand outstretched, like she was greeting any other client and not the guy who'd awakened her to exactly how great sex could be.

"Hey, Rory," she said, sounding coolly professional and nothing like a stunned woman that couldn't help but notice again how blue his eyes were and how his lips were made for other things besides smiling.

Though he wasn't smiling now. He looked . . . horrified.

"You can't be a dialect coach. You're a physical therapist," he said, staring at her in absolute dismay.

So much for connecting that memorable night. She lowered her hand and summoned her inner professional, the one who'd dealt with recalcitrant clients many times.

"It's a specialty field. Only a few physical therapists around the world are interested in dialect coaching. Good articulation involves breathing techniques, core strength, that kind of thing, and being able to combine exercises to focus on those muscle groups is where we come in. So where speech therapists work on actual enunciation, I focus on getting the muscles that help produce speech to work right." She gestured to a nearby plinth and exhaled in relief when he sat. She pulled up a chair opposite. "I think I already mentioned my cousin's setting up this place as a new, innovative center for allied health treatments and wanted me on board, which is why I'm working here for the next six months. My duties are predominantly physical therapy, dealing with orthopedic patients, mostly, but with Pia being a speech therapist, I'm hoping she'll refer some clients my way for dialect coaching."

"I've never heard of any physical therapists in Australia doing dialect coaching," he muttered, glaring at her like she'd fooled him deliberately. "Seems odd when you usually treat sporting injuries and back pain and rehab hip replacements."

"Already told you, this is a specialized field for my profession," she said, keeping the annoyance out of her voice. Why was he judging her? "The way you use your diaphragm to breathe? How your abdominals and back muscles interact to brace your core? All important components in good voice projection."

"I guess that makes sense," he said, but his rigid body posture screamed that he didn't want her anywhere near his abdominals.

"There's no need to feel uncomfortable. I'll refer you to see my cousin Pia. She has an interest in dialect coaching too."

"Thanks," he said, some of the tension holding his shoulders rigid easing. "Sorry for sounding like an idiot, but I was expecting a guy, and seeing you here threw me."

"I go by Sam professionally, something I started when I left uni," she said. "And you're not the only one who's stunned."

Their gazes locked, and a flash of heat so powerful lit Samira from the inside out, making her fingers curl into her palms to stop from pressing her hands to her burning cheeks.

The corners of his mouth curled upward. "Maybe the universe is trying to tell us something?"

"Yeah, don't have casual sex."

She sounded brusque, almost prudish, and inwardly cursed her inability to flirt. Not that she should flirt with him. Though technically, he wasn't a client . . . once she fobbed him off onto Pia. Because no way in hell could she work with this guy. Every time he looked at her, she had erotic flashbacks of his mouth, his tongue, his hands . . .

"As I recall, the sex was pretty spectacular."

His mouth eased into a wolfish grin that made the heat in her cheeks intensify.

"So spectacular you ran out before I could wake," she said dryly, wondering in what kind of universe the hottest guy she'd ever met, and had sex with, showed up at her workplace.

She didn't believe in karma like her mom did. Perhaps she should. That way, Avi's pecker would've fallen off around the time he got that nineteen-year-old pregnant and ruined their marriage.

A strange expression flitted across his face, part embarrassment, part regret. "I contemplated leaving my number on that note."

"Then why didn't you?"

"I—I don't have time for a relationship."

Admiring his honesty when most guys would've lied, she snapped her fingers. "Turns out, neither do I."

He squared his shoulders and eyeballed her. "But I'm totally available for booty calls."

She laughed at his boldness. "I might take you up on that, if you're lucky."

"You do that."

Before she could move, his hand snaked out to capture hers, his thumb stroking the back of it in slow, sensual sweeps that made her sigh.

"I'll be honest with you. I've got a major audition coming up, which is why my agent booked me in to see a dialect coach. And I'm hectic with this kids program I'm helping set up, so I don't have a lot of downtime at the moment."

His thumb swept over the underside of her wrist, like he was testing her rampaging pulse. "But that night we hooked up was beyond hot, and I'd like to do it again."

Excitement streaked through Samira's body, and it took every ounce of willpower not to march over to the door and flick the lock. And when he picked up her hand, brought it to his mouth, and pressed a hot, openmouthed kiss to her palm, she moaned.

"We can't do this here," she murmured, wishing with every cell of her horny body that they could.

"I know."

He curled her fingers over her palm, as if to treasure that sexy kiss, and released her. "If you could send through that referral to your cousin, that'd be great."

"Okay. Give me a sec."

Somehow, her legs worked in sync with her befuddled brain as she crossed the room to her desk and picked up the phone. When she risked a glance over her shoulder, Rory stood where she'd left him, grinning at her with the confidence of a guy who knew exactly how much he rattled her.

When Pia answered, she put on her best professional voice. "Hey, Pia, I have a client here who needs some dialect coaching. Can you see him?"

"Isn't he booked in to see you?"

"Yes, but there's a clash."

"I see."

Pia's silky tone alerted her to the fact her cousin had seen right through her invented excuse. "I'm free now, so sure, I can see Rory Radcliffe, but rest assured, Cuz, once he leaves, you and I are going to have a little chat."

"Thanks, I'll send him out to you," she said, hanging up before Pia could say anything else.

Surely her cousin couldn't have figured out Rory Radcliffe was *the* Rory she'd praised for his exceptional prowess? There were thousands of Rorys in Melbourne, but by Pia's tone, she knew.

Flummoxed by this all-around bizarre day, Samira swiveled to face Rory, only to find him a few feet away. Too close. Not close enough.

"You're in luck. Pia can see you now. Just head back to reception and she'll be waiting."

"Great."

Before she could say anything else, he swooped in for a kiss, an all-too-brief graze of his lips against hers that left her wanting so much more.

"What was that for?" she finally said when he kept staring at her mouth like he wanted to ravish it.

"A reminder to make that booty call."

Feeling ridiculously happy and off-kilter, Samira watched his very hot booty all the way out the door.

Belatedly realizing she didn't have his number.

Nine

Nice to meet you, Rory. I'm Pia. Please have a seat."

He shook hands with the stunning Indian woman in the white coat he'd seen earlier and sat next to her desk. She looked nothing like the countless speech therapists he'd been dragged to as a kid. With her long black hair styled in glossy waves and perfect makeup, she looked like a lead from the Bollywood films he watched occasionally.

"Did Sam tell you that technically I'm not a dialect coach and it's not my area of specialty?"

He nodded, increasingly intimidated he'd be seeing a speech therapist for his coaching. He should be relieved he wouldn't be having to sit through torturous sessions with Samira when all he could think about was being inside her, but Pia would pick up on his stutter, and being Samira's cousin, she'd tell her.

Stupid, because it shouldn't bother him. But it did, and he didn't want the polished, sexy Samira knowing he had a flaw.

"Are we bound by client-therapist confidentiality?"

She nodded, a glint of knowing in her eyes. "Absolutely."

"Good, because I know Samira. We're, uh, friends, and I know she's your cousin, so I would prefer anything th-that happens in here s-stays between us."

Great, just being in the presence of a speech therapist brought out his stutter. Fuck.

"You control your stutter well," she said, homing in on it like the professional she was. "It's difficult to detect unless you're an expert."

"I put in enough hours trying to master it growing up," he muttered, hating talking about his stammer as much as hearing himself trip up when the letters ran into one another.

"Good for you." Her gaze glowed with admiration. "So tell me why you need dialect coaching."

"The short version is, I'm up for an audition to host a new reality show on TV. It's the kind of part I would never consider, but I need the money."

"Okay," she said, steepling her fingers on her desk like some Freudian analyst. "Have you done many speaking roles before?"

"None," he begrudgingly admitted, feeling totally out of his depth and sounding like it. "I'm a stuntman that eschews speaking roles for obvious reasons."

"Learning lines can be like singing; you won't stutter."

"It's a risk I haven't been willing to take."

She pinned him with a curious stare. "Then why now?"

His gaze skittered away to fix on the framed diploma above her desk. "Already told you, I need the money."

Before she could probe further, he said, "So can you help me?"

After a long pause, she nodded. "Of course. Do you know much about dialect coaching?"

"Not really."

"Technically, the coach helps actors with voice and speech in relation to a specific role. I'll give you training exercises, instruct you in problem areas, and work on lines with you. But most importantly, I focus on your consistency, clarity, and ensuring you're credible with the part you're auditioning for."

Rory nodded while his head spun. Did he actually think he could do this?

As if sensing his wavering confidence, she added, "Basically, it's about getting your vocal character and delivery right for the role."

"Uh-huh," he managed, feeling his throat tightening already with familiar fear.

It had been like this every time he started with a new therapist. The fear of appearing a fool, the fear of being incompetent, the fear of trying his hardest to conquer his stutter yet failing regardless.

As Pia studied him without judgment, he almost balked.

He could walk out of here and not look back.

He could ask his father for the money.

Easier than making an ass of himself in the biggest audition of his life. Or worse, in front of the camera if he actually landed the role.

But asking his father for money came with a price, which was why he'd avoided it for years. He'd rather eat bland ramen noodles and take any stunt role no matter how dangerous than be indebted to a man who never let him forget his failures.

"It can be a lot to take in," Pia said. "Why don't I give you some preliminary information and do some fact gathering from your agent who referred you as to exactly what's needed for the audition, and we'll set up our first official appointment for tomorrow?"

"Sounds good," he said, waiting while she printed out a stack of documents and bundled them into a folder, when what he really felt like doing was bolting out of there without looking back.

He inhaled a deep breath and blew it out. He could do this. Whenever the doubts crept in, and that would be often over the next few weeks, he had to focus on the kids' project and providing Amelia with the money to get their program up and running.

He knew how badly those kids needed help. His empathy was what got him started alongside Amelia in the first place, poring over funding applications and rental spaces and the sheer, overpowering number of poor kids with speech problems.

Rory couldn't let them down.

He always paid his dues.

"Thanks," he said, taking the folder she held out to him. "What time tomorrow?"

"Does three suit?"

"I'll be here."

He managed a terse nod as he left her office. Thankfully, Samira wasn't anywhere to be seen, and as he strode from the flashy building, his funk over the dialect coaching eased as he wondered if she'd actually take him up on that booty call.

Ten

"Y ou are so busted." Pia pinched Samira in the same spot she used to when they were kids, between her armpit and her fifth rib, and Samira elbowed her away.

"I have no idea what you're talking about."

A total lie, because after she'd fobbed Rory off to Pia yesterday, she'd bolted and hadn't returned her cousin's texts or calls since. They had ranged from a slightly curious **IS HE THE RORY?** to **NICE BOY TOY** to **U BETTER SPILL** to a rambling voice message this morning, "Sam, you better tell me everything about Rory Radcliffe, or I'm going to tell your mom you're screwing a *gora* when she's hell-bent on setting you up, and you know what she thinks of Aussie guys for her precious Indian princess. Call me."

An idle threat, because Pia wouldn't rat her out. Not when her mother had invited what seemed like the entire Indian community in Dandenong to an informal supper to welcome her home tonight.

As Samira glanced around the smallish backyard of her child-hood home, crammed with about seventy people dressed in their Indian finest, she hated to think what a formal affair involved.

The women wore stylish *salwar kameez* and saris in the most vibrant colors: emerald warred with peacock blue, daffodil with magenta, crimson with chartreuse, in a silk free-for-all that dazzled the eyes.

She glanced down at her sedate burgundy sheath dress and grimaced. She'd never hear the end of it, even though she'd told her mom years ago she didn't want to wear Indian garb.

The men wore suits, but one joker had actually come dressed in a tux. Over-the-top, much? As if sensing her critical gaze, he eyeballed her across the crowd and raised an eyebrow in silent challenge. She had to admit he was good-looking, with thick black wavy hair framing high cheekbones and a strong jaw, but it was his eyes that captured her attention the most: a unique pale gray.

When she didn't look away, he smiled, the whiteness of his teeth vivid against his olive skin. Had to be a dentist. And considering his age, which she pegged around late thirties, he could be one of her mother's setups. The thought alone was enough to send her scuttling for the kitchen on the pretext of helping her mom prepare food.

"Hey, where are you going?" Pia grabbed her arm, and Samira shrugged it off with a sheepish grin.

"Mom needs help—"

"I need to find out about Rory," she said, wiggling her eyebrows suggestively. "There's no way you would've pushed someone that cute onto me, especially when you're wanting to expand your dialect coaching expertise, so he has to be the one you screwed. Though what are the odds of him being a client?"

"A million to one," Samira muttered, still in shock over seeing Rory yesterday but inherently glad. The way she'd reacted when he'd touched her, when he'd kissed her . . . she'd felt no guilt at all looking up his number from the initial referral and programming it into her cell.

Not that she'd contact him. She wasn't the booty call type. But surrounded by prospective dates her mom would painstakingly introduce her to, it felt good to have some kind of safety net, like the blankie she used to clutch as a kid for comfort.

"He's incredibly hot." Pia fanned her face. "Seriously, Sam, when I said you should have a no-strings-attached fling with a boy toy, you couldn't have picked any better."

Of course, that's the moment her mom bustled out of the kitchen and spotted them.

"What is this boy toy fling business? Who's having a fling?" Kushi stared at Samira and wrinkled her nose. "Please tell me you're not going to cause a scandal at your homecoming supper."

Pia sniggered while Samira put on her best demure voice. "No scandal, Mom. Need some help in the kitchen?"

Kushi nodded and beckoned them, a cloud of *besan* flour puffing the air as she waved her hands around. "If you girls could take the snacks around, that would be most helpful. Then I can put the sweets on the long table near the veranda, and everyone can help themselves."

"Sounds like a plan, Auntie," Pia said, before leaning over to Samira and whispering, "Don't think your interrogation is over yet, young lady."

Samira rolled her eyes. "You're younger than me, and this is so over."

"Pity you didn't come into work today. I had an appointment with Rory this afternoon."

Samira's heart leaped even as she mentally chastised herself to know better. "So?"

"So . . . when you saw him yesterday, did he mention anything about you two hooking up again? Did you discuss it? Are you going to—"

"Girls, hurry please, our guests are hungry."

Samira had never been so happy to obey a summons from her mother, and she headed for the kitchen, after poking out her tongue at Pia, who did the same in return.

Only two years separated them in age, but they'd been like this since they were kids, closer than sisters. She didn't know what she would've done without Pia's support when her marriage to Avi imploded. She'd been a mess, and her cousin had got her through the worst of it with copious chick flicks, double chocolate fudge brownies, and margaritas. She may feign indignation at Pia's teasing, but she knew without a shadow of a doubt if her mom tried to fob off some wealthy Indian snob onto her later, Pia would be there for her.

The moment she stepped into the kitchen, Samira's stomach rumbled as the fragrant aromas of mustard oil and onions tickled her nostrils.

"That smells so good, Auntie." Pia snaffled a *pakora* off the nearest platter, earning a slapped wrist from Kushi for her trouble.

"You two eat later, guests first," Kushi said, pointing toward the backyard.

Pia winked, stuffed the fried onion snack into her mouth, and plucked another to hand to Samira, who quickly ate it.

"Naughty girls," Kushi said, her voice thick with emotion as she pinched both their cheeks. "It's good to see you two together again."

Samira could only muster a mumbled, "Yeah," as unexpected emotion clogged her throat. Pia picked up a huge platter of *pakoras* and headed for the door, but not before Samira glimpsed the sheen of tears.

As if sensing a blubber-fest in the making, Kushi shooed them away. "Go. Mingle. Feed the crowd."

As Samira picked up a large dish piled high with *vada*, Kushi touched her arm. "*Betee*, there's someone I'd like you to meet later—"

"This platter is heavy, Mom. Got to dash." But she'd barely made it out of the kitchen when the dork in the tux appeared in the doorway like some misplaced wedding guest who hadn't got the memo about the smart casual dress code.

"Ah, Manish, how fortuitous. I was just about to tell my Samira about you." Kushi beamed as Samira resisted the urge to bury her face in the *vada*.

She'd been through this rigmarole before. The less-than-subtle introductions where the guy had been clued in by his parents, the feigning of surprise, the awkwardness of making small talk with a guy she had no interest in, the sleaze of a guy who thought she'd be an easy target, because why else would a woman need a setup?

Fifteen years ago, she'd been young and naive and eager to please her mom, so she'd allowed herself to get swept along with the unrealistic romance facilitated by Kushi and Avi's parents. Her dad hadn't approved, but he'd seen how much it meant to Kushi to see her happily married, so he'd backed down, leaving her mom to propel her headfirst into a relationship she'd neither wanted nor been ready for.

Back then she'd fallen for Avi because she'd believed in the power of love. She'd craved it, a long-standing yearning that began by sneaking Mills and Boons out of the local library as a teen and encouraged by the clueless girls at her high school who regularly expounded their theories on love and sex.

Samira had been woefully innocent and stupidly trusting. Thankfully, she was older and wiser now.

"Nice to meet you, Samira," Manish said, his voice surprisingly confident and mellifluous for a guy who'd worn a tux to a backyard supper on a Friday night.

"You too." She forced a smile under her mother's watchful eye, rewarded by a slight nod from Kushi.

"Need a hand?"

Okay, so Manish had manners. None of the other Indian guys her mom had tried to set her up with before Avi had ever offered to help her with anything.

"Thanks," she said, relieved when he took the heavily laden platter from her hands. All the easier to escape. However, she should've known her mother wouldn't make it that easy.

"Good, now you can take the dipping chutneys for the *vada*," Kushi said, thrusting a smaller platter into her hands before she could protest. "Off you go."

She shooed them out of the kitchen, and Samira blew out a frustrated breath as they stepped onto the veranda.

"You don't have to accompany me, you know," Manish said, staring at her with that way-too-astute gray gaze. "If the hungry hordes want chutneys, you can put them on the table and they can wander over."

Samira struggled to hide her surprise. Another point in his favor. He didn't expect her to trot alongside him like a subservient maid. And though she'd wanted to escape the potential awkwardness a moment ago, she didn't mind being polite and offering guests dipping sauces with their snacks.

"It's okay. I'll do one circuit of the yard, and then you're on your own."

He chuckled, the corners of his eyes crinkling into fine lines and adding to his handsomeness. She may have sworn off Indian men a long time ago, but this one was nothing like Avi. She guessed her mom had done her homework this time around.

"I can live with that." He waited for her to step past him. "After you."

Taking a deep breath, Samira allowed herself to be absorbed into the crowd. She'd expected to face an interrogation of monstrous proportions from the local community and a barrage of match-making suggestions. Instead, the worst she copped were a few side-long glances and some whispers after she passed by.

Then again, nobody had a chance to say much with Manish greeting almost everyone by name and asking after their children/grandchildren/neighbors as he plied them with *vada*.

"Were you a caterer in a previous life?" she asked as they headed back toward the kitchen, platters empty.

He quirked an eyebrow, just like he had when they'd first laid eyes on each other half an hour ago. This time, it looked less insolent and more charming. "What makes you think I'm not one now?"

"The tux, for one."

His other eyebrow joined the first. "You don't like it?"

"It's overkill."

"Maybe I'm heading to a James Bond look-alike party after this?"

So he had a sense of humor to go with the manners and the looks. She wouldn't be swayed.

"Are you?"

"No, but I wish I was." He screwed up his nose. "There's a doctors' fundraiser in the city after this I couldn't get out of."

Of course Kushi had chosen a doctor. *Ding, ding, ding,* she could almost hear her mom setting up the wedding chimes.

"Too bad you'll be missing out on dessert. Mom makes a killer *jalebi.*"

"I'm more a *gulab jamun* kind of guy."

Typical, obsessed with balls. Then again, she was partial to the golden fried dumplings soaked in sugar syrup too. It wasn't his fault she was a confirmed cynic when it came to Kushi's fix-ups.

She made a grand show of looking at her watch. "You don't want to be late."

"Trying to get rid of me?"

He leaned in close, and for an insane moment, Samira almost wished she'd feel a spark. Not that she wanted to get married again or stay in Melbourne permanently or get caught up in an Indian matchmaking frenzy, but Manish had been nothing but funny and polite, and it would be easier on everyone if she liked him in that way.

But not a zing or a zap as his breath fanned her cheek, nothing like her body's reaction to Rory.

"Can I be honest, Manish?"

He straightened, and she glimpsed the disappointment in his eyes that she didn't want to flirt. "Sure."

"You seem like a really nice guy, but I'm in Melbourne to work for the next six months, and I'm not interested in a relationship."

"Too bad," he said, eyeing her with something akin to hope. "We're both in the medical field, we're similar ages, we could've been good together."

"Good on paper according to our family's astrologers, you mean?"

He laughed again. "If your mom's anything like my grandmother, you know this won't be the last time we'll be 'encouraged' to meet."

"Yeah, I know, but at least we both know where we stand now."

"For the record, I won't hold it against you if you change your mind." He tugged at his bow tie. "After all, who can resist a doctor in a tux?"

She made a buzzing sound. "Wrong on so many levels."

"Don't say I didn't warn you." He shrugged, his grin oddly endearing. "Until we meet again, Samira."

Samira watched the not-so-dorky doctor with the killer sense of humor do the rounds saying his goodbyes, while her cell with Rory's number in it burned a hole in her pocket.

He was too young for her, he was all wrong for her, yet she couldn't deny that for the first time in her life she should quit thinking about doing the right thing and do the exact opposite.

Eleven

Samira had stuffed the last plastic bag into the trash when the first wave of nausea hit.

Her stomach churned like she'd drunk week-old lassi, and sweat broke out over her face. The pungent smell of garbage wasn't helping, and she backed away from the trash can quickly.

However, a second wave swamped her, more powerful than the first, and she staggered toward the front step of the veranda, grabbing at the balustrading to prevent from falling.

"Hey, you okay?"

Of course, dashing Dr. Manish had to be leaving at that moment, and she managed a mute nod before slumping toward him.

"Easy, I've got you." He lowered her to the nearest step as her head swam and she struggled not to barf all over his shoes. "When I said you'd fall for my charms, I didn't expect you to actually swoon or to have it happen so quickly."

In response, Samira vomited on her mother's prize rosebush. Not a dainty vomit either; a full-on, multicolored puke that went on too long and left her swaying and clinging to whatever she could hold on to: in this case, Manish's arm.

"Did you even notice I held back your hair like a true gentleman?"

"Stop trying to make me laugh," she said, punctuated with a groan that had her clutching her stomach again. "I feel awful."

"What did you eat?"

"Not much. An onion *pakora*, maybe two." The thought of any kind of food made her stomach roil, and she wished he'd hurry up and leave so she could nurse her humiliation in peace.

"Could be a virus," he said. "There's a nasty gastro going around; the hospital ER has been inundated."

It wasn't a virus, but no way in hell would she tell him the real cause of her barf. This happened occasionally courtesy of her oligomenorrhea. She didn't mind the infrequent periods and could handle the cramps, but the hormone spikes that induced nausea were the pits. She didn't always vomit, thank goodness, but this spike must've been a doozy.

"I'll be fine," she said, struggling to her feet, grateful for the support of his arm. "Nothing a good lemonade won't fix."

"Barley water, don't you mean?"

The thought of the boiled barley water her mom used to make her drink as a kid for good gut health made her want to barf again.

"Stop. You're killing me."

"Only because I'd get to revive you with mouth-to-mouth."

"Oh my God, you did not just say that."

"I think I did, but hey, at least you're smiling."

"It's a grimace," she said, liking his quick wit more by the minute, even in her puke-induced haze.

At that moment, her head spun again, and she clutched at him, hating herself for showing weakness. Ever since she'd divorced Ari and fled to LA, she'd turned her back on the fragile woman she'd been and embraced her inner tigress. Who had sadly morphed into a pathetic pussycat about five minutes ago.

"Let me take you inside."

She could've protested but didn't know if she'd manage to make it feeling so light-headed, and thankfully, by the time he led her into the lounge room, she felt better.

"Anything I can get you?"

"No, thanks, I'll be okay."

He eyeballed her with startling intensity. "You know you can call me, right? For my medical expertise, of course."

"Of course," she said, offering a smile, wishing she could feel something for this sweet guy.

He strode to the door where he paused. "Seriously, Samira, despite that little speech you gave me earlier, if you want to hang out as friends while you're in town, just give me a call."

He grinned and made a corny cocked gun with his thumb and forefinger. "Your mom has my number."

She smiled as he waved, thankful she'd managed to maneuver through her mom's first matchmaking attempt and come out unscathed.

If only the same could be said for Kushi's inappropriately fertilized rosebush.

*R*ory glared at the immaculately trimmed rosebushes in his father's manicured garden, remembering the time he'd hacked off the flowers in a rare show of rebellion. He'd been seven at the time, struggling at school, being teased incessantly for stuttering and missing his mom. She'd left years earlier, but the fragrance of roses never failed to remind him of her.

"Here you go."

He turned and accepted the boutique beer his father held out to him. Predictably, Garth Radcliffe had a glass with a double shot of aged whiskey in his other hand. He'd never seen his father drink anything else.

"Thanks." Rory raised his beer bottle. "Cheers."

"Cheers." His father downed the whiskey in two gulps. "What brings you by on a Friday night?"

Melbourne's most prominent barrister never minced words. He also never showed affection or emotion or abided weakness of any kind. And while he hadn't ever said it, Rory knew his father viewed his stutter as a weakness.

"It's been a while." Four months to be exact. "I wanted to touch base."

Translated, Rory had undergone a session of dialect coaching with Pia and was in a serious funk, because the more time he spent with the speech therapist, the more his fear would grow that he'd never nail the audition in four weeks, and the speech program for underprivileged kids wouldn't get off the ground.

That was what his impromptu visit to his father was about: giving himself a massive wake-up call that if he didn't get the host gig for *Renegades*, he'd be back here having to grovel to a man who'd never let him forget it.

"You want something." Garth pinned him with a steely glare that had intimidated many of the best lawyers in the country. "Let's not pretend otherwise."

"Nice to see you too, Dad."

Rory took a slug of beer to swallow the bitterness of being viewed as some usurper when he'd never asked his father for anything. He'd learned in his teens that anything his dad gave came at a price, and he didn't want to pay it anymore.

"If you want to get into the economics field, I have connections—"

"I'm happy . . . doing what I'm . . . doing."

Rory paused between the difficult D words because he'd be damned if he stuttered in front of his father. He'd tolerated a lifetime of pitying stares or worse, having Garth finish his sentences for him. He particularly hated that, like his father didn't have the time to hear him out.

"I'll never understand how throwing away your degree to tumble around a movie set like some circus clown makes you happy, but each to their own."

For the first time since he'd set foot in his father's multimillion-dollar mansion in upscale Brighton, Rory felt some of his tension dissipate.

He'd heard that same spiel from his father countless times over the last five years since he'd eschewed his economics degree in favor of acting. Even though Amelia had made it more than clear to Garth that the deep breathing, repetition, and practice involved in acting could only help his stutter, his father had scoffed. Besides, how could working as a stuntman improve his speech when he never talked on camera?

Deep down, he knew his father's disdain and lack of faith in him was a major driving force to win the role of hosting *Renegades*. It was why he'd come, when visiting his father never ended well. He may need the money desperately to fund the start-up foundation for those migrant and refugee kids, but a small part of him couldn't wait to wipe the smirk off his father's face.

"And I'll never understand how you can stand up in court every day defending a bunch of lying criminals, but hey, we do what we have to do."

Rory drained the rest of his beer and placed the empty bottle on a nearby mosaic-encrusted table. "Thanks for the beer, Dad."

His mock salute earned a frown. "It would be nice to see you around here more often."

"And it would be nice to have a father who actually respected my choices and supported me, but we don't always get what we want, do we, Dad?"

As the deep groove of disapproval slashing his father's brow deepened, Rory strolled down the steps without looking back.

Yeah, visiting dear old Dad had achieved what he'd set out to do.

Given him a swift kick in the head as a reminder of why he had to nail the *Renegades* audition.

Because no way in hell he'd ask his judgmental, narrow-minded, emotionless drone of a father for money.

Ever.

Twelve

Rory had to admit the coaching sessions with Pia were working. His confidence increased every time he conquered one of the vocal exercises she gave him, and he'd put in a lot of extra hours practicing at home. Between training his diaphragm and working out at the gym, he'd been suitably distracted.

Because every time he entered the posh health center for an appointment with Pia, he hoped he'd run into Samira.

She hadn't called like he'd hoped—he'd seen his referral from Chris, and it had his cell number on there, which meant she could get it if she wanted—so rather than lament it, he'd focused on the task at hand.

But after a particularly grueling session with Pia where he'd ended up stumbling over his words more than usual, he needed a distraction of a different kind. It had been a week and a half since he'd hooked up with Samira, and while he'd mentally chastised himself the last ten days—he had to focus and not allow a sensational one-night stand to derail his focus—he'd worked hard and could do with a little relief from the frustrations of screwing up his session with Pia.

Not that he expected to have sex per se, but he remembered how hanging out with Samira for that one night had taken his mind off the stress of the *Renegades* audition, and he could do with that same feeling now.

Before he could second-guess his impulsivity, he strode down the corridor toward her office. The lights in the foyer had been dimmed, and the CLOSED sign had been flipped on the glass doors out the front, which meant he was probably the last client in the building. Surely she wouldn't be consulting at six if the rest of the center had closed?

Mentally rehearsing what he'd say to her so he wouldn't stumble over his words, he stopped outside her office and knocked on the door.

He'd keep his greeting light and breezy, and try not to remember the last time he'd been in her office, when he'd kissed her in the hope she'd want to do a lot more of it. They shared a real spark, and he wondered what would've happened if he'd left his number the morning after their hookup. Would she have taken it as a sign he was keen for more and contacted him? Or would she have chalked up their raunchy night to a one-off and not bothered regardless?

The fact she hadn't called pointed toward the latter, and while he'd initially taken their meeting again here as a sign, maybe he should just quit while he was behind.

Besides, he didn't date. Dating set up expectations and soon led to a relationship, and he'd deliberately shied away from emotional involvements for the simple fact the closer he got to a person, the more relaxed he became in their company, the more he had to talk, and the more he stuttered.

A stupid reason for not getting involved; he knew it. But he'd never met anyone who he'd been willing to take the risk for. He'd gone out with a woman once for three dates in a week, his record. He'd thought they had a spark, but when she'd pushed him for details of his family history and his job and a myriad of other things, he realized how relationships involved a hell of a lot of talking and he'd ended it.

He wasn't a man whore, but having a string of brief sexual encounters with women who knew the score suited him much better; encounters like he'd had with Samira.

So why was he really here, pushing his luck, hoping to hook up with her again?

The door opened as he half turned away, and in that moment when their eyes connected and he glimpsed genuine happiness in her eyes, he knew he'd made the right decision in chasing her up tonight.

"Hey."

Not quite the scintillating greeting he'd hoped for, but at least he didn't stutter. Because there was a high chance of that, considering his excitement level shot into the stratosphere the moment he saw her.

Samira was even more stunning than he remembered. Her eyes were truly beautiful, their unique hazel sparking green and gold as she stared at him, one eyebrow arched. Her skin glowed like she'd just finished a workout, and his mind immediately stumbled into the gutter as he imagined the kind of workout he'd like to have with her.

Her arched eyebrow edged higher. "What are you doing here?"

He inhaled slightly, let it out, calming, centered. "I've just finished a session with Pia, it's been a long week, and I thought you might fancy a drink?"

The words ran into one another too fast, and he hoped she'd take it as a sign of his eagerness to hang out with her rather than anything else.

She hesitated, gnawing on her full bottom lip, and damned if he didn't get a hard-on as he remembered what else she could do with those lips.

"Okay," she eventually said, opening the door wider. "I have to finish up a few things, so why don't you wait in here?"

She didn't sound overly enthusiastic, but her gaze roved over him, hungry and possessive, like she too remembered . . .

"Hey." She snapped her fingers in front of his face. "You know a drink is just a drink, right?"

"Yeah, why?"

"Because you've got this look . . ." She trailed off, the tip of her tongue darting out to moisten her bottom lip—definitely not helping the hard-on situation. "And the last time we were in a bar, it didn't stop there."

"I liked hanging out with you that night." He held up his hands, showing he had nothing to hide. "So that's what tonight's about, an impulsive decision to drop by and see if you're free for a drink, that's it."

To his surprise, she stepped in close, reached over his shoulder, and pushed the door shut. Her faint jasmine fragrance washed over him, and he gritted his teeth against the urge to haul her into his arms.

Their gazes locked, and she inhaled sharply, the soft hiss of her breath as she released it the only sound in the silence. He could've sworn electricity arced between them, potent and lethal and bound to scorch him.

He wanted to close the distance between them and kiss her senseless. Hell, he wanted to do a lot more than that, starting with laying her on the exercise plinth and doing creative things with those colored exercise bands.

But he could see the skepticism in her eyes, like she knew his real reason for stopping by was a booty call. And while he'd like nothing better, and deep down that was exactly why he'd dropped by, he wanted to be better than that.

For what reason, he couldn't fathom. He couldn't date her, they never had to see each other again unless they accidentally bumped into each other in the corridors here, and they shared nothing but an intense physical connection. Once.

So why was he trying to impress her with this upstanding act when he wanted her so badly his balls ached?

Mentally kicking himself, he broke eye contact, and she stepped away, giving a little shake of her head as if she couldn't believe they'd come so close to giving in to baser instinct again.

"Take a seat. I shouldn't be too long," she said, pointing at a sofa not far from her desk.

Glad she turned away so she couldn't see him adjust himself with the boner situation going on behind his fly, he watched her stride to her desk. She wore stylish navy pin-striped wide-leg pants, a fitted white shirt, and black patent leather pumps, a simple work outfit that shouldn't have been remotely sexy yet was. The way the pants hugged the curve of her ass, how the small heel added a sway to her hips . . . man, at this rate he'd be so hard he'd be unable to walk.

When she reached her desk, she glanced over her shoulder,

a puzzled frown creasing her brow when she saw he hadn't moved. Mustering his best acting skills, he grinned and headed for the sofa, relieved when she didn't make a comment about his rather stilted gait.

She sat at her desk while he perched on the sofa and picked up a brochure, not giving a flying fuck about ergonomic chairs or exercises to improve posture but needing the distraction so he wouldn't watch her.

He stared blankly at the diagrams featuring people sitting at desks, but the sound of her fingers clacking against a keyboard drew his attention, and he watched her. He couldn't see much beyond a half profile, her tongue poking out slightly as she typed. She sat straight, shoulders back, just like one of the diagrams for perfect posture in the brochure. It thrust her breasts forward, drawing his eyes there, as he remembered feasting on them, sucking on her spectacular nipples . . .

Stifling a groan, he rested his head on the back of the sofa and covered his eyes with his forearm. Damn it, he needed to stop fantasizing about her, and the only thing guaranteed to douse his libido was to think about the *Renegades* audition.

Chris had been on his back about it, checking in every second day to ask how the dialect coaching was coming along. He had no idea why his agent did it, because he never gave him anything beyond "fine" and "good." But considering the money Chris would earn from his cut if Rory actually landed the hosting role, he guessed that explained his agent's exuberance.

"You okay?"

He lowered his forearm, shocked to find Samira sitting beside him on the sofa. He'd been so deep in thought he hadn't noticed the silence when she stopped typing or heard her move.

"Yeah." He straightened, hating being surprised like this. It didn't give him time to formulate responses in his head. He often mentally rehearsed what he'd say to people before actually saying it, and having her sneak up on him took away his chance to do it.

When he didn't say anything else, she cocked her head slightly to one side, as if she couldn't quite figure him out. Good.

"You are nothing like other guys I know."

"That's a good thing, yeah?"

She took a while before she nodded, continuing to study him with that probing stare. "Most guys can't shut up. They want to talk about themselves, a lot, plenty of inane chatter about their job, their car, and their football team. Yet you're . . . quiet."

She was way too intuitive, and he needed to stop her delving into the reasons for his preference for silence.

"Haven't you heard the quiet ones are the worst?"

Scooting closer, he snagged her hand and raised it to his lips. Her eyes widened as he pressed a kiss to the back of it, before nibbling on her knuckles, pausing to flick his tongue in the dips between.

She groaned, and he was on her, pressing her back into the sofa, kissing her with every ounce of pent-up frustration from thinking about her all week.

Her mouth opened beneath his, her tongue searching for his, demanding, commanding. She kissed like she fucked, with wanton abandonment and sheer enjoyment. Like she couldn't get enough. Like she wanted him as badly as he wanted her. Big turn-on. Huge.

When he covered her body with his, grinding his rigid cock against her sweet spot, she stilled and broke the kiss. Her chest heavied with her rapid breathing, her eyes glazed and wide.

"The door's unlocked," she murmured, placing her hands on his chest to push him away. "I can't do this; it's unprofessional."

"Yeah, of course, sorry." He pushed off her and helped her into a sitting position, wishing he hadn't lost his head but a small part of him not regretting it at all. Guess he'd answered the question of whether he wanted more than the one-night stand. He craved another hot encounter with the sexy brunette so much he'd almost devoured her in her office. "When you say you can't do this, do you mean here or in general?"

He saw in her eyes the battle she waged. Lust with sensibility. Desire with logic. But when the corners of her mouth curved in a coy smile, he knew he'd like her answer.

"Here," she said, her hand snaking out to take his. "But if you recall, my apartment's not that far, so why don't we go have that drink?"

Rory didn't have to be asked twice.

Thirteen

*I*t had been a long week.

Samira had treated way too many arthritic backs when she'd anticipated a lot more soft-tissue injuries for hot Aussie rules football players. She'd spent an inordinate amount of time setting up rooms for other allied health professional staff that hadn't started working at the center yet. And she'd fallen into bed exhausted most nights after dodging her mom's calls to set up another meeting with Manish.

Though she'd attributed her ongoing fatigue to residual jet lag, she knew better. Tossing and turning while remembering a scorching one-night stand that had the potential to turn into more wasn't conducive to good sleep. So when the object of her disrupted slumber knocked on her office door, what was a girl to do other than invite him back to her place, again?

They barely made it into her apartment before he had her up against the wall, his deliciously hard body pressing against hers, setting alight every nerve ending, making her skin hypersensitive. She wanted to claw off her clothes, and his, her hands plucking ineffectually at his cotton T-shirt because she didn't know where to grab first.

"Sexy as fuck," he murmured against her neck, alternating between gentle bites and sensual sweeps of his tongue, his use of the f-bomb ratcheting up her desire, if that was possible.

She'd never done the dirty-talk thing, and there was something raw and natural about him that called to her.

She loved living in LA, but most of the guys she'd dated had been well-groomed, well-spoken, and hooked on the wellness regimen that the beautiful people favored. Many of them had been fake, their obsession with manscaping and fast cars an instant turnoff.

Rory was so far removed from those guys, she knew that was part of the attraction. The other parts . . . She slid her hand between their bodies to cup his groin, letting out a little squeal when he bit down on her trapezius particularly hard.

"Sorry," he said, not sounding sorry at all, and she deliberately squeezed him, earning a loud groan.

"Bedroom?"

"Here's fine." She unzipped him and slid her hand inside, emboldened, eager.

He returned the favor, unzipping her pants and pushing them down along with her panties, his hands impatient, his fingers plucking at elastic, until she kicked them away and his hands cupped her ass, lifting her slightly.

She liked that he was a man of few words, and she could tell what he wanted by touch, so she slid her hand inside his jocks, wrapped her hand around velvet hardness, and eased him out.

"Condom. Wallet. Back pocket," he said, and she didn't waste any time in getting him sheathed.

She'd barely rolled the latex all the way to the base of his penis when he lifted her higher, leaving her no option but to wrap her legs around his waist.

Her breath hitched as he nudged her entrance, teasing, waiting, until she locked eyes with him, and what he saw must've driven him to slide in to the hilt.

Heat streaked through her at the first thrust, and the next, and the next. Over and over, the exquisite pleasure of having him fill her.

His lips sought hers, his kisses sensual and soul drugging as he picked up the tempo, angling his hips so each thrust grazed her clit.

Considering her raunchy memories of their one night together, it didn't take long for her to cling to him, whispering "more" as a monumental orgasm clawed at her.

With another thrust, she came so hard she bit into his shoulder, and he followed a second later on a low, guttural groan that raised the hairs on the back of her neck.

She'd never had this kind of sex before, had never been so horny for a guy, and as he gently lowered her and her feet touched the ground, she wondered about the prudence of turning a one-night stand into two . . . but with him still inside her and the after-shocks of her pulsating muscles setting up a delicious heat between them, she didn't particularly care.

*R*ory didn't do this.

He didn't linger after sex with a woman he barely knew, and he certainly didn't stand in her kitchen chopping onions for scrambled eggs. Yet there he was, in Samira's apartment, doing exactly that. It should've given him hives. Instead, the repetitive soothing action of the sharp knife dicing through the layers calmed him.

It helped that she didn't mind talking enough for the both of them.

"Once those onions are done, dice the tomato next, then the cilantro, and you're ready to learn the art of creating the best Punjabi scrambled eggs you've ever tasted."

She brought her fingertips to her lips and kissed them with a flourish, making him laugh. She had this way about her, an easygoing lack of self-consciousness that he admired yet envied.

What would it be like to feel that comfortable in your own skin? To appear completely at ease standing in a kitchen wearing a long T-shirt over knickers while beating eggs with a fork? To make conversation without having to overthink every goddamn word? To share an impromptu dinner after great sex and not feel the slightest bit awkward?

If he ever broke his relationship rule, she'd be a primary candidate. Then again, what was the point? She'd be leaving at the end of her six-month stint at the health center, and the last thing he needed was to let down his guard for the first time in his life, fall for her, only to be left broken when she headed back to LA. He was many things; a masochist wasn't one of them.

"You really are a man of few words," she said, picking up a dishcloth. "I'm hoping it's you being an introvert and not because you find me a boring conversationalist."

"You're fantastic, and I think I demonstrated fifteen minutes ago exactly how stimulating I find you."

She blushed the same shade as the tomato in her hand, which she tossed him and he caught. "That's sex, and yes, I think we've established how good we are at that."

"Just good, huh?"

She rolled her eyes. "Great. Amazing. Stupendous. Better?"

"Getting there." He winked, tossed the tomato, and caught it. "Yeah, I'm quiet. I prefer to listen."

Her eyes narrowed in suspicion. "Are you real or some superhuman male deposited here from another planet?"

"Some parts of me are superhuman, if your moans of approval are any indication," he deadpanned, earning a flick of the dishcloth on his ass.

"Just chop," she said, amusement crinkling the corners of her eyes. "For what it's worth, I don't reveal the secret of my Punjabi scrambled eggs to just anybody."

"So I guess that means you like me for more than my superhuman co—"

"Dice," she said, pointing at the tomato, her blush intensifying as she turned the stove knob to light the gas.

Grinning, he focused on the task at hand so he wouldn't dice a fingertip along with the tomato. She had that effect on him, her sense of humor as beguiling as the rest of her. And even though they'd only hooked up twice, and she was transient, and he couldn't afford to get too distracted from nailing the *Renegades* audition, he couldn't help but wish they could do this for longer.

"Why is someone like you single?"

Fuck, the question popped out before he could get his brain into gear, something that never happened.

She paused, pouring oil into a frying pan and adding a dob of ghee, before answering. "I could ask you the same question."

"That's easy. I'm not a relationship kind of guy. I live in a tiny flat, my work is intermittent, and I travel around a lot for it." He shrugged. "Not exactly stable material."

She whirled the pan in circular motions to spread the oil and ghee while eyeing him speculatively. "I was married, once, many years ago. It lasted eighteen months. When the divorce came through, I moved to the US because my dad's from there, so I got a green card, started working, and never looked back."

Her admission surprised him. She didn't sound bitter. In fact, she sounded almost blasé, like it meant nothing. While he'd never contemplated marriage and never would, he was pretty sure if his imploded, he'd be more cut up. Then again, she'd said many years ago . . .

"You must've been a child bride."

"Something like that," she said, turning away to focus on the stove. "Can I have the onion please?"

Nice deflection, and he didn't push for answers, no matter how curious. He handed her the saucer with diced onions and watched as she tipped the onion into the pan, deftly flicking the pieces around with a wooden spoon.

"Tomato," she said, and he handed her the next saucer, wishing he hadn't opened his big mouth and changed the playful mood to wariness.

With the both of them reverting to silence, the sizzle of frying onion and tomato the only sound in the kitchen, an awkwardness he didn't like extended between them.

This was why he shouldn't speak. On the rare occasions he tried to make conversation, he inevitably screwed up.

"These eggs are my mom's recipe," she said, soft, uncertain. "The guy I married was her choice."

His eyebrows shot up. "You had an arranged marriage?"

"Sort of." She added a pinch of garlic powder to the pan, and half a teaspoon of garam masala. "He was Indian, came from a solid family, had a good job, and was handsome. I was young and craving a fairy tale from watching one too many Bollywood movies, and I ended up falling for him after Mom gave me a none-too-gentle shove in his direction."

She poured the eggs into the pan, the wooden spoon moving faster now, stirring around and around. "He cheated on me after a year of marriage."

"Bastard."

He never understood the whole cheating thing. If you wanted to play the field, why settle down? Easier to stay single than end up hurting someone. The dickhead must've been a real prick to do a number on someone like Samira.

"My sentiments exactly." She switched off the stove and started dishing the fragrant eggs onto two plates. "I blamed Mom a long time for pushing me toward Avi. I've avoided Melbourne for that reason. We're not as close as we once were, but I'm hoping we can get past it this trip."

Surprised she continued to share private revelations, he asked, "How often do you come home?"

"The last time was five years ago, for my dad's funeral."

She handed him a plate, picked up the other, and gestured to the small dining table in the corner. "So now that you know why I prefer to stay single, let's eat."

He could've left it at that, but he wanted to know more, against his better judgment.

"Sorry about your dad. But one jerk shouldn't taint your view of relationships." He picked up his fork and stabbed at a piece of egg. "You're spectacular and deserve to be happy."

"Thanks, Dr. Phil," she said, raising a glass of water in his direction, and he chuckled.

"On that note, I'll shut my mouth, revert to that silence you love so much, and eat."

As he lifted the fork to his mouth and got his first taste of Punjabi eggs, he hoped his eyes didn't roll back in his head. The incredible combination of sautéed onion, tomato, and cilantro along with the eggs and spices burst on his tongue, and he moaned in appreciation.

"This is fantastic," he said, shoveling another two forkfuls into his mouth in quick succession.

"Tell me something I don't know." She smiled at his compliment and proceeded to eat as fast as he did. A woman with healthy appetites. He loved it.

When he regretfully pushed his empty plate away, he patted his stomach. "Thank you. That was absolutely delicious. You'll have to give me the recipe."

"Sure." She winked. "But then I'll have to kill you, and if I don't, my mom will."

"But she'll never know."

The cheeky glint in her eyes faded, and he instantly knew he'd said the wrong thing again.

He wasn't a "meet the parents" type of guy, especially when they weren't even dating, but by her reaction, he got the distinct impression she was either ashamed of him or had major hang-ups with her mother beyond blaming her for choosing a shitty husband for her.

Inwardly cursing his never-ending ability to get words wrong even when he was so sure they were right, he stood and started clearing the table. As he reached for her plate, she covered his hand with hers.

"Leave it. We can do the dishes later."

He dragged his gaze from her hand to her eyes, her somberness not encouraging. "Later?"

"Don't you want seconds?"

"But there aren't any eggs left—"

"Exactly."

She stood, intertwined her fingers with his, and eyeballed him with an unspoken challenge he was all too willing to accept as they headed for the bedroom.

Fourteen

This time, when Rory woke in Samira's bed, he didn't slink away. Not that he wasn't tempted, considering she captivated him just as much when she slept, with small puffs of air blowing out of pursed lips and her eyeballs' rapid movement making her lids quiver, but they'd connected beyond the sex last night when she'd revealed all that stuff about being married, and slipping away would be a shitty thing to do.

But staying around until she woke and agreeing to brunch were poles apart. Saturday mornings were reserved for mega workouts and studying the requirements on stunt jobs for next week. But his schedule was annoyingly clear considering he needed the money, and he could always hit the gym later. Besides, he'd had a good cardio workout several times last night, three to be precise, and there was nothing like sex with Samira to get his heart pumping.

"What are you thinking about?"

He grinned at her from across a small table in an Indian café off the main drag in Dandenong. "Do you really want to know?"

She held up her hand, her eyes glittering with remembrance. "You don't have to spell it out."

"Then why did you ask?"

"Because I spent a great night with a hot guy and I'm in a cheeky mood, so sue me."

He laughed and she joined in, and he wished he could attribute the weird feeling in his chest to heartburn, but they hadn't eaten yet.

When he'd turned up at her office last night, he hadn't expected to connect this way. The sex had been as good as he remembered, and it should've ended there. But with cooking dinner together, spending the night, and sharing this late breakfast, Rory knew they'd moved beyond the "just screwing" phase into something . . . more. He didn't know what it was, and he had no idea how to label it, but they were in some weird dating limbo land where he wanted to see her again but was terrified by the urge.

"So you think I'm hot, huh?"

"Like you need the validation." She rolled her eyes. "You asked me last night why I was single, and I asked you the same." She poked him in the biceps. "So what gives? You mentioned all that stuff about your job and small apartment, but what's the real reason?"

No way in hell would he tell her why he steered clear of relationships, so he deflected by pointing at his chest and pulling his shoulders back. "Why would I deprive so many women of this by taking myself off the market?"

She laughed as he'd intended, and he breathed a sigh of relief. She'd already mentioned he was a man of few words, and he didn't need her knowing why. Though interestingly, sitting across from her at the dining table last night and now, he realized he hadn't been so self-conscious. He wasn't weighing every word carefully before speaking or tensing in case he slipped up. She made him feel at ease in a way he hadn't experienced since . . . well, ever.

Thankfully, their order arrived and prevented her from asking any more questions he'd rather not answer. He'd never heard of Indian dishes like *upma* and *idlis*, being a chicken tikka and *rogan josh* man, but they smelled delicious, and he was looking forward to trying his first vegetarian South Indian breakfast.

"Would you like a little of everything?"

He nodded and held out his plate, watching as Samira placed two white saucerlike cakes and a spoonful of chutney on it, along with several large spoonfuls of a grainy concoction.

"The *upma* is made from roasted semolina, with curry leaves, onion, chili, mustard and cumin seeds, and *chana dahl* mixed through it. It's amazing."

She looked so animated, so enthused, he wanted to drag her across the table and devour her rather than the food she'd described.

"The *idlis* are made from a special rice and *urad dahl* ground together, fermented, then steamed." She pointed to the dollop of red on his plate. "And that's coconut chutney. It's so good."

"Thanks," he said, surprised to find himself salivating, and after he forked some *upma* into his mouth, he knew why. If the aromas of sautéed spices weren't tempting enough, the explosion of flavor made his taste buds dance.

He must've made a weird noise, because he glanced up to find her staring at him with a beguiling mix of approval and admiration.

"Told you so," she said, grinning. "Try the *idlis*."

When he picked up a knife and fork to cut it, she shook her head. "Like this."

She broke off a piece with her fingers and dunked it in the

chutney before popping it into her mouth. Her blissful expression made him hard in an instant.

"That good, huh?"

"Better," she said, with a wink, and he forced himself to focus on eating rather thinking about other ways he could put that ecstatic expression on her face.

He found the *idlis* rather bland, but the chutney was delicious, and he cleared his plate quickly, to find she'd done the same.

When the waitress placed stainless steel mugs of steaming masala chai in front of them and cleared their plates, Samira said, "I know I've already said this, but one of the things I like most about you is your ability to enjoy this"—she waved her hand between the two of them—"without endless chatter. It's refreshing."

If she only knew that the source of her admiration for his preference for silence came from necessity rather than any grand plan on his part.

"I don't see the point of talking for the sake of it," he said, hoping she couldn't read the truth on his face. "Listening is much better."

She sighed, the corners of her mouth curving. "You may just be the unicorn of men."

"Because I'm rare or because you think I have a mighty horn?"

She laughed so loud several people at nearby tables turned to stare, but she didn't care and neither did he. There was something about this spontaneous woman that captivated him.

Which meant he should run for the hills before it was too late.

Samira knew bringing Rory to Dandenong was a big risk. Any number of her mom's acquaintances or the dreaded auntie brigade—a group of local elderly Indian women who judged everyone and found them lacking—could spot them together and carry the news back to Kushi before she'd finished her masala chai. But she didn't care. In fact, a small part of her had done this defiantly, almost daring fate to catch her sharing breakfast with a young Aussie guy far removed from Kushi's version of the perfect man.

She could've ditched him after breakfast, but she didn't want to, and not from any nefarious reason to flaunt him in the face of tradition. No, there was much more behind her invitation to him to accompany her on a stroll around her old stomping ground, and it revolved around how damn addictive this guy was.

She'd never met anyone like Rory before. He had this way of looking at her that made her feel like the only woman in the world. And his silent strength made her want to delve beneath the surface while enjoying the calmness he emanated too.

She wasn't a big talker herself and hated when guys she'd dated would overpower the conversation every time. With Rory, he made her appear garrulous, and she liked it. The best thing was, rather than worrying about whether he was hiding some deep, dark secret, she was enjoying living in the moment.

Nothing could come of this. They were opposites in every way; he was too young for her, and she'd be leaving in just over five months. So who cared if her one-night stand had morphed into two? Maybe more if she was lucky, considering his expertise between the sheets?

That was why she'd agreed to his offer to have a drink last night, knowing they'd end up having sex. But she hadn't expected to open up to him about Avi or hint at her mom's involvement in keeping her away from home. Those damn good listening skills of his had got to her, yet after she'd blabbed, she hadn't felt so bad. In fact, he had this way about him . . . like he empathized.

He'd made her feel so good last night, it had seemed natural to invite him to have breakfast and spend more time together. She'd half expected him to refuse, and when he didn't, she'd experienced a buzz of happiness she hadn't in a long time.

"I haven't been to this part of town in years," he said, taking hold of her hand as they strolled along Walker Street past Indian clothing stores, sweetshops, and a barber. "It's incredibly cosmopolitan."

"You sound like the tourist, not me," she said with a laugh. "At least, that's what I feel like considering I haven't been back home for so long, and even then it was only a flying visit."

She expected him to probe, to ask more about why she hadn't been home since her dad's funeral, but once again he remained silent, leaving her to divulge as much or as little as she wanted.

"I've lived in Dandenong for twenty-five years and LA for twelve, yet America feels more like home. What does that say about me?"

His grip on her hand tightened. "You're thirty-seven?"

Oops. She'd been so caught up in her thoughts, she'd let that gem slip inadvertently. "Yeah. I'm old."

"You're spectacular." He tugged on her hand until she fell against him, and he pressed his mouth to hers in a scorching kiss that made her weak-kneed.

When he released her, she swayed a little, unable to keep the grin off her face. If she needed the validation the age gap didn't matter to him, she'd just got it.

Capturing her chin, he tipped it up to eyeball her. "I like you, Samira. I want you to know that, and this has been the best first date I've ever had."

Her throat tightened with emotion, and she swallowed before saying, "Right back at you."

And she meant it.

But she wanted to make inroads with her mom this trip. She wanted to mend fences and ease old animosities.

So how would Kushi feel when she discovered her precious daughter was not only shunning her mother's choice of man but had chosen a decade-younger Aussie stuntman to date?

Fifteen

Samira had never been more tempted to head back to the city with Rory and spend the rest of the day with him. But after last night and their leisurely morning, which had morphed into a pretty special first date, she needed some space before she did something silly: like tie him to her bed for the next five months.

She'd been with the guy twice now and shouldn't be feeling this . . . dazzled. She didn't believe in love at first sight or soul mates or any of that romantic crap. But hanging out with Rory made her feel good in a way she hadn't experienced in forever.

The way he'd reacted to her age, like it meant nothing, surprised her. She'd expected a withdrawal of some sort, a hesitation, at worst an excuse to cut short their morning. Instead, he'd held her hand like he didn't want to let go and had been all too keen to share a *falooda*, her favorite Indian drink, at one of the many sweetshops she remembered from childhood, where they'd lingered, laughing over his mispronunciation of *gulab jamuns* and *rasgullas*.

It was so easy being with him. She'd never dated an Aussie guy even though she'd grown up here, because she'd had to concentrate on her studies in high school and uni, and then dated a few of her mom's "suitable choices" before she'd married Avi. Her mom would've burned her best sari if she'd brought an Aussie home back then. Which begged the question, how would Kushi react now?

No way was she ready to find out, so she bade farewell to Rory at the station and headed to her mom's, battling the usual guilt. She'd been so busy at work she hadn't visited all week; though that could have more to do with the fact the few times they chatted on the phone, Kushi kept badgering her about Manish. She had to agree Manish was a nice guy, but considering he'd seen her barf the first and last time they met, she wasn't in a hurry to catch up, no matter how much Kushi insisted.

Parking outside her childhood home, she wondered if she'd done the right thing. Rory had seemed keen to spend the day with her, and dropping him at the station had been tough. How had he gotten under her skin so fast? Before she could second-guess her impulse, she slid her cell from her bag and brought up his number. She could text but had a sneaking suspicion what she wanted to say would come out all wrong. At least if she screwed up while talking to him, he couldn't look back and see evidence of her idiocy in print.

Gnawing on her bottom lip, she hit the "call" button.

"Hello?" His deep voice sent a shiver of longing through her, which was totally crazy considering she'd had her fill of him well and truly last night.

"Surprise." Damn, she sounded too perky and quickly tempered her enthusiasm with a calmer, "I thought it only polite to ring and make sure you haven't been accosted by any punks on the train."

He laughed, and her skin rippled with awareness. "Babe, the train's only just pulled out of the station. Give the gangs a few minutes to pull out their weapons."

"Don't joke about that," she said, hating the thought of anything happening to him. Ludicrous, to care this much about a guy she barely knew, but she couldn't help it. She was smitten. She blamed the phenomenal sex. It addled her brain.

"You started it with that feeble excuse for calling me."

"Can't you give a girl a break?"

"I thought I already did last night." He lowered his voice. "Several times."

Her thighs clenched. "Aren't you remotely interested in how I got your number?"

"From my agent's original referral, I'm guessing. I've been waiting for your call ever since."

"You could've got my number from Pia."

He made a cute snorting sound. "Too icky, mixing business with pleasure."

"Fair point."

"So do you want me to swap trains at the next station and come back? Because like I said, I'm more than happy to extend our first date into an all-day affair that lasts well into the evening . . ." He ended on a seductive purr that made her want to say *hell yeah*, but she really owed her mom a visit. "I like you, Sam, and I'm hoping our first date can extend to another?"

"Only if you're lucky."

She cringed at her flippant response. She'd rung him because she already missed him, and now she sounded like she didn't give a crap.

"You know where to find me," he said, amusement lacing his words like he could see right through her gaucheness. "And now I have your number, so I don't have to pine away if you don't contact me again; I can call you."

"Promises, promises."

She tried to sound seductive. It came out lame, and she resisted the urge to hit her forehead against the steering wheel. "I really did have a good time last night and this morning, and I just wanted you to know that."

"Then we definitely need to do it again soon."

The train must've passed through a tunnel, as reception dropped out for a moment, long enough for Samira to know she had to end this call now, before she did something silly like invite him back to her place again tonight.

"Thanks again, Rory."

"No worries. See you soon."

She hit the "end call" button and slumped back against her seat. Maybe she should've stuck to texting after all, because in trying to say how much she'd enjoyed hanging out with him, she'd ended up sounding like a schoolgirl with a major crush. Not that far from the truth, and she pondered anew how her mature, independent self had reverted to about sixteen on that call just now.

Cringing, she got out of the car and walked up the cracked concrete driveway. As she neared the house, she heard voices from the backyard. Oh no. Her mom wouldn't have . . . would she? Trepidation made her shoulders tense as she rounded the back corner of the house, hoping Kushi hadn't taken matters into her own hands and invited Manish over.

However, when she lifted the latch of the door hanging on

loose hinges and pushed it open, she breathed a sigh of relief. Kushi had just poured chai for Pia and her mother, Sindhu, and three sets of eyes swung her way.

"Samira, my girl, come and have some tea." Kushi beamed, and Samira's guilt increased tenfold. She really needed to make more time for her mom. They'd made a start on mending their relationship the first night she'd arrived back, and she needed to build on that.

"Hey, Mom." Samira strode across the garden and hugged Kushi, who clung to her a moment longer than expected. Yeah, she definitely had to make more of an effort.

"Auntie, so good to see you." She bent down to hug Sindhu, who patted her cheek.

"You naughty girl, you haven't come to see me since you've been back." Sindhu waggled a finger in her face. "Do not turn out like this daughter of mine, all work and no play."

"Wow, thanks for the support, Mom." Pia rolled her eyes, perfectly rimmed with kohl in a way Samira had tried to emulate many times and failed.

"Pia's doing amazing things at the health center," Samira said, squeezing her cousin's shoulder as she slid into the seat next to her.

"Yes, yes, I know," Sindhu said, her praise begrudging while she glanced at her daughter with obvious pride. "She's a good girl."

"And don't you forget it, Mom." Pia tugged on the end of Sindhu's sari, creating a gap between the silk and the choli, revealing a few rolls that indicated her cuddly aunt still favored highly sugared Indian sweets. "Samira's just as busy as me, so leave her alone."

"These hardworking girls . . ." Kushi tut-tutted as she poured Samira a cup of chai. "At least your Pia is married. My Samira needs a good man in her life."

"Mom, I'm right here." Samira waved her hand in front of Kushi's face. She swatted it away.

"Tell her, Sindhu." Kushi poked her sister in the ribs. "She won't listen to me."

Her aunt shot her a fond look. "I'm not interfering. My match-making days are over."

"Thanks, Auntie." Samira blew her a kiss, knowing her mom wouldn't be deterred.

"That Manish is such a nice boy—"

"I'm starving, Mom. Got any snacks?" From years of experience, Samira knew the only way to distract her mother was to mention food, and it worked like a charm when Kushi stood.

"I've got leftovers in the fridge," Kushi said.

"I'll help." Sindhu stood, and the two of them walked toward the kitchen, their heads bent close and muttering something Samira assumed had to do with her lack of a man.

"When are you going to tell them about your boy toy?"

"Stop calling him that."

Pia's eyebrow rose at her snark. "It's a term of endearment."

"His name's Rory, and if you want me to keep you posted on proceedings, you better start using it." Samira feigned nonchalance designed to distract. "Besides, there's nothing to tell."

Samira picked up her chai and took a sip when Pia said, "I saw you two last night."

The chai caught in her throat, and she coughed several times while Pia smirked.

"Where?" she finally managed to get out.

"Leaving the center together, and from your haste and your horny expressions, it looked like you couldn't wait to find somewhere more private."

Samira bit back a grin. "There's no such thing as a horny expression."

"Sure there is, and you two could've been poster models for it." Pia crooked her finger and leaned over. "Quick, tell me everything before the busybodies return."

Samira could fob off her cousin's curiosity, but it was nice having someone to confide in, considering she was in the midst of her first full-blown crush in forever.

"He came back to my apartment, we had amazing sex again, we made Punjabi eggs together, he stayed the night, and I took him for Indian brunch not far from here, then we strolled around Dandenong for a bit."

By the time she'd finished, Pia's eyes were wide and her mouth hung open a tad.

"Wow. Are you two dating?"

The million-dollar question, because in what warped universe did a one-night stand with a decade-younger guy turn into any kind of relationship?

"Sort of."

Pia's eyebrows shot up. "What does that mean?"

Before she could formulate a response, Kushi and Sindhu bustled out of the kitchen carrying a platter each and bearing down on them.

"This conversation isn't over," Pia hissed under her breath. "But for what it's worth, I'm proud of you, Cuz. He's hot."

A blush heated Samira's cheeks as she remembered exactly how accurate that description of Rory was. Hot and then some.

But as she nibbled on a vegetable samosa and listened to her mom and aunt swap gossip about the latest scandal in the local Indian community, she couldn't help but wonder if she was reading too much into this thing with Rory. They may have spent two nights together and had a first date this morning, but they could never have anything more than a fling. And while some lighthearted hookups were exactly what she needed, for the first time in a long time she wondered if her mom had the right idea . . . What would it be like to have more?

Sixteen

The train and tram trip from Dandenong to Carlton took about an hour, giving Rory plenty of time to think. If last night with Samira and the way she'd opened up had been a surprise, this morning had blown him away. She'd come alive as they'd strolled the streets where she'd grown up, her enthusiasm rubbing off on him in a way he hadn't expected. He didn't get excited about much these days, beyond a sexy brunette who'd got under his skin.

He couldn't believe she was thirty-seven. Not that it mattered. He'd been out with women older and younger, and while he'd technically never dated anyone beyond a night or two, he knew none of them came close to Samira.

It irked that they hadn't arranged to meet up again when they parted. He'd hoped she'd say something, because he sure as hell wouldn't. Not that he didn't want to, but he'd become particularly tongue-tied at the station, wanting to articulate how much fun he'd had hanging out with her but lacking the words. But then she'd called, and everything had been okay. They'd both been flippant and teasing, but he knew she wouldn't have called so soon if she didn't feel the same buzz he did.

Spending the night with her had been rare enough for him; hanging out for the entire "morning after" never happened. It had been the best date he'd ever had. It felt so natural, so easy, but that should make him extra wary. The more comfortable he felt with her, the higher chance he'd become a stuttering mess.

Though he wasn't a complete fool. If they continued to hang out like he wanted, he would slip up, and she'd learn his secret. If it happened after he nailed the *Renegades* audition, he'd feel better somehow, like he was more her equal. Because right now, with her job and her lifestyle and her age, she had it all over him, and he felt like he didn't quite match up.

And he hated feeling not quite good enough. He'd had enough of that shit from his dad.

Samira would never deliberately do it, but first would come the pity, then the questions, then the changes: the waiting for him to complete sentences with the slightest hint of impatience, the occasional awkward glance away when he couldn't get a word out, or the worst of them all, trying to finish a word or sentence for him. Fuck, he hated that the most.

So while he had no clue where things stood with Samira, he'd stop overthinking it, and what better place to do that than the rec hall?

Amelia wouldn't be here today, though she dropped in occasionally on a Saturday afternoon like he did to build informal relationships with the kids. Building trust was the first step toward encouraging them to take part in the program once it was up and running. Being migrants and refugees, most of their parents hadn't heard of speech therapy or they viewed health professionals skeptically.

That was where he came in. If the kids bonded with him over shooting a few hoops or kicking a footy, and he opened up about his own therapy, they'd be more likely to welcome Amelia's intervention when the time came.

Pushing open the wire door that led to the courts, he spotted a motley crew of boys and girls aged from eight to sixteen. He knew most of them but spied a few new faces. Out of the group of eighteen, at least six kids could do with speech therapy. Two with stutters, four on the spectrum. Those kids tended to hang back and not engage with the others.

He knew the feeling.

It didn't matter that he'd attended one of the best private schools in the city; kids still mocked the same the world over. It had been easier to shut his mouth than be ridiculed for it, and while he may have been tall and strong for his age when he hit his early teens, it didn't make the bullies back off. If anything, they taunted more, hoping he'd lose his cool and end up fighting. He never had, but most days the punching bag in his workout room at home copped a beating.

He'd been to these courts several times now, and most of the kids knew him, but that didn't make them any friendlier. Considering some had come from war-torn countries and witnessed horrific atrocities, he didn't blame them for their mistrust of adults in general. But he persisted because he wanted them to have every chance of treating their speech impediments.

One of the kids, Davey, a boy of about nine, spotted him and waved. He felt sorry for Davey because Ds were particularly difficult for stutterers, so the simple act of introducing himself to anyone was tough on this kid.

Rory strolled over to the outskirts of the scuffed court where a half-hearted game was in progress, the older kids jostling for position and shooting hoops.

"Hey, Davey, how are you?"

"G-g-good," the kid said, avoiding his eyes like he usually did, as if ashamed of his affliction.

"Shot any hoops yet?"

Davey shook his head, taking any opportunity to use a gesture rather than speak. Rory had done the same at a similar age. It had infuriated his father. But what was the point of speaking when it would earn him a pitiful glance or a sentence finished by someone else? Later, in his teens, he'd let his fingers do the talking, the middle one in particular.

"Want to join in the game?"

Another shake of the head, but Rory caught the longing glance Davey sent the other kids. One of them tripped, and the others laughed uproariously, but it was good-natured as they helped the kid to his feet and continued playing.

"Sure? It looks like fun."

Davey reluctantly dragged his gaze from the kids to focus it on him, and Rory hated the pain in his wide eyes. "I c-c-can't c-call out for the b-ball. It t-takes t-too long b-b-because I t-talk like this. K-k-kids d-don't like it."

Rory's chest tightened, an ache that spread and made him want to rub it away. He knew the desperate yearning to be part of the gang but also the fear of being ridiculed that came with it.

He'd had no friends at school and didn't have any now beyond acquaintances from the movie industry. His fault, for deliberately distancing himself from anyone before they got too close, a relentless cycle of holding people at bay for fear of slipping up, stupid and self-flagellating, because real friends wouldn't give a fuck if he stuttered or not.

But it was all on him. His insecurities, his hang-ups. He knew he had to get past them, and in a way that was what spending time with Samira was about. She was easy to be with, and she liked his quietness rather than pushing him out of it. It gave him time to open up if he wanted to, and he liked having that choice.

"You know Amelia can help with that, right? Once she starts her program, you should join."

Davey shrugged, disinterested, kicking at pebbles under his feet.

"She helped me."

Davey's gaze flew to his. "Really?"

"Yeah, I stutter."

Davey's eyes narrowed in skepticism. "No, you d-don't."

"Yeah, I do. But I did a lot of speech therapy, and Amelia taught me loads of stuff, which means I can control it most of the time."

"Wow." Davey visibly brightened, pulling his shoulders back, standing taller. "I w-want to t-talk like you."

"Work hard with Amelia and you can, buddy." Emotion clogged Rory's throat at the hope lighting Davey's eyes. "Tell the others too, okay? Amelia's really cool, and she has other therapists to work with her too."

"Will you b-be around?"

He hadn't intended to. Rory envisaged handing over the money and only popping in occasionally. But if his presence helped kids like Davey, he'd be here every week if he could.

"Sure, I'll drop in as much as I can when I'm not working," he said, holding up his fist, waiting until Davey did the same and bumped it. "It's going to be okay, mate."

And for the first time since he'd met this kid, he saw that Davey believed him.

He liked bonding with these kids and giving them hope. But it would mean jack if he failed the *Renegades* audition and couldn't come up with the ten grand Amelia needed.

He already knew how important the audition was, but now more than ever he had to nail it. These kids depended on it.

He wouldn't let them down.

Seventeen

Samira may not believe in fate, but that old karma train had pulled into her station.

She stared at the patient referral from an inner-city hospital; in particular, the referring doctor.

Dr. Manish Gomes.

Considering there couldn't be too many doctors in Melbourne called Manish, she assumed this was either a cosmic joke or Manish's way of getting her to contact him.

The patient had postsurgical complications for a fractured tibia and had just left after an intensive session. She'd usually touch base with the referring doctor if a case was particularly involved like this one, but reaching out to Manish seemed like playing right into his hands.

If this was a game, that was. Perhaps this was a coincidence? Busy doctors in city hospitals signed off on referrals all the time; it didn't necessarily mean he'd wanted her to call him. Regardless, she never took shortcuts on patient care, and contacting Dr. Gomes would be the right thing to do.

Blowing out a breath, she picked up the phone and dialed the number on the bottom of the referral. A direct line, considering it didn't match the hospital number at the top of the form. Hoping to leave a message, she waited as it rang five times; voice mail would kick in any moment. After all, what were the odds of actually catching a doctor in his office on a Monday morning?

Odds not in her favor, apparently, when he picked up. "Dr. Gomes speaking."

Her heart sank. She knew the voice. It was him. Mom's Manish, the man of her dreams, whoop-de-do.

"Hi, Manish, it's Samira."

"Hey. So you got my referral?"

So much for coincidences. He'd wanted her to call him, the rat fink.

"I did, thanks. The session went well, but I wanted to touch base to see if you had any other concerns about the patient?"

"No concerns, other than that you didn't call me."

She bit back a grin at his low chuckle. She may not have a spark with this guy, but he had a knack for making her laugh.

"I've been busy."

"You're avoiding me, even though we agreed to be friends."

She had no response, other than *hell yeah.*

"Mondays are manic here at the hospital, but I've got a forty-five-minute scheduling gap in an hour. Want to grab a coffee?"

Samira glanced at her appointment calendar on the screen in front of her. She'd asked the receptionist to block out the afternoon to catch up on paperwork. Yet she hesitated. A guy saying he wanted to be friends and actually being okay with it tended to be miles apart. She'd been through it before, where they'd use friendship as an excuse to get into her panties.

But considering her mom knew Manish, she doubted he'd be that underhandedly sleazy. Plus he didn't give off that vibe. Besides, having a coffee with him would come with an added bonus: she could tell her mom about it and Kushi would lay off . . . for a day or so at least.

"Sure. Where shall I meet you?"

"There's a café in Southbank about halfway between us. Bobbie's. Do you know it?"

"I'll find it," she said. "See you there in an hour."

"Great," he said. "Now I know how easy it is to schedule a coffee date with you after one referral, I'll be sending all my patients requiring physiotherapy to you in the future."

She smiled at his lighthearted flirtation. "You do that, buddy, but this is a one-off. I need a caffeine fix, that's all."

"Keep telling yourself that, Samira."

With another chuckle, he hung up, leaving her staring at the phone, bemused. She didn't think Manish would be persistent, as she'd already made it clear she wasn't interested in him in that way. But maybe she'd given him the wrong idea in calling? If so, she'd set him straight. She had eyes for one guy at the moment, and despite only seeing him on Saturday, she wanted to see him again.

On impulse, she picked up her cell from the desk. After her bungling call last time, she'd stick to texting this time. But when she glanced at the screen, a little red dot glowed above the "message" box. She occasionally checked her cell between patients but had been too busy all morning. It could be her mom or Pia or anybody, but her heart pounded as her thumb stabbed at the little green button and she spied Rory's name above the message.

Her lips eased into a smile as she read the first line: **I MISS U**

The feeling was mutual, and she liked that he didn't play games like some guys, who'd never admit they missed a woman they were dating in a million years. She read the rest of his text.

> U BUSY? I AM.
> BUT NEED TO T UP ANOTHER DATE SOON.
> I'M PINING 4 U.

Samira unconsciously pressed a hand to her heart. It was the most romantic text she'd ever received, and she thought it was cute that he was far more eloquent in text than verbally.

With a big grin on her face, she fired back an answer:

> MISS U 2.
> V. BUSY, WILL B IN TOUCH,
> ANOTHER DATE SOUNDS GR8.

She deleted the two kisses at the end and settled for a loved-up emoji with three hearts floating around a blushing, smiling face, because that was her all over every time she thought about him; warm and fuzzy, like one of those cartoon characters from her childhood with hearts for eyes.

Crazy, because he was all wrong for her. Kushi would not approve of Rory, and a small part of Samira wondered if that was part of the attraction? Before she remembered his startling blue eyes and his lazy grin and his stubble and his muscles and his very impressive . . . No, she liked Rory for a multitude of reasons beyond his obvious attributes.

The sooner she had a quick obligatory coffee with Manish, the better, so she could rejig her calendar and fit in a very important date with the guy who'd piqued her interest without trying.

Here you go, one skinny cappuccino." Manish placed the takeout mug in front of her and sat opposite. "Sure I can't tempt you with one of these?" He picked up a ginormous blueberry muffin and brandished it.

"No, thanks, I'm good." She picked up her coffee. "At least I will be once I drink this."

"Tough morning?"

"Just busy. You know how it is."

"Yeah." He grimaced. "We had a multiple-vehicle pileup on the Ring Road this morning, which meant ER went into overdrive."

"So you're an ER doctor?"

He nodded, those peculiar gray eyes clouding with worry and something else she couldn't identify but looked a lot like guilt. "Yeah, it's stimulating work, but you can't save everyone, and that sucks."

His empathy made her like him a little more. She'd worked with many doctors over the years, and most developed a hardened shell to deal with the constant deaths they saw every day. But she glimpsed real emotion in his eyes, like he seriously cared.

"You love your job."

The corners of his mouth quirked in a wry grin. "Guilty as charged. I'm married to my work, which is as good an excuse as any when my grandmother starts pushing me toward every eligible Indian girl in Melbourne."

She chuckled. "What does your mom think?"

A shadow passed over his face, and he glanced away to stare at the Yarra River several feet from their riverside table. "She died not long after I graduated from uni, and Dad died when I was a kid, so Izzy, my gran, raised me."

So much for light coffee conversation. Samira had put her foot in it. "Sorry to hear about your folks. Does your gran know my mom?"

He nodded. "She lives in Noble Park, so stands to reason they'd cross paths at the many interminable Indian dances."

Samira smiled. "Were you dragged along to those as a kid?"

"Hell yeah," he said, his vehemence breaking the tension as they both laughed. "Izzy would dress me up in a suit complete with vest and make me dance with all the girls in their spangled *salwar kameez*. I hated it."

"The food wasn't bad though," she said, remembering that her passion for samosas often led her to wander through a giant town hall, watching dancers bounce around to Bollywood beats, on the lookout for leftover snacks on tables that she'd snaffle and scoff in the corner. "But the karaoke was the worst."

They laughed in unison, and once again Samira was struck by how nice this guy was. "So what's this coffee date really about, Manish?"

"Blunt, I like that." Respect glinted in his eyes. "And my friends call me Manny."

"So sharing a coffee constitutes friendship?"

"It does." He picked up his takeout mug and tapped it to hers. "Here's to a no-pressure, no-arrangements, no-hookup friendship."

"I'll drink to that," she said, taking a sip of her cappuccino but still thinking this guy was too good to be true.

"Though I'm always up for reviewing our stance on the no hookup?"

He wiggled his eyebrows suggestively, and she laughed.

"I'm seeing someone."

The moment the words tripped from her mouth, she realized how much she liked hearing them. Sure, she and Rory may not have stipulated exactly what was going on between them or established whether they were dating, but she'd like to, and saying it reinforced that.

"Lucky bastard." He took a giant bite out of his muffin, chewed, and swallowed. "Is he Indian?"

"No."

He winced. "Sister, you're in for a world of pain."

"Don't I know it."

They grinned, and she waited until he'd finished another bite before asking, "From your surname, I take it you're Anglo Indian?"

"Yeah. Mom and Dad were Anglo Indians from Goa. Izzy is Goan, too. I was born in Chennai; they migrated here when I was a few months old."

His mixed heritage explained the gray eyes.

"I'm a half-and-half too. You've met Mom, and Dad was American."

"What a spectacular mix it is, if I do say so myself."

They locked gazes and . . . nothing. Not a hint of sizzle or attraction like she had with Rory. Kushi would be disappointed with their lack of spark. Manish was easy on the eyes, had a sense of humor, and was a doctor: perfection in any woman's eyes, but Samira felt nothing but friendship for the handsome medico.

"I have to get back to the center," she said, standing. "Thanks for the coffee."

"Anytime, friend."

She hesitated, unsure whether to bring up her mom's matchmaking but thinking it prudent in case Kushi misconstrued this meeting. "Just so you know, I'm going to tell Mom we met up to get her off my back. So if she tells your gran and they book the wedding reception hall, don't freak out."

He chuckled and stood. "So you're using me as your dating beard. Nice." His eyes twinkled with amusement. "I'll play along, but you know giving your mom a hint of anything between us is going to encourage her."

Samira sighed. "Maybe, or I'm hoping she'll back off with the nightly phone calls where she extols your virtues at great length."

"I am a pretty good catch." He squared his shoulders in a mock superhero pose that had her laughing.

"Then why are you single?"

The amusement in his eyes faded, and he masked it with an exaggerated eye roll. "Because I haven't met the right one, of course."

He sent her a pointed glare, and she held up her hands. "Don't look at me. I'm all wrong for you."

"Pity. Just imagine, we could've had a merging of medical minds." He winked. "And a merging of other parts—"

"Stop right there, mister. Being friends means no lame-ass flirting, got it?"

"Yes, ma'am." He saluted. "And for the record, I'm not interested in you as more than a friend either, but it's fun to wind you up."

"Idiot," she muttered, softening it with a touch on his arm. "Thanks again."

"Anytime."

She watched him stride away, wending his way through Southbank's lunchtime crowds, relieved they'd established a friendship and craving Rory more than ever.

Eighteen

After coffee with Manny, Samira didn't head back to the health center as planned to catch up on paperwork. Instead, she sought the sanctity of her apartment, where she pondered her irrational urge to call Rory while trying to get patient files in order.

Bizarre that she felt disloyal after spending thirty minutes with Manny, and while there was absolutely nothing between them and she'd reiterated that, she still felt like she'd cheated somehow. Totally idiotic.

That was one of the things she'd never been able to fathom about Avi; how he could leave their bed in the morning and go directly to that teenager's place on his way to work. She hadn't wanted to know any of the gory details of his affair, but he'd been almost gleeful when he'd told her the news of his impending fatherhood and that he was leaving her for a nineteen-year-old. Bastard.

She'd been gutted by his cheating and distraught their marriage had ended so soon. It may have taken her a long time to get over it, but Avi had done her a favor. Not being able to give him a baby he so desperately wanted would've ultimately caused a breakdown in their marriage. If he couldn't wait eighteen months for her to fall pregnant before sticking it to another woman, their marriage would've been peppered with infidelities, and she would've hated that.

She'd been young and impressionable and hopeful back then. At thirty-seven, she was older and wiser and wouldn't put up with crap from a guy.

As much as the news of Avi expecting his second child had affected her when she'd found out, she wondered why the long gap between kids. His eldest would be . . . what? Thirteen or fourteen by now? She wouldn't wish reproductive challenges on any couple, but maybe karma had caught up with her philandering ex and baby number two might not have been so easy to conceive?

Hating that she'd allowed thoughts of her ex to intrude, she refocused on her work. However, after staring aimlessly at a patient file for ten minutes, she gave up and shut down her laptop. She knew what would help this strange unease plaguing her.

Seeing Rory.

He made her feel carefree in a way she hadn't experienced for a long time, and right now she could do with some of that. She hoped their second date would be sooner rather than later. She picked up her cell and fired off a text.

MY SCHEDULE OPENED UP.
I'M HOME. U FREE?

She just wanted to spend some time with him, but her text sounded like an invitation for a booty call. Not such a bad idea, but she'd never done anything so brazen.

When his response pinged a moment later, she jumped.

B THERE @3

Glancing at the time in the corner of her cell, she noted she had twenty-five minutes to wait. After firing off a quick GR8, she headed for the shower, where she lathered off her busy morning, shaved her legs, and slathered on body lotion before slipping into a strapless cotton sundress as the buzzer rang.

After instructing downstairs security to bring him up, she paced a few feet, nerves making her tingle with anticipation. She didn't do this, invite guys she'd barely started dating up to her apartment during the day knowing it would end in sex. She didn't lust much as a rule, discounting her crushes on Chris Hemsworth and Tom Hiddleston. But there was a world of difference between fantasizing about unattainable movie stars and having a walking, talking fantasy that knew how to pleasure her exactly right.

A throb between her legs alerted her to why she'd done this. It had only been two days since she'd seen Rory, but she missed him. And she wanted him. Real bad.

A soft knock sounded at her door, and she padded toward it, inhaling and exhaling with every step. When she opened the door, her breath whooshed out of her lungs. Rory. Wearing a tight black T-shirt, black jeans, and a sexy smile that indicated he knew exactly why she'd asked him over.

With a nod of thanks to the security guard, she opened the door wider and waited until Rory had entered before slamming the door and whirling on him.

"Is this what I think it is?" His bold gaze raked over her, and she felt it like a physical touch, as if he'd caressed every inch of exposed skin. "A g-good old-fashioned booty call?"

Looked like she wasn't the only nervous one, and in response she took his hand and led him to the bedroom, anticipation thrumming through her veins.

"Technically, it's our second date, but hey, booty call works for me too," she murmured, letting out a little squeal as he nipped at her neck and palmed her ass.

She wanted this. Wanted him.

All afternoon.

As Rory lay flat on his back, his hands behind his head, staring at Samira's bland beige ceiling, he wished he could de-stress with mind-blowing sex all the time.

If hanging out with the housing commission kids in the morning hadn't been difficult enough, getting a phone call from his agent with the news he'd now be up against one of the biggest reality TV hosts for the *Renegades* gig had really put him in a shitty mood.

Samira's text had been a godsend, and he'd hightailed it to her apartment. He'd expected to sit around, chatting, having a few laughs. He'd hoped for the sex later. To his surprise, she'd skipped the chatter and gone straight for the good stuff. Could she be any more perfect?

"Here you go." She padded back into the bedroom holding two glasses of water, incredibly sexy in a large blue T-shirt with USA emblazoned on the front, which skimmed her upper thighs. "Screaming your name is thirsty work, so I really needed this."

He laughed, more relaxed than he'd been since . . . he had been here on Saturday morning. He shouldn't get used to this. It wouldn't last. But for now he'd enjoy it.

"You're good for my ego," he said, scooting up into a sitting position and accepting the glass of water she held out to him. "And I hate to pick you up on a technicality, but I think you were moaning my name rather than screaming."

"I'll save that for the next round." She smiled and clinked glasses as she slid back into bed beside him. "If only all Monday afternoons could be this good."

"You didn't have any patients booked in today?"

She shook her head. "I had a busy morning but blocked out the afternoon to catch up on paperwork."

"How's that working out for you?"

She ogled his chest in blatant appreciation. "Freaking great."

He chuckled, loving the banter between them.

"How was your morning?"

He gulped the water, draining the glass, giving himself time to compose an answer. While he couldn't tell her the whole truth about why the speech therapy program was so important to him, he could give her a snippet or two.

"I hang out with some kids at the housing commission flats in Carlton sometimes. They have tough lives, and it's good for them to have a mentor."

Her eyebrows rose, her eyes glittering with admiration. "That's pretty cool."

He shrugged, like it meant little, when nothing could be further from the truth; helping those kids master their speech meant everything to him. "I was lucky enough to have a privileged up-bringing, so it's good to give something back. That's why I want to nail the upcoming audition too, so I can help fund some programs for them."

She eyed him like he was too good to be true, and increasingly uncomfortable under her obvious admiration, he changed the subject. "I also got a call that turned my morning to crap."

"What happened?"

"You know how my agent referred me for dialect coaching for the big role I'm up for? Well, Benedict Dixon is up for it too."

She screwed up her nose. "He sounds familiar."

"He's hosted a couple of big reality shows."

"Ah . . . so he's got the edge on you?"

"Shit yeah." Rory sighed. "But I need this role, and I'll do anything I can to score it."

"Things going okay with Pia?"

He nodded, glad they weren't discussing him. Pia had assured him about client confidentiality, but they were cousins and he'd wondered. "She's great. But a million things can go wrong on the day, and I might screw up the audition."

Namely, by his nerves getting the better of him and turning him into a stuttering mess.

"For what it's worth, I have full confidence in you," she said, leaning over to brush a kiss across his lips. "You are amazing."

Feeling ten feet tall with this woman, he said, "Pity I can't audition my prowess."

"Yeah, pity," she murmured, trailing a fingernail from his sternum to his belly button. "Speaking about prowess . . ."

As she tugged the sheet off and slid lower, Rory knew a little afternoon delight was just what he needed to shake off this funk.

For a guy who looked like a movie star and had a body she couldn't get enough of, Rory's insecurities surprised Samira. He rarely talked about his work. Then again, he didn't talk much at all, and she'd dominated their conversations the last two times they'd been together.

As for wanting to help out those kids, if she didn't already like him more than was good for her, a glimpse of his altruism would've tipped her over the edge. Like he just had with his tongue. And his very talented appendage.

"What are you thinking about?" He traced the gap between her brows with a fingertip, where she often glimpsed the start of frown lines. They made her self-conscious. With him, he made her feel so beautiful she didn't care.

"You and your many talents." She wiggled her eyebrows and he chuckled.

"We're pretty great together."

"Yeah," she said, wondering if he meant out of the bedroom too. She didn't want a full-blown relationship, but grabbing coffee with Manny earlier had cemented one thing. She really liked Rory and wanted to spend more time with him. "Speaking of being together, I know neither of us is wanting anything long-term, but how about hanging out?"

"Dating, you mean?"

Loath to make it official but knowing she had to acknowledge they'd be more than "hanging out," she nodded. "Yeah, though I have to warn you, my mom's trying to match me with this Indian doctor, and while we're nothing more than friends, we might cross paths occasionally."

Rather than her declaration intimidating him, an eyebrow arched in amusement. "Sounds like you've already seen him?"

An embarrassed blush flushed her cheeks. "Mom invited him

to my welcome-home party, where I told him I wasn't interested. Then he referred me a patient today and we caught up for coffee."

His other eyebrow rose. "You sure this guy knows you're not interested and that referral wasn't just a sneaky way to see you?"

Flattered by the hint of jealousy in his tone, she shook her head. "I told him I'm seeing someone." She broached the short distance between them to whisper in his ear, "That someone is you."

"And don't you forget it," he said, flipping her onto her back so quickly she squealed.

His hands were everywhere, stroking and caressing, his mouth hot and frantic as it claimed hers, and for the third time since he'd arrived on her doorstep, he pleasured her until she could focus on nothing but him.

When he shifted his weight off her, she rolled onto her side to face him. "I like being with you. A lot."

Too much too soon? Maybe, but he cupped her cheek, his palm warm, while his steady gaze tried to convey a message she hoped she read correctly.

"Same here." He hesitated, as if wanting to say more, before giving a little shake of his head. "I'll be back in a sec."

He pointed to the condom and dropped a lingering kiss on her lips before getting out of bed and striding into the bathroom. The sight of his taut, bare butt had her itching to crawl all over him again once he took care of practicalities.

She'd barely had time to snuggle under the sheets, close her eyes, and replay their last sensual encounter in every glorious detail when his loud "fuck" had her sitting bolt upright at the urgency in his tone.

"What's wrong?"

She wrapped a sheet around her and followed him into the bathroom, grateful he'd turned on the muted mirror lights and not the all-too-illuminating fluorescents. She may be comfortable with him in bed, but she didn't think either of them was quite ready for her thirty-seven-year-old body in the harshest unflattering light.

"Condom broke." He pointed to the discarded rubber in the trash, panic paling his cheeks, accentuating his vulnerability, his age.

"Don't worry." It wasn't like she could get pregnant or anything. "I'm clean and it's not the right time of my cycle."

She actually needed to have a cycle for that to happen.

"I'm clean too," he said, his relief obvious by the return of his trademark smile, the one that made her realize he was naked, they were in a bathroom, and the marble-and-glass double shower stall was less than two feet away.

"We could get cleaner." She sent a pointed look at the shower.

"Great idea."

He whipped the sheet out of her hands before she could blink, bundled her into the shower, and turned the jets to warm.

Make that hot, very hot, as his hands and mouth played her body for all it was worth.

Nineteen

*E*xpanding her physical therapy practice in LA to include alternative therapies had been a goal of Samira's from day one. Her interest in dialect coaching had come from a conversation with Pia years ago, and she'd run with it. She'd had several clients over the last eighteen months, actors and actresses wanting an extra boost for competitive Hollywood roles.

She knew it was a fairly new field in Australia, one that physical therapists were rarely involved in, so when she spied a new referral for a client requiring dialect coaching first thing on Tuesday morning, she was ecstatic. Pity her first referral hadn't worked out. Then again, she'd rather have Rory in her bed than in her office.

Until she glimpsed the name and realized the implications of helping this particular client.

Benedict Dixon.

Well-known host of reality TV shows.

And Rory's biggest rival for the audition he wanted to nail to help those poor kids financially.

Crap.

However, she was a professional, and as she spent the next hour honing Benedict's diaphragmatic breathing and demonstrating techniques using a strong core for voice projection, she focused solely on the job at hand. It wasn't until he'd left her office with a sheet of exercises and another appointment that the guilt set in.

Stupid, because she had nothing to feel guilty about. He'd been referred to her; she had to do her job. Worse, she couldn't tell Rory about it because of therapist-patient confidentiality, and she would never betray her code of ethics. Instead, she had an odd feeling she was betraying Rory.

Needing to off-load to Pia, she stepped out of her office and strode toward the foyer. Only to find Rory and Benedict in some weird standoff, their buffed bodies radiating tension as they acknowledged each other with a tense nod before shifting away.

Samira breathed a sigh of relief when Benedict left, short-lived relief when Rory fixed an accusing gaze on her.

He strode toward her, purpose in his step, thunder in his eyes. "You're coaching that dickhead?"

Bristling, she nodded. "It's my job."

"But you know . . ." He trailed off, his lips compressing into a thin line.

"Know what?"

"He's my rival, and I need to land that gig."

Yeah, she knew, but she didn't need him ramming it down her throat. "I'm a professional. So when a referral comes in, I do my job."

He glared at her like he wanted to say more but couldn't come up with a polite way to do it.

"Is he any good?"

"I can't talk to you about this," she said, shaking her head, hating that he was putting her in this position.

"I need to nail that audition," he said, through gritted teeth, the muscles in his shoulders bunching with tension. "It's vital."

"So you do your best. What's my working with Benedict got to do with it?"

"Benedict," he mimicked, with a scowl.

For a moment, she thought he might be jealous, but that was plain crazy. She'd never sleep with a client, which was exactly why she'd referred him on to Pia in the first place.

"We need to stop discussing this." She held up her hand. "It's got nothing to do with us."

"So there's an us?"

He made it sound like the most outlandish thing in the world, and the tenuous grip she had on her temper snapped.

"Grow up."

He gaped, and she spun on her heel and stalked back to her office, slamming the door for good measure.

Twenty

After his session with Pia, Rory had felt pretty bloody good about himself. He'd nailed every exercise she'd set as homework, and she'd praised him for his enunciation, which was clearer than last week's. So it seemed surreal when he'd seen Benedict Dixon coming out of Samira's office, all smiley and chummy. His momentary surge of jealousy had been stupid, though that hadn't got him half as riled as the moron's usual condescension. His good mood had been eradicated as soon as Benedict opened his mouth.

"What are you doing here, Radcliffe?"

Rory had resisted the urge to punch him in the mouth once before when the guy had made fun of his stutter, yet anytime their paths crossed, the urge returned. "Not much."

The jerk hadn't bought his blasé act for a second. "I'm getting dialect coaching for a big role." He smirked. "Not that you'd know anything about big roles."

"And you do?" Rory barked out a laugh. "Keep telling yourself that, mate."

Anger made Benedict's jaw jut. "I host TV shows rather than waste my time doing he-man stunts."

In the past, Rory wouldn't bother responding. But as he caught sight of Samira staring at them with curiosity, he had to shut this dickhead up once and for all.

"Some of us aren't built for stunt work," he drawled, sending a pointed glare at Benedict's biceps. The guy obviously worked out—he had to, in order to keep landing hosting gigs—but his muscle definition had nothing on Rory's. "And from what I hear, the producers of *Renegades* are looking for someone with an impressive physique."

This time, when Rory laughed in obvious dismissal of Benedict as a threat, he flushed a furious puce. "Brains will always trump brawn."

"So I'm guessing my economics degree might come in handy after all?"

Surprise glinted in Benedict's eyes, before they narrowed with malice. "You're a smart-ass."

"And you're just an ass."

"Fuck you," Benedict muttered under his breath, making Rory's hands curl into fists.

He'd never forgotten their first run-in four years ago, when Rory had plucked up the courage to audition for a speaking part in a local sitcom. He'd avoided speaking roles until then, but Amelia had encouraged him, and not wanting to disappoint her, he'd stepped up.

It had been an unmitigated disaster. His nerves had got the better of him, and every technique Amelia had ever taught him to manage his stutter had flown out the window, leaving him a blathering mess. His humiliation had been witnessed by Benedict, who'd thought it hilarious to mimic him as he'd stridden off the stage, his cheeks burning, his pride shattered.

He'd hated him ever since.

As if nailing the *Renegades* audition hadn't been important enough for the housing commission kids, the moment he'd learned Benedict Dixon would be up for the same role, it had become imperative he land it.

Not that he could tell Samira any of that, and he'd stupidly taken his foul mood out on her. The shock of learning she was Benedict Dixon's dialect coach had shaken him, and he'd behaved like an idiot.

"So there's an us?" had been the dumbest response, designed to hurt her as much as her cool indifference had hurt him.

But hers had been based in professionalism. What was his excuse?

Yesterday afternoon at her place had been phenomenal, and they'd confirmed they were dating. And what had he done? Flung it back in her face like a jerk. He'd been so tempted to go after her and apologize earlier but had needed time to cool down. Bad enough he had a meeting scheduled with his agent to get the latest update on the *Renegades* role hot on the heels of running into his rival; he couldn't afford to show up rattled. So he let her go, giving them both time to cool it before he reached out.

For now, he had to focus and get the lowdown on the biggest role of his career.

He entered the café on South Wharf and spotted Chris, talking on his phone. Chris caught sight of him and waved him over, and as Rory made his way to the table, he wondered how far he could push for information.

He liked Chris, despite them being opposites. Chris was flashy, confident, and garrulous, the perfect pushy agent. He'd intimidated Rory at first, but he'd soon learned in this industry an agent was essential to getting regular work, and he'd appreciated Chris's enthusiasm and dedication to his clients.

When Rory reached the table, Chris hung up and stuck out his hand. "Hey, mate, how's it going?"

"Good."

Rory sat, and a waitress instantly appeared to take their order: a short black for him, a skinny almond latte for Chris. His agent always ordered the weirdest drinks.

"How are the dialect coaching sessions coming along?"

"Great."

Chris chuckled. "You're a man of few words. I hope you're going to say more at the *Renegades* audition."

"Of course."

Rory would recite the alphabet backward a hundred times to guarantee he got the gig.

"You know how I mentioned Benedict Dixon is your biggest rival for the role?"

Rory immediately tensed at the mention. "Yeah."

"Turns out he's not so popular with some of the channel executives at the moment. Something to do with chatting up one of their daughters." He shook his head and wrinkled his nose like he'd smelled something bad. "Anyway, he's going all out to land this gig as a bit of a comeback for him, so just thought I'd warn you to put in as many hours as you can with the dialect coach to get up to scratch."

"Thanks for the tip."

Great, that was all he needed, for the dickhead to be down on his luck courtesy of a screwup and even more determined to land the role.

"The producers are planning on pitching *Renegades* as a mix between *Survivor* and *The Amazing Race*, so if you haven't seen either of those in a while, it wouldn't hurt to put in some study hours and watch some reruns."

"Done."

Looked like he had a date with his TV for a marathon, considering he hadn't watched either show in ages.

Chris snapped his fingers. "One more thing. I've managed to get a look at the audition short list, and to be honest, the other three guys going for it don't have the right vibe. So it looks like it'll be down to you and Benedict, and despite his recent indiscretion, with his track record, he's going to be hard to beat."

"Thanks for the vote of confidence," Rory deadpanned, earning a bark of laughter from Chris.

"I wouldn't have put you up for this role if I didn't think you'd be perfect for it." He held up his clenched hand for a fist bump, and Rory obliged, even though he found the gesture as annoying as his agent's penchant for fancy-schmancy drinks. "You've got this."

Actually, he didn't, and the thought would keep Rory up nights until the audition.

As much as he wanted to reach out to Samira, maybe he should focus on the audition. Watch the reruns. Practice his dialect exercises. Get in the zone.

It didn't sit well that she'd think badly of him, so he'd fire off a curt apologetic text, but for now he had to concentrate on nailing this audition, no matter how much he'd like to be curled up with her once they got past their hiccup.

Twenty-One

So much for getting Kushi off her back. Mentioning she'd had coffee with Manny on Monday ensured Samira had fielded phone calls from her mom every day this week. By Friday night, she'd had enough and needed to tell Kushi the truth.

Considering she hadn't seen or heard from Rory beyond a short text, **SORRY FOR BEING A DICK**—though he hadn't written "dick" but had used an eggplant emoji instead—**AM BUSY, TALK SOON**, since their argument at the center on Tuesday, what exactly was the truth?

She'd thought they were dating, meaning his flyaway jibe "so there's an us?" hurt more than it should. They'd fallen headlong into a few steamy liaisons courtesy of an unforgettable one-night stand, and all that mushy stuff they'd said about dating had probably been nothing more than pillow talk.

Okay, so maybe she was making light of the situation because he'd really hurt her. And she wouldn't be hurting unless she hadn't fallen for him a tad. He'd crept under her skin faster than she could've anticipated, and not seeing him since their verbal altercation had left her grouchy all week.

She'd told Kushi she'd stop by after work around seven, but by the time she'd stopped off at the Punjab sweetshop to grab her mom's favorite *besan laddoos*, it was almost eight when she pulled into the drive. To find both sides of the street jam-packed with parked cars.

It could be one of the neighbors having a get-together, but the moment she stepped from the car and heard the loud bhangra music coming from her childhood home, she knew her mom had ambushed her again.

If Manny was here, it would be the last straw.

However, as she let herself into the house and followed the raucous laughter coming from the family room at the back, she wondered if that would be such a bad thing. That way, she could show Kushi that Manny was nothing more than a friend and to stop meddling. As long as Manny didn't mention anything about her seeing someone . . . That would send Kushi's matchmaking radar into overdrive, and no way in hell would her mom approve of Rory.

She may have given up seeking Kushi's approval a long time ago, but she didn't want them to end up fighting over her choice of man, even for a short-term fling, not when they were tentatively reestablishing some kind of relationship.

As she entered the kitchen and spied a roomful of aunties, she breathed a sigh of relief. No Manny. A relief short-lived when Kushi caught sight of her and bustled toward her, her eyes gleaming. Samira knew what that glint meant: Kushi and the aunties were in full matchmaking mode. Though these gossiping women being here was a surprise. What were they doing here, looking like they belonged? Their bags lay strewn over the floor, knitting spilling from some, while those that weren't squeezed into the sofas were lounging on beanbags they'd struggle to get out of. They looked way too comfortable, and Samira hoped she could encourage her mom to get rid of them ASAP so she could unwind.

"Darling, so glad you came to see your old mother." Kushi enveloped her in a hug, the familiar aromas of fenugreek and coconut oil clinging to her.

"Mom, I thought it would be just you and me tonight," she said, handing over the box of sweets. "It's been a long week, and I want to relax."

"You work too hard, *betee*." Kushi pinched her cheek before opening the box to peek inside. "My favorite. We'll save these for later." She placed the box into a nearby cupboard. "Now come. The aunties didn't have a chance to talk to you at your welcome-home supper. They're dying to hear all your news."

From what she could remember, these women had never been her mom's friends. In fact, Kushi had been an introvert who had preferred cooking for her cosmopolitan neighbors rather than inviting the judgmental Indian aunties around. Samira knew them because they were ever-present at every Indian function, casting their shrewd, beady-eyed glares over everyone, coolly assessing everything from appropriate fashion to potential husbands.

When she'd married Avi, the aunties had been invited, but she'd always wondered why, as they didn't socialize with them. It made Samira contemplate how her mom had become so close to these dominating women that she'd gathered them here to assist with her matchmaking. Particularly as she'd bet they would've alternated between pitying her mom for having such a wayward daughter and gossiping behind her back when Samira had divorced Avi and fled Melbourne.

Mustering a tight smile, Samira entered the family room and made her way along the three sofas, greeting each of the matronly women. Four wedged on each sofa, three sprawled on beanbags, all eyeing her with blatant speculation.

Samira had borne the weight of Indian expectation before. These women had been as delighted as Kushi when she'd agreed to marry Avi all those years ago. None of them were blood related, but each held sway within their large Indian families and beyond. Samira didn't like how many in the local community deferred to them as being doyens of Indian culture. While they'd celebrated her marriage, they'd shunned her just as quickly after her divorce. Never mind that she was the innocent party and Avi was a lying, cheating scumbag. They'd judged her and found her lacking. Escaping the endless pity and stares had been one of the motivating factors in fleeing Melbourne.

After she'd endured the hugs and cheek pinching, she chose a seat in the farthest corner, wishing she could slink out the front door and not look back. She would've loved a glass of wine, but she gratefully accepted a masala chai from her mom, along with a small plate covered in potato *bhondas*.

"Eat. Drink," Kushi said, running a hand over her hair. "You look worn-out."

"That's why I wanted it to be just us tonight, Mom," she murmured, leaning over to add, "How soon can we get rid of the battle-axes?"

Kushi covered a snort of laughter with her hand. "Be nice. All their daughters are married, so they have nothing better to do than interfere."

"Hell," Samira muttered, flashing a grin when the nearest auntie eyed her suspiciously.

The leader of the aunties, a formidable sixty-something woman called Sushma who'd successfully married off her four daughters to a gastroenterologist, an obstetrician, a chemical engineer, and a barrister, respectively, clapped her hands to get everyone's attention.

"On behalf of your aunties, Samira, we would like to say how happy we are to have you back in Melbourne, and how we're willing to do whatever it takes to see you happily married."

Hell, indeed.

Sushma picked up her teacup and raised it as if it were the finest champagne. "We know pickings can be slim at your age, but if you're willing to settle, I'm sure we can come to a beneficial arrangement for both parties, all things considered—"

"Mom, something's burning." Samira stood abruptly, almost upending her *bhondas* in the process and not caring. She couldn't spend one more minute listening to this drivel. "Excuse me, aunties."

She marched into the kitchen without a backward glance, feeling the judgmental stares boring into her back and ignoring the disgruntled mutterings. Didn't these women have anything better to do? And how could her mom let them interfere in her life when she'd effectively turned her back on all this over a decade ago?

It might've been fatigue after a long week at work, it might've been the residual aftereffects of her falling-out with Rory, or it might've been plain old anger at the busybody biddies in the family room, but tears stung her eyes, and she brushed them away with the back of her hand.

She heard a door close before a hand landed on her shoulder.

"I'm sorry, *betee*, you know they can be blunt."

"Rude, more like it," she muttered, turning to face her mom, who appeared surprised by the sheen in her eyes but wisely didn't say anything. "How can you stand it?"

Because Samira knew without a doubt if the aunties had confronted her so soon after not seeing her all these years, they must be constantly giving Kushi grief over her unmarried daughter. Happiness in their community consisted of seeing all their children attend university to gain appropriate degrees before being married off to prosperous partners, followed by becoming grandmothers to equally clever grandchildren.

Samira may be a successful physical therapist and had accumulated a healthy nest egg courtesy of her hard work, but without a man to put a ring on her finger, she was equated with failure. These women had lived in Australia for decades; when would they leave the traditions of the past behind and move into the twenty-first century?

"I tolerate them because I worked hard for their acceptance," Kushi said with a fatalistic shrug. "They belittled me when I married your father, for going against tradition, and I was effectively ostracized." She gestured toward the closed door leading to the family room. "When he died, they surprisingly rallied around me when I needed them most."

A hint of accusation hung unsaid in the air. *I needed them because you weren't around.*

In that moment, Samira understood. She'd virtually abandoned her mom not long after her dad's funeral. Not because she couldn't cope with the sly stares and gossip mongering but because deep down a small part of her still blamed Kushi for the fiasco that had been her marriage. But in hanging on to her resentment, she'd left Kushi alone at a time her mom needed her most. She should be ashamed of herself. She'd been selfish, fleeing back to LA to nurse her own grief, oblivious to her mom's.

"I'm sorry, Mom," she said, enveloping Kushi in a hug. She didn't need to elaborate, and they clung to each other for a while before Kushi eased away, dabbing at her eyes with the corner of her sari.

"I'll get rid of them so we can talk."

"That'll be nice," Samira said. "Tell them I'm on a call and can't say goodbye."

"I didn't teach you to lie." Kushi waggled her finger, but a smile tugged at her mouth. "But after what that tactless Sushma said, I'll gladly do it."

They shared a conspiratorial smile before Samira ducked out of the kitchen and into her childhood bedroom to wait out the interminable farewells. She knew it would take a while, as Kushi exhorted her guests to take home any leftover food and the aunties pretended to refuse but would leave with foil-wrapped parcels regardless.

She closed the door and reached for the light switch, illuminating a virtual time warp.

Nothing had changed.

Emotion welled in her chest as she spun a slow three-sixty, taking in the batik bedspread, the bookshelves crammed to overflowing, the anatomy textbooks stacked in a corner. She'd favored a yellow-and-white color scheme in her teens, with fake bunches of daisies and daffodils in tall vases bracketing either end of her desk, where she'd spent countless hours poring over online study guides for her physical therapy exams.

Taking a deep breath, she opened the wardrobe, not surprised to see a rainbow-colored *salwar kameez* pushed to one side. Kushi had bought her one every six months in the hope she'd change her mind about wearing Indian garb, but she never had; it hadn't stopped her mom from buying more.

Slamming the door shut, she whirled back to face the room, unprepared for the flood of nostalgia that made her want to crawl under the covers and hide out for a week.

She'd lived at home until her marriage to Avi and hadn't set foot in this room since the night before her wedding. When they'd separated, she'd rented a tiny one-bedroom flat in Carnegie until she'd fled Melbourne altogether, so being here thrust her back to a time she didn't welcome.

She'd been starry-eyed that last night in here, dreaming of having a happily ever after with her Bollywood prince. Avi had been so suave, so self-assured, she'd never doubted they would have a wonderful marriage. After all, she'd been the one against it from the start, bucking tradition and her mom's choice of groom, only to be wooed by his persistence and charm.

She'd been a virgin before she'd married, so she had spent her last night in this room hot and bothered, dreaming about her first time with Avi. She'd been so naive for twenty-two, her head filled with romantic notions and unobtainable fairy tales.

She may have blamed Kushi for pushing her toward Avi, but she'd also blamed herself for being so caught up in the whirlwind that she hadn't stopped to question anything. She'd sugarcoated Avi's faults, labeling his arrogance as confidence, his sleaziness flirtatious, his selfishness self-assuredness. He'd professed to love her, and she'd believed him, because for the first time in her life she'd felt a part of something bigger, embraced by the Indian community that had often eyed her sideways for the simple fact she had an American father.

She'd hated their stupid reverse racism, and the aunties her mom had ushered out the door had been a big part of that. Having her mom admit they'd ostracized her when she'd married someone outside her culture made sense of why they never socialized with her family. She'd assumed Kushi preferred being at home, but to learn the real reason . . . it made her mad. Especially as Kushi had turned to them in her hour of need because her own daughter hadn't been around.

Her mom may have embraced them after her dad died because she felt alone, but Samira couldn't imagine these judgmental women would've been truly supportive. She couldn't remember them being at her dad's funeral or his wake. Then again, her mom had wanted to keep both private, and only her parents' closest friends had attended, her dad's mostly. Nobody apart from Sindhu and Pia had attended from her mom's circle. And Samira had been too wrapped up in her own grief to find out why.

Craving a glass of wine more than ever, she edged the bedroom door open and listened. Farewells faded down the corridor, and when she heard the familiar creak of the front door as it shut, she breathed a sigh of relief and exited the bedroom.

"You can come out now," Kushi said. "They're gone."

Samira didn't want to delve too deeply into her mom's friendships. It was none of her business, because as Kushi had said, these women had been around for her when Samira hadn't. But she needed to make it clear she wouldn't stand for any interference regarding her love life while she was in town, and the sooner Kushi conveyed that message to the Bollywood battle-axes, the better.

"I'll make some fresh chai," Kushi said, linking her arm through Samira's. "Or would you prefer something stronger after that ordeal?"

Samira smiled, knowing her mom didn't drink but would have a ginger wine stock, her dad's favorite.

"Chai is fine." She leaned into her mom, glad for their renewed closeness. She hadn't expected Kushi to take her side in what just happened. In fact, when she'd walked in on the aunties, she'd suspected an ambush.

But she'd been wrong, and having Kushi stand up for her meant a lot. It gave her hope that once she came clean about Manny, her mom would take the news well.

"I can do it," she said, moving toward the cupboard above the stove where Kushi stocked her spices.

She'd learned how to make masala chai from a young age because she loved the tantalizing aroma of crushed cinnamon, cloves, and cardamom when they simmered together with pepper, nutmeg, star anise, and tea leaves. Kushi made her own blend by grinding the spices together and kept them in a small red-and-gold tin with a sizable dent in it. Samira had mentioned replacing it once, but her mom wouldn't hear of it. In fact, she'd become quite upset, so she'd backed down.

"You sit. I'll make it," Kushi said, guiding her toward a chair at the small dining table where they'd shared so many meals over the years. "You look tired. Is Pia working you too hard?"

Samira knew the dark circles under her eyes she'd tried to hide with concealer were a result of losing sleep over her stupid argument with Rory rather than working too hard, but one revelation at a time. She'd come here to discuss Manish. She doubted Kushi could cope with learning about Rory too. Not that there was much to tell anymore.

"I'm enjoying the work," she said. "I've even got a client requiring dialect coaching, which is part of my specialized field back in LA."

She'd almost said "back home" but stopped herself at the last moment. Kushi may have understood her desire to leave her home city, but she never approved and often badgered her into returning during their phone calls.

"And what about Manish? Have you seen him again since your date?"

Great, her mom had given her the perfect opening to segue into the discussion they had to have.

"No, Mom. And it wasn't a date."

"You spent time with him; it is a beginning," Kushi muttered, pouring the steaming chai into two cups before waddling toward the table and setting them down. "He is a lovely man and so perfect for you—"

"I've heard those exact words from you before, Mom, and they turned out to be untrue."

A blush stained Kushi's cheeks as a frown creased her brow. "Manish is nothing like that horrid Avi."

Samira agreed, but she needed to put a stop to her mom's matrimonial hopes once and for all. "How do you know? Did the aunties extol his virtues and you believed them?"

Kushi tut-tutted. "Leave the aunties out of this."

"No, Mom, because we need to have this conversation, and it's long overdue."

The frown between her mom's perfectly threaded brows deepened. "No good can come of dredging up the past."

"This is about the future." Samira laid a comforting hand on her mom's forearm. "I like Manish. He is lovely. But there's no spark between us and we both know it, so we've agreed to be friends."

Disappointment clouded Kushi's eyes. "But love can grow—"

"Mom, it's not going to happen. Last time, I got swept up in a fairy tale and living up to expectations. This time, I'm older and wiser and will choose my own men, okay?"

"Men?" Kushi shook her head and slipped her forearm away to fold her arms across her chest. "You should be past the dating stage. You should be looking toward the future." Her glance slid away. "What about babies—"

"Enough." Samira held up her hand, ignoring the inevitable twinge of pain whenever the subject of children came up. Her mom knew how difficult it had been for her trying to conceive, and those problems would only be exacerbated now because of her age. "The only reason I told you about meeting up with Manish for coffee is so you would back off. Instead, he's all you've talked about for the last week when we've chatted on the phone. So from now on I'd appreciate if you don't push it, okay?"

Kushi's lips compressed in a mutinous line Samira had seen many times before. Her mom wouldn't give up until Samira had a shiny gold band on the ring finger of her left hand. "Friendship can grow into love, but you need to be open to it."

Samira sighed and reached for her tea. Sipping the fragrant brew should soothe her. It didn't, because the moment her mom had mentioned being open to love, an image of Rory popped into her head, and she knew all the chais in the world wouldn't dislodge it.

Twenty-Two

As Rory strode out of Pia's office for the last time, he knew he had to get his nerves under control or he'd be shot at the audition in two hours.

He had this. Pia had said as much. They'd worked their asses off, and he had to admit his confidence had skyrocketed as a result. But all the dialect exercises and practice in the world couldn't change one salient fact.

He had to get up in front of a camera and recite from a script without stumbling.

Hard enough for anyone without a speech impediment, but for him? No matter how hard he tried, he couldn't forget the first and only time he'd done this before, when Benedict Dixon had been witness to his humiliation. And now the dickhead would be present again, though this time he wouldn't see it firsthand; Chris had assured him of that. This role was too big and nothing like the bit part of his first audition where it had been an open set.

Two hours. One hundred and twenty minutes to get his head in the game.

Which meant of course he'd run into Samira.

He'd managed to avoid her and clamp down on the urge to call her since he'd sent that pathetic apologetic text after their confrontation two weeks ago. Once the audition was done, he'd planned on saying sorry in person. But until then, he had to focus.

She stiffened when she caught sight of him in the dimly lit corridor, her hesitation giving him a chance to study her. Man, she looked even hotter than he remembered, with those big hazel eyes and tousled brunette bob and curves he remembered all too well highlighted by a simple black knee-length dress.

Nailing this audition was imperative, and putting their fledgling relationship on hold had been part of his preparation, but seeing her again acted like a sucker punch to the gut, leaving him winded and slightly breathless.

"Hey," he said, raising his hand in a casual wave, relieved when she crossed the short distance between them.

"How are you?" One of her eyebrows rose, as if daring him to give some trite response.

"Nervous as hell," he said, the truth spilling from his lips, but he didn't care. Nothing he said now would change the fact he had to nail the audition of his life in two hours and he'd treated this gorgeous woman appallingly because of it.

"The audition's today," she said. A statement, not a question. Then again, she'd already know, considering she'd been helping Dixon. But he couldn't think about that now. It would only derail his carefully prepared mental plan to deal with the upcoming audition.

"Yeah, I'm heading home to change, then going to the studio."

"Good luck," she said, sticking out her hand for him to shake it like some goddamn acquaintance.

"Thanks." He took her hand and tugged, her body slamming flush against his as he covered her mouth with his.

She gasped in surprise, and he took advantage of it, his tongue seeking out hers, elated when she gripped his shirt and pushed him up against the nearest wall like she wanted to clamber all over him.

He groaned a little, or that might've been her, as the kiss deepened. Hot. Long. Sexy as hell.

She broke it off, her breathing ragged as she smoothed down his shirt where she'd bunched it before stepping away.

"That's one hell of a good luck wish," he said with a grin.

"I should be mad at you." She thumped his chest. "And I have been. But I know this audition is important to you, and I hope you kill it."

"Thanks."

He wanted to tell her everything right then. Why the money from this job was so important, why the housing commission kids needed the speech therapy program, why he empathized.

But he had to get his head back in the game, starting now.

"Pity you didn't sabotage my rival."

Predictably, shutters descended over her eyes. "He's a client, so you know I can't discuss him with you."

"Yeah, I know." He swiped a hand over his face. "Sorry for being a schmuck."

A soft sigh escaped her lips. "I'm guessing you have reasons for overreacting the way you did to me coaching him, and for avoiding me after that amazing afternoon we spent together at my place, but I'm too old to play games."

She brushed a soft kiss on his cheek. "I really do wish you all the best with the audition."

With that, she left him standing in the corridor, torn between wanting to run after her and run from her as fast as he could because of the unexpected feelings rioting through him.

Twenty-Three

I am so sick of you using me," Manish said, with a wink as he puffed out his chest. "The least you can do if you're going to treat me as a plaything is use me for my body."

Samira rolled her eyes but smiled nonetheless. "You're an idiot."

"But you like me anyway, huh?" He wiggled his eyebrows, and she barked out a laugh.

"You know what this lunch is about, so behave." She grimaced. "My mom doesn't need the slightest sign of encouragement."

"Relax, I've got this." He held up his hand to count off points on his fingers. "No flirting. No meaningful eye contact. No touching. No encouraging. No problem."

If only it would be that easy. Samira had facilitated this lunch to prove to her mom once and for all there was no future with Manish beyond friendship. Because despite their chat after the aunties debacle, Kushi had persisted in calling her every night, and the conversation eventually steered in the direction of Manny being marriage material.

She'd had a gutful.

As if she wasn't nervous enough about this lunch, she'd had to run into Rory just before leaving the center. Considering his lack of contact, she should've slugged him. She'd almost convinced herself their interlude meant nothing and chalked it up to a little homecoming fling. But seeing him again had blown that preconception, as her body flooded with heat at remembrance of exactly how great her home-*coming* had been each and every time they got together.

Then he'd kissed her as if to prove it, and she'd been a goner. She still wanted him as bad as ever. But she'd been right about one thing: she was too old to play games, so she'd let him get whatever audition funk was plaguing him out of his system, and if he wanted to contact her after that, he knew where to find her.

First, she had a lunch to endure.

"What are you thinking?" Manny tapped her temple, and she swatted his hand away.

"How I'm an idiot for entrusting such an important task to a joker," she said, eyeballing him.

He laughed and held up his hands. "I'll be good, promise."

"You better be, otherwise this friendship is over." She poked him in the chest. "Seriously, my mom has to get the message to stop meddling after this."

"Don't worry. I've got this. Moms love me."

"That's what I'm afraid of," she muttered, as they entered a café not far from her apartment.

She would've preferred having lunch there before realizing that would send Kushi mixed messages: insisting Manish was a friend while inviting him to a cozy lunch for three at her place. So she'd settled on impartial ground, and this way, if things got too tense, she could make a break for it.

"There's your mom," Manish said, placing a hand in the small of her back before realizing how that looked and dropping it. "Sorry," he murmured. "Force of habit being a gentleman."

"I am in so much trouble," she muttered, deliberately putting some distance between them as they made their way toward the back table she'd reserved where her mom currently had her nose buried in the menu.

When she reached the table, she said, "Hi, Mom," and bent down to kiss her cheek.

"My darling," Kushi said, standing and enveloping her in a hug, while murmuring in her ear, "He's so handsome and tall—"

"And you know Manish," Samira said, breaking the embrace before her mom could extol the virtues of Manish any longer.

"Hello, Auntie." Manish stepped forward and took her mom's hands, squeezing them tight, before releasing. "It's good to see you."

"And you, Manish. How is your grandmother?"

"She's doing well, thanks for asking."

The overt politeness made Samira grit her teeth as they sat, and an awkward silence descended.

"Samira tells me you two caught up for coffee a couple of weeks ago," Kushi said, her beady-eyed stare swinging between the two of them, looking for the slightest hint of anything beyond friendship.

Manish nodded. "That's right. I referred a patient to her, so it was a professional melding of minds."

"Oh."

Kushi visibly deflated, and Samira bit back an inane giggle.

"Yet she invited you to lunch today?" Kushi squared her shoulders, preparing for matrimonial battle. "And with her mother, no less."

"Mom, as we've already discussed, Manny is a friend."

"Manny?" The glint in her mom's eyes showed she'd plow on undeterred. "You have a sweet nickname for him already?"

"All my friends call me Manny," he said, and Samira shot him a grateful glance. "Your daughter is lovely, Auntie, and we're becoming good friends, but that is all."

Samira almost felt sorry for her mom as the light in her eyes faded. "Friendship can be the start to so much more—"

"Not in this case, Mom."

"But I don't understand . . ." Kushi shook her head. "You two make such a great couple."

As Kushi's lower lip wobbled, Samira realized this lunch wouldn't solve anything. Her mom wouldn't give up until Samira told her the truth. She didn't want to. It would only make things worse, ramping up her mom's badgering to monstrous proportions.

But it was wrong to try to involve Manny in this. He was a good guy; just not the guy for her.

"Mom, I'm seeing someone."

Kushi's eyebrows shot up. "Who? Do I know him? Does he have a good job? Do I know his family?"

"Oh boy," Manny muttered, and when Samira met his gaze, they burst out laughing.

"What is so funny?" Kushi tut-tutted. "I am an old woman. You shouldn't keep secrets from your mother." She waggled her finger. "Tell me about this man."

"That's my cue to leave." Manish stood and clasped Kushi's hands again. "Auntie, your daughter is a smart woman. I'm honored to be her friend, but she can make her own decisions when it comes to men."

Samira wanted to hug Manny as her mom gaped, not used to being chastised by her choice of prospective groom.

"Thanks, Manny," she said, standing to give him a quick hug. "And I owe you lunch since you won't get to eat this one."

"Call me," he said, with a smile, before mouthing, "Good luck."

"I'm going to need it," she said softly, before turning back to find Kushi watching their exchange with a strangely smug expression.

"What, Mom?"

"Protest all you like, but you two are good together." She added an emphatic nod. "I just know it."

Sighing, Samira said, "Mom, do you want to come back to my place so we can talk? We can order takeout."

"Fine," Kushi said. "Why don't we take some of those vegetarian focaccias back to your apartment?" She pointed at the glass display. "That way we won't waste time deciding on food and you can tell me all about this mystery man."

"Okay."

As Samira placed their orders and paid, she hoped to God she'd done the right thing in deflecting Kushi's attention off Manish by bringing up the guy she was sort of dating.

Because she had a feeling her mom wouldn't understand her infatuation with Rory, not one little bit.

Y ou haven't lost your chai-making skills," Kushi said, draining her cup before placing it back on its saucer. "Do you drink it often in LA?"

Try never, but Samira would keep that gem to herself. "I'm usually too busy, so I grab takeout coffees."

Kushi shook her head, her eyes narrowing slightly in judgment. "You young people are in too much of a hurry. Rushing here, rushing there, little wonder you don't have time for finding a husband—"

"Mom, has it ever occurred to you that my experience with Avi scarred me so badly I may never want to get married again?"

Kushi's lips compressed in tight disapproval.

Samira sighed, softening her approach. "I haven't had a serious long-term relationship since Avi. In fact, the longest I've lasted is four months, and that's with a guy I broke up with just before coming home."

"Four months?"

Samira shouldn't find her mom's incredulity funny, but Kushi's expression was a mix of shock, dismay, and sadness.

"He wanted to move in together, but I didn't love him, so I ended the relationship. That's why I'm enjoying my current situation with Rory."

"Rory?" Predictably, Kushi zeroed in on the one fact hinting at his cultural background. "Rory does not sound Indian."

"That's because he's not," she said, adding a spoonful of sugar to her chai when she usually didn't take it; anything to sweeten the mood. "He's Australian."

"Aiy, ya, ya." Kushi gripped the table so tight her knuckles stood out. "I have a bad feeling about this."

"Well, I don't, because he's sweet and fun to be with and exactly what I need."

"But there's no future." Kushi gave the table a little shake for emphasis, sloshing chai from Samira's cup into a saucer. "Why waste your time?"

"How do you know there's no future?"

The moment the question slid from her lips, Samira felt guilty. She shouldn't raise her mom's hopes. Of course there could never be a future with Rory. They were too different, the age gap too great, and they lived on opposite continents. But she didn't like having her choice dismissed so summarily. It wasn't like her mom's choice last time had been so great.

Kushi released the table to reach over and clasp Samira's hands in hers. "*Betee*, I don't want you going through the same hardships I did."

Of all the things her mom could've said, she hadn't expected that. "What do you mean?"

Kushi's gaze slid away, furtive, before she shifted in her seat, squaring her shoulders as if coming to a decision. "Why do you think I only considered Indian men for your first marriage and I persist in pushing you in Manish's direction now?"

Samira had always assumed it had been about tradition, but by her mom's downcast expression, there was more to this.

"You're very culturally aware, Mom. Tradition is important to you, so isn't that why?"

Kushi shook her head, her mouth downturned in sadness. "I loved your father, I truly did, but I often wonder if I made the right choice in defying my parents by marrying him. If I'd known how cast-off I'd be . . ."

Her mom made an odd garbled sound, halfway between a sob and a choke. "I already told you about the aunties, but back then it felt like the entire Indian community shunned me. They judged my choice and found me lacking. And in those days, locals weren't so welcoming of foreigners, so being cast out of my social circle left me with no friends, no family apart from Sindhu, and treated like a leper by the people I'd come to depend on."

"That's why you invited all our neighbors over for meals." Samira squeezed her mom's hands, hating the overt pain evident in every crease of her lined face. "I always wondered why you interacted with virtual strangers more than the aunties. And we didn't socialize with them much beyond the big functions." Samira hung on tight to her mom's hands. "I thought you were introverted. I wish I'd been more observant and less self-absorbed."

"I didn't want you to see my pain." Kushi managed a wan smile. "You were my world, and I didn't want you to suffer their judgment like I did. Love isn't enough in the face of ostracism like that, and while I adored your dad, I didn't want that for you. It is easier, culturally, if marriage partners come from the same background, and that's why it is preferable you have an Indian husband."

While she understood her mom's rationale, she didn't agree with it, because Samira had felt just as isolated as her mom growing up. She'd watched the aunties dote on one another's children at functions and always wondered why she'd been on the outside. Her school had been multicultural, and she'd craved friends with a mixed Indian background like her, but the aunties' daughters had virtually ignored her. It all made sense now, but she needed to couch her objections carefully.

"I understand you're coming from a position of caring, Mom, but things are different now. Intermarrying is common, especially here in Australia and the US."

Kushi's eyebrows rose, and shock made her reel back. "You're thinking of marrying this Australian man you barely know?"

Samira sighed. "No, but I told you about him so you understand once and for all that I won't bow to expectations again like I did the first time around."

Kushi's expression fell further, if that were possible, as she released her hands. "But I thought you were happy with Avi. You seemed so in love."

"Honestly? I think I was more in love with the concept of being in love rather than any real, deep-seated emotion for Avi." Samira shrugged, as if how far she'd fallen for Avi meant little when in fact

she'd been gutted when their marriage fell apart. "I wanted the Bollywood fairy tale, and I thought I'd got it. But being pushed toward
Avi all the time, having you wax lyrical about his many good traits
even before I'd met him, built him up in my head so it almost
seemed inevitable I'd fall for him."

"You are still blaming me." Tears filled Kushi's eyes, and Samira's
throat tightened with emotion.

"No, though I have to admit I did for a long time, and that's a
major reason why I stayed away for so long. But I understand now.
You did it from a place of genuine caring, not wanting me to go
through what you did."

Ironically, she had anyway, as the Indian community had
looked down on her for divorcing Avi almost as if it had been her
fault. Her new start in LA had a lot to do with feeling alienated
within her community, and she hadn't looked back. So why did her
mom think she'd welcome being dragged back into all that traditional expectation rubbish now?

"I hope you understand, Mom, there's no future with Manish
beyond friendship, and you need to let me live my life the way I
want to and with whoever I choose to live it with."

Kushi visibly deflated, her shoulders slumping, her torso appearing to fold in on itself, as if all hope had been driven from her.
"I don't understand, Samira, but I will respect your wishes."

"Thanks—"

"But you need to know I wasn't joking earlier when I said love
can grow from friendship, so I will continue to hope you see sense
and pursue a relationship with that lovely Manish."

Samira bit back a laugh. Of course her mom wouldn't give up.
But for now, with their revelations and some kind of acceptance, it
would have to do.

Twenty-Four

Rory arrived for the audition thirty minutes early. Interesting that the small, nondescript studio tucked away in the back streets of South Melbourne held the key to his future. More to the point, the future of those poor kids.

But he couldn't think about that now; it would only add to the pressure already building in his chest. He sat in the car, practicing the breathing techniques Pia had shown him, knowing it would be easier to calm his nerves here, alone, rather than inside the studio. Besides, the last thing he needed was to run into Dixon; that would undermine his meager confidence completely.

He'd been riding high after his final session with Pia, then he'd seen Samira, kissed her, and his concentration had been shot to shit. He'd been right to avoid her the last two weeks; she was a major distraction, wrapped up in one very attractive package.

But after this audition, he had every intention of making up for lost time with her.

With five minutes to spare, he strode into the studio, relieved to see the waiting area empty. Chris had warned him both the producer and the director would be at the audition, and he'd have to read from cues. He'd been relieved to hear that. Reading was much easier for him than ad-libbing. Less chance to stumble and screw up.

He'd done everything Chris had asked of him, down to wearing a more casual outfit of jeans and a chambray shirt rolled up at the cuffs—the perfect *Renegades* host attire, apparently.

It should've given him more confidence. It didn't, because as the studio door opened and a hipster guy with a too-long beard and shaved head beckoned him inside, every single technique he'd learned from Pia over the last few weeks faded into oblivion, leaving him light-headed and unsure.

However, as he entered a small room, with a stage and a cue machine at the front, and only two men in their forties sitting and facing the stage, an odd thing happened.

He didn't have to perform in here. He didn't have to try too hard. He had to channel everything he'd learned and just be himself.

"Thanks for coming in, Rory." The director, a seasoned veteran of a long-running Aussie soap opera, stood and extended his hand. "I'm Sherman Rix, and this is Allan Stuart."

"Nice to m-meet you."

Dammit. Rory felt the blood surge to his face at his stumble, but thankfully, neither man reacted, probably putting it down to nerves.

"Take a seat, Rory," Allan said, shaking his hand too. "We like to have an informal chat first."

The heat in his cheeks intensified. So much for reading off a cue then getting the hell out of here. He'd been naive to think this audition would be easier without having to learn lines. Or maybe he'd tried to downplay the possibility of curveballs to clamp down on his nerves.

Whatever, he was so screwed.

"You come highly recommended for this part." Sherman swiped at an electronic tablet, probably skimming his CV. "Chris is a respected agent."

"We've worked together for a few years now," Rory said. "He's a good guy."

Sherman's impressive bushy brows drew together. "Yet he hasn't put you forward for any speaking parts before this?"

Shit. Here came that first curveball. So he trotted out his prepared spiel in case he was faced with this very question.

"I've preferred stunt work to give me a good grounding in the industry. I've always been better at hands-on learning."

"Admirable," Allan muttered, eyeing him with speculation. "So why would an economics major who graduated top of his year at university choose to do stunt work instead?"

Another question he'd prepared for, phew. "Because movies are magical, and driving cars at top speed beats sitting behind a PC all day."

Sherman laughed. "Ain't that the truth."

Approval glinted in Allan's eyes. "I'm an accountant myself but couldn't stand working a nine-to-five job behind a desk for more than six months."

"So how did you get into this business?"

Allan grinned. "Shouldn't we be asking you the questions?"

Rory hesitated, hoping he hadn't screwed up, but the men laughed again.

"Relax, Rory, we're just messing with you. Having this kind of informal chat is exactly what we wanted, to see how personable you are, how you'll come across chatting to the contestants on the show, that kind of thing."

Trepidation tightened his throat. "So there'll be a lot of that on the show?"

He'd spent endless hours watching every *Survivor* rerun he could, taking note of exactly how much talking the host had to do. It had been comforting to see that the bulk of it was left to the contestants, with the host mainly introducing the challenges and asking brief questions at the tribal council. He'd envisaged *Renegades* being similar.

"You'll be reading from cues mostly, as we've found it's easier to have scripted reality than a free-for-all," Sherman said. "But you'll be filming in the outback for months at a time, so we'd be foolish to choose a host who couldn't interact with the crew and contestants socially as well."

"Makes sense."

Rory grew uncomfortable under the scrutiny as both men continued to study him.

"You certainly have the look we're after," Allan said, staring at him with cool, impartial assessment. "Strong. Rugged."

"Uh, thanks," he said, as Sherman snapped his fingers.

"Don't get us wrong, Rory, we're not going to objectify you, but it doesn't hurt when the host looks like you and wears tight T-shirts to draw in a greater female audience."

He tapped his tablet screen. "From our research, this kind of outback reality show tends to attract predominantly male viewers, and we want to broaden our audience."

Being told to wear tight T-shirts to accentuate his pecs and biceps sure sounded like objectification to him, but if it meant landing this role and a healthy paycheck, the tighter the better.

"It also helps that you have stunt experience," Sherman said. "Where we're filming, in far north Queensland, can be a challenging environment, and we want a host who's . . . how can I say this politely . . . not too precious?"

He must've looked confused, because Allan added, "Some industry types, especially in hosting roles, can be all about ego, and we want someone down-to-earth."

Rory nodded and bit back a smile. They could've been describing Benedict Dixon to a tee. He'd been dreading this informal chat at the start of it, but it looked like he'd impressed without trying or having to say too much.

"Do you have any questions for us?"

He'd prepared these carefully and rehearsed them out loud in front of the mirror so felt confident in asking.

"How soon will filming commence?"

"Location scouting will take place soon, with actual filming starting about six weeks later, though our timelines are fluid and prone to change," Allan said. "Will that be a problem?"

"No, not at all."

So much for spending more time with Samira. It looked like their fledgling romance was destined to fail no matter how much he wished otherwise.

"And how long will I be on set?"

"We expect the filming of all episodes to wrap up within three months, giving us time to do extensive editing before it screens."

"Okay." Rory nodded, trying to project enthusiasm when being holed up on a set in the middle of nowhere and forced to make small talk with crew for three months seemed like a life sentence. "Sounds good."

When he didn't ask anything further, Sherman said, "Great. Ready to read for us?"

"Absolutely."

This, he could do. Relieved he'd got through the first part of the audition fairly unscathed, he strode onto the stage and faced the cue machine.

"Ready?" Allan asked, and when Rory nodded, he hit a button that started the cues rolling.

He'd done this very thing with Pia in her office, reading off giant cards, so he soon slipped into the role, injecting the right inflections into his voice, controlling his breathing, allowing the words to free flow without halting.

He had no idea how long he read for, but every time he glanced at the men, they appeared to be leaning forward, wearing matching approving expressions, so he took it as a good sign.

When the cues rolled to an end, he exhaled softly, surprised at how relaxed he felt. The tension had left his spine, and the slight viselike pain at the base of his skull had vanished.

Applause rang out and both men stood.

"That was great, Rory," Sherman called out, and Allan added, "Impressive."

"Thanks," he said, stepping off the stage and heading toward them.

"We're making a decision shortly, so you'll hear from Chris later today."

"Great." He shook their hands. "Thanks for the opportunity."

"I'm sure we'll be seeing you again," Sherman said, and Rory wondered if he imagined the meaningful glance the two men exchanged before he headed for the door.

He had a good feeling about this, but he wouldn't be counting his dollars until he got the call from Chris.

Until then, he needed a distraction.

He knew just the person to provide it.

Twenty-Five

After lunch with her mom, Samira headed back to the health center. She had a stack of patient files to catch up on. Her most loathed task, usually; she'd much rather be treating patients than writing about them. But the monotony of it would be a welcome distraction after the chat with her mom. She really hoped she'd finally got through to Kushi, but she doubted it. Her mom may profess to understand, but she'd seen the gleam in her eyes after she'd hugged Manish goodbye.

Kushi wouldn't give up easily.

She'd been this way with Avi too. Despite her initial protests, her mom kept instigating meetings, and Samira had let his charm get to her a little. That had been all the encouragement Kushi needed, and before she knew it, they'd been dating.

Never again.

Her stomach gurgled, and she pressed a hand to it. She'd been feeling a tad off lately, plagued by intermittent nausea and wooziness, worse than her usual hormonal swings. She hoped she hadn't picked up a gastro bug of some sort; if it didn't let up, she'd have to see the practice's doctor.

"Knock, knock, got a minute?" Pia rapped on her door and stuck her head around it, and Samira beckoned her in.

"Sure. What's up?"

The moment Pia stepped into her office and closed the door, Samira knew this wasn't about work. Her cousin's somber expression and rigid posture sent a skitter of fear through her and had her shooting to her feet.

"Are you okay?"

Pia nodded and managed a wan smile. "I'm fine, but I have to tell you something."

A million awful scenarios flashed through her mind in a second: Dev had a terminal illness, Aunt Sindhu had been in a car accident, her mom had fallen . . . The thought of Kushi gave her a quick wake-up call. This was exactly the kind of thing her mom would do, envisage the worst, predicting the direst consequences without hearing what the other person had to say.

"Come sit." Samira pulled up a plinth, and they sat side by side like they used to on the bench outside Dosa Villas as kids, waiting to be picked up after stuffing as many *idlis* as they could fit into their stomachs after school. She'd never really liked the steamed rice cakes, but Pia had loved them. "What's up?"

"You know how I mentioned our last IVF attempt had failed and we'd wait awhile before trying again?"

Relief filtered through her. Nobody was dying, but by the worry in Pia's eyes, she knew the seriousness of not being able to conceive was just as devastating.

"Yeah?"

"Well, I convinced Dev to try again, so our next IVF attempt is scheduled for late next month, but I want to take some time off beforehand to try alternative therapies to enhance our chances."

"And you want me to step up and manage this place while you're away?"

Pia nodded and reached out to grab her hand. "I know it's a big ask when you're so busy, but I really need to do this."

"Of course I'll do it." Samira squeezed her hand, wishing she could make this whole process easier on her cousin. "So what kind of alternative therapies?"

A sheepish expression replaced Pia's gravity. "It's a wellness retreat for infertile couples, focusing on preparing the body for pregnancy, so they do hypnotherapy, acupuncture, reflexology, meditation, massage, mindfulness . . . crystals."

Samira barked out a laugh. "I know you trying to conceive isn't funny, but crystals?"

Pia laughed too. "I know, the science-trained logical person in me can't believe I'm hoping crystals have electromagnetic charges that encourage a body's processes and therefore help conception, but hey, at this point I'll try anything."

"You know I'll support you through this." Samira leaned forward to give Pia a hug, and as she did so, the room spun, the edges of her vision darkened, and the weirdest floating feeling washed over her.

The next thing she knew, she had Pia and the practice's doctor, Kate Beck, leaning over her as she lay on the floor.

"What happened?" She struggled into a sitting position and blinked several times to clear the fuzziness clouding her head.

"You fainted." Pia slid a supportive arm around her shoulders. "And scared the living daylights out of me."

"Is this a common occurrence?" Kate took her pulse and glanced at her watch, counting the appropriate beats.

"No, but I get crazy hormonal swings that can lead to vomiting, dizziness, that kind of thing. And it's been worse than usual the last few weeks. Or it could be a virus?"

"Possibly," Kate said, releasing her wrist. "But if you think your hormones are haywire, and worse than usual, let's do a few simple blood tests to make sure you're okay."

If there was one thing Samira hated more than her mother's matchmaking, it was needles, but she nodded.

"Come through to my office now, and I'll get it done."

As Kate left the room, Pia continued to eye her with concern. "You sure you're okay?"

"Yeah, I'm fine." Samira stood slowly, determined to hide from her cousin exactly how wobbly she still felt. Pia had enough to deal with at the moment. "It probably is some stupid virus. You know I always catch something when I come back to Melbourne."

Considering she'd only been back once in twelve years, it was lame, but thankfully, Pia didn't push it.

"If you're unwell, maybe now isn't the best time for me to be taking leave—"

"Stop right there." Samira held up her hand. "You and Dev have been trying everything to have a baby, and the fact you're resorting to putting crystals on your chakras or wherever else you'll stick those things means this is important."

Pia barked out a laugh, and Samira patted her arm. "I'll be fine."

Pia's shoulders slumped in relief. "Thanks, you're the best. And for the record, I won't be sticking crystals anywhere they're not supposed to go."

They laughed and headed down the corridor to Kate's office, Samira's legs feeling decidedly wonky.

"Take it easy, okay?" Pia pecked her on the cheek and Samira nodded.

"Go. Organize your bookings for when you're away, and get ready to do handover to me for all the managerial stuff."

"Thanks, you're the best," Pia said as she strode away on those impossibly high heels she wore even at work.

Samira didn't feel the best as she entered Kate's office, and the first thing the doctor handed her was a pregnancy test.

"Before we draw blood, I'd like you to do this."

Samira's loud guffaw earned a raised eyebrow from the unflappable doc.

"I can't be pregnant. I have oligomenorrhea."

Not to mention the more salient fact of an infrequent sex life.

Apart from those memorable interludes with Rory, but they'd used a condom.

That had broken the last time they'd been together.

Laughter bubbled up again, and this time Kate frowned.

In what alternate universe could a woman who had three periods a year, if that, have sex, the condom breaks, and that actually results in a pregnancy?

No way, no how.

"When was your last period?" Kate brandished the pregnancy test in her direction, and Samira took it.

"I can't remember." She screwed up her eyes, trying to think. "I don't mark them on a calendar anymore because they're too infrequent . . . Before I arrived in Melbourne . . . Maybe ten weeks ago?"

"And have you had unprotected sex?"

"No." Samira bristled at the insinuation she'd be so careless and resisted the urge to squirm under Kate's probing stare. "Though I have had sex during that time and the condom broke once, though it was only two weeks ago."

"That could do it." Kate's stern expression eased, and her mouth twitched with amusement. "And the more sensitive tests we perform can actually confirm a pregnancy eight days after conception, so why don't you tell me about these hormone swings and the resultant symptoms."

Reeling from the implications and signs that could indeed add up to a pregnancy, Samira said, "Nausea, mainly. I puked once almost four weeks ago, but I get that occasionally due to hormone imbalance, and that was before the condom broke. Wooziness mostly, and feeling blah, but at random times with no real pattern."

Kate picked up a pen and started jotting notes in a file. "Are your breasts tender?"

"No."

"Any spotting?"

"No."

"Any other odd symptoms?"

Samira shook her head, increasingly relieved. She couldn't be pregnant. It would be too incongruous. "Nothing at all. I'm usually pretty healthy apart from the hormone stuff, so this has to be a virus, right?"

Kate's benign smile did little to reassure her. "Please take the test, then we can talk more."

"Okay." She refrained from adding, *But this is the biggest waste of time ever.*

Her heart tripped with nerves as she entered the small bathroom next to Kate's office and locked the door. She stared at the rectangular box for a few long moments before tearing it open, unwrapping the foil, and grabbing the white plastic stick.

The instructions on the box were simple enough. Pee on the stick. Wait two minutes. Check the window.

However, as she stared at that little window one hundred and twenty significant seconds later, she knew there was nothing simple about this.

Numbness flooded her, quickly followed by shock, fear, and elation.

Two blue lines.

At thirty-seven, without a regular period, a regular man, or regular sex, she'd fallen pregnant.

Twenty-Six

Rory tried calling Samira, but her phone rang out, so he left a message. He didn't want to head home and sit by the phone waiting for a call from Chris like some sad sack, so on impulse he drove toward South Wharf.

He could thank Pia in person and give her a rundown of how the audition went. Crazy, because she probably had patients booked and he could convey his gratitude just as easily on the phone. But he really wanted to see Samira, and even if he had to loiter in the waiting room, he'd do it.

He reached the center in ten minutes and had parked when the phone rang. His heart leaped in anticipation, and he didn't know who he wanted to be on the other end more, Chris or Samira.

One glance at the screen had his hand shaking as he hit the "answer" button.

"Chris. How are you?"

"I'm bloody fantastic, considering I get a cut of your earnings as the host for *Renegades*."

Shock rendered him speechless for a moment. "I got the gig?"

"You sure did, mate. You blew them away at the audition, and they're rapt to have you on board."

"Fuck," he murmured, joy expanding in his chest until he could barely breathe. "I can't believe it."

Chris chuckled. "I knew you could do it. Anyway, go celebrate, and I'll be in touch once I have more information."

"Thanks, Chris, for everything."

"You're the one who did this, mate. I just made a few calls to set everything up. Well done."

When Chris hung up, Rory stared at the phone in his hand, wondering if he'd conjured up the call out of wishful thinking.

He got the job.

He could give Amelia the money she needed to kick-start the speech therapy program.

He could help those kids.

He felt freaking invincible.

Chris had been right about one thing. He had to celebrate. He hoped he could convince Samira to skive off work, because they had some serious partying to do, one-on-one.

He had no recollection of the five-minute walk to the center—because he'd probably floated there—and as he entered, he strode toward Samira's office, relieved to spot her door open and the woman he wanted to see tidying exercise equipment.

"Samira," he called out, unable to keep the grin off his face as he entered her office.

She looked a little pale, but he saw the exact moment she figured out why he was grinning like an idiot who'd just won the lottery.

"You nailed the audition?"

He nodded. "I got the job. You're looking at the host of Australia's newest up-and-coming reality show."

"That's great." She enveloped him in a hug, squeezing so tight he laughed.

"Want to help me celebrate?"

She hesitated, as something furtive shifted in her gaze. "What did you have in mind?"

"What do you think?"

He rested his hand on her waist, before sliding it around to her gorgeous ass in a slow caress.

Her eyes widened, and her lips curved into a coy smile. "Hmm . . . I've got a lot of patient files to complete—"

"I want you, now," he murmured, giving her ass a gentle squeeze. "I'm so damn happy I could burst, and I want to share that with you."

"Okay," she said, pressing her hand to his cheek. "Give me five minutes."

"Make it one." He swooped in to claim her mouth in a scorching kiss that had him hard and craving her more than ever.

He'd made the right decision in coming here.

A sizzling celebration for two would make this day even more memorable.

Samira had been so shocked to see Rory not long after learning the momentous news of her pregnancy that she couldn't think up an excuse fast enough to fob him off. Not that she wanted to, but she needed time to absorb the news that still left her reeling twenty minutes later and had envisaged slinking off to her apartment to sit on the sofa and dwell.

She couldn't tell him, not yet. Maybe sneaking off for some afternoon delight would be just what she needed to take her mind off it and the million questions pinging around her brain.

She hadn't been taking prenatal vitamins. Would that damage her baby?

She'd been drinking alcohol and eating soft cheeses and deli meats. Would that harm her baby?

Would she need to screen for fetal abnormalities sooner rather than later because of her age?

Would her baby be damaged because she'd been so clueless about all of the above?

Interesting, that she was already referring to the baby as "hers" and not "the baby." Because despite all the questions and the shock and her bone-deep fear, she was ecstatic about this pregnancy.

She'd never imagined having a child. Being a reproductively challenged, single thirty-seven-year-old didn't inspire her with confidence, and she'd secretly given up on her dream of ever conceiving.

During her marriage, she'd had an inordinate amount of sex, because procreating had been so important to Avi. He'd wanted to create his own people to show the world how damn powerful he was, and when she'd failed, he'd gone elsewhere for his baby making.

So in what crazy world did she have sex with a guy a decade younger than her a handful of times and make a baby?

"You're distracted," he said, trailing a finger down her naked torso, from her breasts to her belly button. "Hope I didn't disappoint."

"You know exactly how good you are." She rolled onto her side to face him, the afterglow of amazing sex and two orgasms fading as she looked into his startling blue eyes and wondered if their child would have the same unique color.

"Guys have big egos, and we like to be stroked."

"We're still talking about egos, right?"

He chuckled, idly caressing her hip in languorous strokes that made her skin pebble. "I was freaking out about the audition when I saw you earlier today, but even in my nervous funk, all I could think about was how it's been two weeks since we've been together and how badly I wanted to spend some time with you again."

"Wow, that's the longest thing you've ever said to me." She rested her hand against his chest, savoring the crisp hair beneath her palm. "But yeah, I kind of missed you too."

"High praise indeed," he said, his familiar lopsided smile doing weird things to her insides. Or was that their baby already wreaking havoc? "So why didn't you call?"

"I've been busy."

It sounded like the lame excuse it was.

"Your mom still trying to marry you off to that Indian dude?"

"Yeah, we actually had lunch today."

His hand stilled, and a tiny dent appeared between his brows. "The three of you, together?"

"Relax, it's not like it sounds." She reached out, her fingertip smoothing away his frown. "Mom's constantly going on about Manny, so I thought by her seeing there's no spark between us, she might back off."

"Is that what happened?"

"No, so I told her about you to make sure she got the message."

His eyebrows shot up. "You told her about me?"

"Yeah."

His smile returned, part bashful, part proud. "I guess we really are dating, then."

"Something like that."

Would that make it easier for her mom to accept her pregnancy? Doubtful. Being of Indian descent and an unwed mother did not make for a happy baby shower. Kushi would love her grandchild, Samira had no doubt about that, but after their discussion regarding the aunties and how the Indian community had rallied around her after her dad died, would they ostracize Kushi all over again?

Their judgment wouldn't affect Samira all that much; she wouldn't be around . . . That was the moment reality set in.

Her baby had a father.

An Aussie father.

Who resided in Australia.

Would Rory be amenable to her taking the child to live halfway across the world and thus cutting down his access to minimal?

"What's wrong?" His frown had returned, deeper than ever. "Is there something you're not telling me about this Manny guy? Do you have feelings for him?"

"No, absolutely not." She shook her head. "We're friends, that's it. But I've got a lot on my mind, what with Pia leaving me in charge of the center for a few weeks while she takes some time off to be with her husband."

Another complication in this fraught scenario. Pia loved her like a sister, but how would her cousin feel about her conceiving so easily when she'd been trying for years and it still hadn't happened?

Samira had been gutted to learn about Avi's impending fatherhood all those years ago, and she knew deep down his cheating hadn't devastated her as much as the fact that the other woman was having the baby she craved so much.

She knew Pia loved her, but infertility wore a person down, and hearing Samira's news would be a sucker punch. Pia was the most logical, methodical person she knew, and for her cousin to resort to alternative therapies like crystals meant she was desperate. Samira needed her support to get through this pregnancy, but it might appear callous, like she was rubbing Pia's nose in her fertility.

"Is everything okay with her?"

"Yeah, she's trying to have a baby."

Crap, why did she blurt that out? Then again, it gave her a chance to study Rory carefully for a reaction. A wrinkle of a nose, a screwed-up face, any sign he didn't like kids and she could hold off telling him about theirs.

But he looked back at her, his expression thoughtful. "She's great. I really hope it works out for her."

Impressed by his genuine caring, she pressed her palm to his cheek again. "You're a good guy, Rory Radcliffe, and I can't wait to see you on TV."

A cheeky glint lit his eyes. "Why wait, when you can see all of me now?"

With that, he whipped off the top sheet, leaving him gloriously naked.

Yeah, that was exactly what she needed.

She could mull the staggering news of her baby and the consequences for everyone later.

Twenty-Seven

After another glorious night in Samira's bed, Rory headed for the rec hall at the housing commission flats. He'd wanted to tell Amelia the good news in person yesterday but had got sidetracked—and how—with Samira.

She'd been different last night, preoccupied and less chatty than previous times they'd got together. It had made him nervous, because he preferred it when she filled the silences between them. He believed her when she said she didn't like that Manny guy as anything more than a friend, but a small part of him couldn't help but wonder if she was torn over it. It was hard not to bow to family pressure; he should know, considering dear old dad still continued to hound him regarding a change in career. And after not seeing her mom for so many years, it stood to reason she'd want to please her.

Stupid, to have doubts after yet another incredible night together. If she'd told her mom about him, she was into him as much as he was into her. Unless she was using him as an excuse? He hadn't delved into how much she'd told her mom about him. In fact, he'd been so euphoric he hadn't questioned much. He'd been content to celebrate in her arms. A simple man with simple tastes. But would he make life more complicated for her if he pushed for answers regarding their relationship and her mother's acceptance of them as a couple?

As he parked outside the flats, he caught sight of Davey, the nine-year-old with a bad stutter who he'd talked to the last time he'd been out here. He stood on the outskirts of a group of boys who were kicking a can between them, jostling for position, mucking around. Rory paused as he got out of his car and closed the door, stunned by the overwhelming sensation of helplessness.

He'd been like Davey once, always on the outside looking in, craving acceptance, feeling like a freak because he didn't talk like everyone else. What would have happened if he hadn't got help? Considering how gauche he still felt in certain social situations, how he avoided relationships, how inferior he felt to people like his father, he knew exactly what would've happened. He'd still be an outcast, and he certainly wouldn't be fronting a new TV show.

He wanted Davey and the kids like him to have the choices he had, and thanks to the money he could now contribute to the program, they'd have those choices. It made him feel ten feet tall.

Striding toward the rec hall, he waved at Davey, who offered a half-raised hand in return. However, rather than hang back as he'd expected, the kid approached him.

"Hey, Davey."

"Hi."

"I'm here to see Amelia about that speech therapy program I mentioned. Have you enrolled yet?"

Davey nodded, a small smile lighting his somber face. "Y-yes. I w-w-want to t-t-talk b-b-better."

"Good for you, champ." Rory ruffled his hair. "You need to do all the homework Amelia gives you, okay? I didn't like it at first, but when I noticed my speech improving over time, it made me want to work even harder."

Davey gave him a thumbs-up sign and a grin. Rory had often resorted to hand signals rather than talking as a kid too.

"See you around, buddy."

Hoping Davey would take his advice to heart, he entered the rec hall and spied Amelia in a far corner, hanging up some enunciation posters. He'd seen the same ones in her office years ago, with "ph," "th," "kn," and "fr" sounds to be practiced.

"I remember those," he called out, striding across the hall.

"That's because you were the hardest-working student I ever had," she said, sticking up the last one before dusting off her hands. "How are you?"

"Good. Great, in fact." He grinned, and one of her eyebrows quirked. "You still after that ten grand?"

Hope lit her eyes. "You've got it?"

"Yeah. I had an audition yesterday for a really big role, and I got it."

"Congratulations, Rory, I'm so happy for you." She hugged him, before stepping back to eyeball him. "But there aren't too many stuntman roles that pay that kind of money, so where are you really getting it?" Concern creased her brow. "I hope you're not taking a loan for this—"

"I landed the role of host on a new reality show, so no leaping off tall buildings or high-speed car chases this time."

She gaped for a moment, before eyeing him with admiration.

"I'm so proud of you. I always knew you could take on a speaking role."

"I didn't, but this program and the foundation we're setting up is important to me, and I want these kids here to have the opportunities I did."

"You're a good guy, Rory Radcliffe," she said, her words echoing Samira's from last night and making him blush.

"Obviously, I don't have the money yet, but my agent emailed through the contract this morning, and I get ten grand on signing, and more as filming starts, after the first five episodes, that kind of thing, on a sliding scale."

A shadow passed over her face. "Are you sure about this? Ten thousand dollars is a lot of money. You could put a deposit on a home or save it or—"

"I want to do this," he said, his authoritative tone brooking no argument. "Give me the banking details, and I'll forward the money across as soon as I get it."

She flung her arms around him again and hugged tight before releasing him. "So many kids are going to benefit from this thanks to your generosity."

"I'm counting on it." He jerked his thumb over his shoulder toward the doorway. "There's a kid out there, Davey. His stutter is pretty bad, and he's on the outs with the other kids because of it. He's keen to work hard."

"I'll make sure he does," she said, her knowing expression alerting him that she knew why he'd mentioned Davey—because he saw so much of himself in the kid. "Thanks again, Rory. You've really come through for us."

"My pleasure. I'll be in touch." He glanced around the hall, pleased with how everything was coming together from the vision the two of them first had. "And I'm happy to take as much of an active role in the program as you need, like dropping by occasionally to having informal chats with the kids, that kind of thing?"

"Great." Her beatific smile made him feel like he'd hung those posters with sheer willpower alone.

As she returned to her task, he wondered if she knew what a difference she'd made in his life and how this donation was a small gesture of eternal gratitude.

Amelia really had changed his life, and he hoped she could do the same for these less-fortunate kids.

Twenty-Eight

Samira had managed to get through the workday without spilling her secret to Pia. She'd wanted to blab so many times but knew it would be better to wait until they met after work for handover.

Knowing Pia, she'd have a stack of files to go through regarding management of the center, despite her only going away for a month. Besides, Samira wouldn't have to do much beyond oversee any major decisions. Their office manager was extremely competent, and Samira wished she could poach her to run her practice back in LA.

A sliver of unease made her rub her bare arms. Every time she'd thought about returning to LA over the last twenty-four hours she'd had the same reaction. She'd treated this six-month stay in Melbourne as a jaunt, a way to re-bond with her mother while helping her cousin. But LA was her home these days, and she'd looked forward to heading back.

Yet the moment she'd discovered she was pregnant, the ties

that bound her to Melbourne tightened around her, and oddly, they didn't feel so constricting. The baby's father lived here. Her mom lived here. Her best friend/cousin lived here. A support network a single mother needed.

But could she do it?

Move back to the city she'd fled because an entire community had judged her and found her lacking?

Have her mom love the baby but give her side-eye because of who the father was and their lack of wedding rings?

Give up the comfort of having an ocean between them when her mom's matchmaking grew unbearable?

She knew Kushi. The minute she learned about this pregnancy, she'd be booking the town hall for a reception. Not that her mom needed an excuse, but having a child on her own without being married would plunge Kushi back into matrimonial machinations; and the rest of her cronies too. Not too many babies were born in the local community without both parents wed. And those who were would be gossiped about over countless cups of chai.

Interesting, that when the news of Avi's infidelity had broken and she'd left him, it seemed like she'd borne the brunt of the gossip. Never mind that Avi's first child had been born out of wedlock. His family had such a huge standing in the Indian community, they'd glossed over that salient fact and thrown a lavish traditional wedding the month after her divorce had been finalized.

Not that she cared what the local community thought of her, but Kushi did, and the fact her mom might be ostracized again after Samira left was a sobering thought.

"Hey, what's up with you?" Pia breezed into the conference room and shut the door. "You look like this." Pia pulled a weepy face. "Trouble in paradise?"

"Nothing like that . . . How did you know I've been with Rory again?"

Pia grinned and tapped her temple. "He called me this morning to thank me for all the dialect coaching and to tell me he got the job."

"But how did you know—"

"I saw you two sneaking out of here yesterday afternoon, and I figured you 'celebrated.'" Pia made cutesy quotation mark signs around the last word. "How's it going with you two?"

"Good," she said, nerves making her palms clammy. She needed to tell Pia about the pregnancy, but she knew firsthand how hard it was to hear about other women's fertility when struggling with your own.

They may be cousins and best friends, but deep down, Samira knew this would test their bond.

"Good seems pretty tame considering how fast you two wanted to get somewhere more private yesterday."

Samira's cheeks flushed. "He's great, actually. We have a lot of fun together."

"So that's what you're calling it these days." Pia snickered before nodding her approval. "He's a nice guy. Perfect fling material while you're in town."

Samira had to tell Pia that Rory was more than a fling. He was the father of her child. She dragged in a steadying breath and blew it out. "Yeah, but is he daddy material?"

Pia's eyes widened with shock before she gave a short laugh. "You're crazy. Why would you consider trying to get pregnant with a guy you won't see again when you head back to LA?" Her gaze slid away. "Not to mention the fact you had major problems conceiving years ago with Avi and you're older now—"

"I'm pregnant," Samira blurted, unable to keep the news in a second longer. "I know it's madness because I rarely get periods and we used protection, but the condom broke, and I'm reeling from the shock, but I'm happy too, and I had to tell you."

All the color drained from Pia's face as she stood ramrod straight, her fingers curling into fists before unfurling, over and over, like she wanted to pump blood to the rest of her body.

Pia's stricken expression and rigid posture made Samira wish she'd couched the news in better terms, but what could she say other than the truth? "I know it doesn't make sense considering how hard I tried to conceive with Avi, but who knows, maybe there's something to Mom's belief in fate or karma or whatever, and this is the right time for me?"

Pia's pallor hadn't improved. If anything, she looked worse, and Samira took a step toward her. Her cousin flinched, and Samira stopped, unsure whether to approach to give her a hug or not.

"I know this is a shock—"

"What do you mean you're pregnant?"

Pia spoke slowly, enunciating every single word with icy emphasis, her tone frigid. Her catatonic, unblinking stare unnerved Samira, but she'd had to do this, had to tell her cousin everything; it would be better than Pia finding out from someone else, and Samira had no doubt that could happen once she told her mom and the Indian grapevine got hold of the news.

"It's nuts, I know—"

"No, you don't know." Pia stalked toward her on wooden legs, her steps jerky, before pulling out the chair next to Samira and collapsing onto it. "You have no fucking idea how nuts it really is."

Samira startled and reached out to comfort Pia, only to have her scoot away like her touch was abhorrent.

"I know this must be tough on you—"

"Tough?" Pia snorted, an ugly sound ripped from deep within. "Tough doesn't begin to describe how I feel right now."

Samira had expected Pia to have a hard time with the news of her pregnancy, but she hadn't expected this cold disdain, like she'd somehow done this deliberately to hurt her. But then she glimpsed the truth in Pia's eyes.

Pain. Potent and raw. Complete and utter devastation.

"I'm sorry—"

"Don't you dare apologize," Pia barked out. "I know I'm being a bitch, but I can't handle . . . I mean, I can't deal . . ." She let out a sob that raised Samira's hackles.

This time when Samira stepped forward and reached for her, Pia allowed her to bundle her into her arms, as she heard a whispered, "It should've been me."

Samira's heart ached for her cousin as she held her tight, waiting until her tears subsided before easing away.

"It will happen for you—"

"Please don't give me platitudes right now." Pia shrugged off Samira's arms and stood, backing away. "I need time to process."

"Okay."

As resentment replaced the sorrow in Pia's gaze, Samira wished things could be different. She hadn't expected Pia to be over the moon about her pregnancy, but they'd been best friends for a long time, and Pia hadn't even offered congratulations. In fact, Pia was so consumed by self-pity and resentment she'd pretty much forgotten how Samira had once yearned for a child and how shattered she'd been when she couldn't have one.

Considering her oligomenorrhea, conceiving naturally at her age was nothing short of a miracle, and a part of her wished Pia would acknowledge that rather than . . . blaming her.

"I have to say, it's pretty irresponsible of you, what with you taking on the role here for six months and—"

"Are you kidding me?" Samira shook her head, unable to bite her tongue a moment longer. "You're telling me off like I'm a child for something that is so incredible for me I can hardly believe it?"

She pressed her hand protectively over her stomach, an instinctive reaction she'd seen other mothers-to-be do and had been envious of each and every time. "I was worried about telling you my news, but I also hoped you'd share in my excitement. You know how much this means to me . . ."

She trailed off as Pia's lips compressed in disapproval. "What do you want me to say?"

"That you're happy for me? That you love me and you'll support me through this? That you'll be here for me?" Samira flung her arms wide. "I need you—"

"And I already told you, I need time," Pia muttered, shaking her head. "I can't do this right now."

With that, Pia spun on her heel and marched to the door, leaving Samira stunned and incredibly hurt.

"Pia, please . . ."

In response to her plea, Pia slammed the door.

Twenty-Nine

Rory may never have had a real relationship, but when Samira called asking him to meet at her place ASAP, he knew something was drastically wrong.

She exuded a vibrancy he loved, and that carried through to her voice, whether she was discussing her work or LA or her family. But she'd been subdued on the phone, and her request had a hint of plea about it. It scared him. Just his luck when he was on top of the world professionally and personally, something had to go wrong.

Was she dumping him before they'd barely started up? Crazy, considering their afternoon together yesterday and the way they'd left things this morning. They were dating. Officially. So why would she do a backflip so soon?

He'd made it to her place in record time and tried not to appear too cagey as the security guard who took him up to her room kept casting suspicious glances his way. He knew why. He fidgeted whenever he was nervous, so the constant watch checking, belt tightening, finger flexing must make him look like someone up to no good.

When they reached her door, he stabbed at the bell, trying to ignore the guard's stare. She took an eternity to answer, and when she opened the door, the dread in his gut solidified into a solid ball of worry.

Bloodshot eyes. Red-tipped nose. She'd been crying.

"Thanks, mate, I've got it from here," he said to the guard, who waited until Samira gave a nod of approval before striding away.

"Are you okay?" He took her into his arms without waiting for a response, hoping a hug could do more than words ever could. Besides, if he held her, he wouldn't be tempted to blab, *Are you dumping me?*

"Hmm," she mumbled against his chest, squeezing him tight.

When she showed no signs of wanting to let go, he held her tighter. How many times had he craved a comforting hug when he was younger? Too many, courtesy of his dad's callous indifference, especially when he asked questions about where his mom was. He'd given up asking after a while; because of his nerves, he'd inevitably stutter worse than usual and would earn one of his dad's impatient glares, and he hated those as much as his lack of answers.

After what seemed like an eternity, her grip loosened and she eased out of his arms. He braced—for her to avoid his eyes or for a cold expression—but to his relief, she slipped her hand into his and tugged him toward the sofa.

"I have to say, you're kinda scaring me," he said, sitting next to her. "What's going on?"

"I had a massive fight with Pia." She gnawed on her bottom lip, disappointment in her eyes. "It wasn't pretty."

Thankfully, he didn't blurt the first response that came to mind: *Is that all?* They were family, so he figured this wouldn't have been their first falling-out. But she was seriously rattled, so whatever was said, it must've been big.

"You two are close, yeah?"

She nodded, staring at their clasped hands rather than meeting his gaze. "Best friends as well as cousins, so I expected more from her . . ."

She shook her head and raised it but still couldn't meet his eyes. "I told her something earth-shattering, and while I didn't expect her to like it, I expected more support."

Earth-shattering? That didn't sound good. Was she sick? Leaving early? At least he could strike dumping him off his list of suppositions; considering they'd barely got together officially, breaking up definitely wouldn't classify as earth-shattering.

"Family can be hard to deal with at times."

Didn't he know it.

She cast him an odd look. "You never talk about yours. What are they like?"

"Mom left when I was a kid, almost four, so I barely remember her. Dad and I aren't close."

Thankfully, he couldn't see pity in her stare, merely curiosity. "No other extended family? Cousins?"

Her sudden interest in his family confused him. Then again, maybe she was trying to deflect attention from hers and would rather focus on his.

"No, both my parents were only kids, and all my grandparents are dead."

He'd hated grandparents' day at school because he had nobody. Other kids who didn't have grandparents had one of their parents turn up, or a close relative. His father had always been too busy with "important legal work," so Rory would sit quietly in the back corner of the class, trying to force a smile when other grandparents politely inquired about his latest art project or portfolio because they felt sorry for him.

Though it could've been worse. In third grade, his teacher from the previous year must've given his dad a subtle hint about his lack of attendance, because his father had actually sent one of his PAs from work. Rory had met her only once previously. It had been beyond embarrassing, and he'd remained mute rather than attempt to answer her faux-interested questions, because he knew his nerves would exacerbate his stutter and he was bad enough in front of strangers.

"So it's just you and your dad?" She hesitated, gnawing on her bottom lip. "It's a shame you're not close if it's just the two of you."

"I'm pretty sure you didn't ask me over to talk about my crappy relationship with my dad," he said, not willing to discuss the many reasons he didn't get on with the illustrious Garth Radcliffe. "So is your argument with Pia the only reason you're so upset?"

"Who says I'm upset?"

Her response came out a tad high, and he raised an eyebrow, earning a bashful smile. "Okay, you got me. I have something to tell you, and I'm hoping you won't freak out."

Intrigued, he squeezed her hand. "I pretty much guarantee there's nothing you can tell me that will make me freak out. I'm a laid-back guy."

"Yeah, but this is big . . ." She huffed out a breath, and as her gaze collided with his, he glimpsed genuine fear.

"I know we haven't been dating long, but I'm here and I'm listening." He raised her hand to his lips and pressed a lingering kiss to the back of it. "Tell me."

She stared at the back of her hand, wide-eyed, as if she couldn't quite believe he was real, before gently withdrawing her hand from his to clasp both of hers in her lap. Tight, by the skin stretched taut across her knuckles.

The silences between them before today had been comfortable. That was one of the things he liked about her, that she didn't expect him to talk to fill the quiet. She let him be. But this bordered on awkward, and as he reached out to touch her arm in reassurance, she eyeballed him and blurted, "I'm pregnant. And it's yours."

Rory heard the words, but he didn't compute them above the roar in his head. He'd never wanted kids. Stuttering could be hereditary, and no way in hell he'd risk passing on this bloody affliction to a child of his.

Pregnant.

With his kid.

Fuck.

"I know it's a shock—"

"Are you going to keep it?"

She recoiled as if he'd slapped her, and he regretted speaking before engaging his brain. He didn't mean it to sound so callous, but it was a legitimate question, considering she was carrying their child and it was ultimately her choice whether she wanted to or not.

She nodded, her neck stiff, her lips thinned with disapproval. "I had fertility issues in the past. I didn't think I could have a baby. And I'm thirty-fucking-seven, so yes, I'm keeping the baby."

He couldn't recall hearing her swear before, so the fact she did now meant he'd seriously pissed her off. He didn't know what she wanted from him. He would support her decision and offer whatever financial support he could, but he didn't want a child. He couldn't go through the heartbreak, and the accompanying guilt, if the one thing he passed on genetically was the one thing he loathed about himself.

"Okay," he said, sounding like it was anything but, and she wriggled back on the sofa, disappointment etched across her face.

"I don't expect anything from you." She stood, her movements jerky, like she couldn't quite coordinate her muscles to work in sync. "And I'm exhausted. So let yourself out, and we'll talk more about it, if you want to, another time."

She stalked toward her bedroom, her back rigid. He should go after her. He should reassure her everything would be okay. He should say something to erase his stilted, unenthusiastic response a few moments ago.

Instead, he sat there like a dummy, regretting a lot of things, most of them centered on a broken condom and the far-reaching consequences for them all.

Thirty

Since her divorce and fleeing Melbourne, Samira had been proud of her independence. She didn't need anybody. She did everything on her own: building her physical therapy clinic from scratch, buying her apartment, dating if and when she felt inclined.

But two hours after Rory left, she still lay on her bed, curled on her side with her legs drawn up, craving comfort. Pia would be the person she'd usually reach out to, but her cousin had left her in little doubt how she felt about this baby.

Her mom would be the next obvious choice, but after dealing with Pia's reaction and then Rory's, she couldn't face Kushi's disapproval too. She needed to be in a stronger state emotionally when she told her mom the good news. And it was good news. Sensational, in fact, because once she'd got over the initial shock, she couldn't help the elation filling her, expanding like her belly soon would.

That was what nobody had understood about Avi's betrayal. His cheating had been bad enough, but the thought of him having something she'd wanted so badly . . . it had gutted her.

Maybe she'd already sensed his withdrawal from their marriage early on and she'd thought having a baby to love would soothe some of her loneliness. So when he told her the truth, she'd mourned for the baby they never had more than the loss of her marriage.

Now, she'd have the baby she'd always wanted, without the encumbrances or expectations of a partner. Because Rory's response to the news told her exactly how much of a part he wanted to play in their child's life: absolutely none. He'd been stunned, understandably, but the first question that popped out of his mouth about whether she would keep the baby or not spoke volumes.

He didn't want to be a dad.

And she didn't need him to be.

But she'd been disappointed, nonetheless. She'd hoped he'd hold her in his arms and tell her how excited he was. In fact, a small part of her had envisioned him being so swept up in her euphoria he'd try to convince her how they could make this work. Co-parents. A team. Pathetic, considering she'd given up on fairy tales around the time she realized her marriage didn't live up to the Bollywood hype.

Her cell buzzed with a text, and her heart leaped. Seeing either Pia's or Rory's name on the screen would cheer her up.

However, when she glanced at the screen and saw "Manny," her hope deflated. She speed-read his text.

HAS YOUR MOM BACKED OFF?
OR R U FALLING IN LINE WITH HER PLANS AND
FALLING 4 MY CHARMS?

For the first time all day, the corners of her mouth twitched into a semi-smile.

She fired back: **BIGGER PROBLEMS THAN U.**

She expected to see tiny moving dots on the screen to indicate he was responding, so when the cell rang, she jumped.

When she answered, Manny said, "I thought talking would be easier than typing with my gammy thumbs."

"How can a doctor have gammy thumbs?"

"Probably signing all those exorbitant paychecks before I cash them."

This time, her smile turned into a short laugh.

"So what's happening? What are these big problems?" He cleared his throat. "I hope I didn't make things worse for you by showing up to lunch. Is your mom still hounding you to make an honest man out of me?"

"No, that's not it."

She couldn't tell him, not before she'd told her mom. Then again, it could be good to get an impartial opinion from a person not emotionally invested in the outcome of her pregnancy.

The crazy thing was, she'd never contemplate telling anyone so early into this pregnancy. She hadn't had any tests yet, beyond a blood test to confirm it. Any number of things could go wrong between now and her first scan at twelve weeks, which was when most excited parents blabbed the happy news.

But she'd been lying here for the last two hours wishing she could talk to someone about this, someone who would offer comfort rather than judgment.

"You're awfully quiet," he said. "You know, despite all my teasing about falling for me, and the fact we haven't known each other long, you can talk to me as a friend."

"I'm pregnant."

A long silence, finally punctuated with a low whistle. "Congratulations."

He sounded like he meant it, warmth tempering the surprise in his voice.

"You're the first person that's said that to me," she said, and burst into tears.

"Hell, are you okay?"

She hiccupped in response and grabbed a handful of tissues from the box on her bedside table to dab at her eyes. "Yeah, just a tad emotional."

"Want me to come over?"

Yeah, she did, but it wouldn't be fair to him. Because for all his jokes and banter about their friendship, she couldn't forget that a small part of him must've been interested in her as prospective marriage material to agree to meet in the first place, and she didn't want to take advantage of the tentative friendship they'd established.

"Thanks for the offer, but I'll be okay. It's just a lot to take in, you know?"

"Actually, I don't, but if you're knocked up, I'm here for you." He paused. "I assume that guy you're seeing is the father?"

"Yeah."

"Are you going to tell him?"

She swallowed down a sob that bubbled up again. "I already did."

"And?"

"He's not thrilled."

"Prick."

Surprised by the vehemence in his tone, she said, "I told my cousin Pia too, and she went ballistic."

"Why?"

"Because her husband's sterile and they've been struggling with infertility for years."

"Ah . . . that must be tough."

"It is, and I get it, but she's my best friend, and I thought she'd be here for me . . ." Samira swiped at her eyes again. "She'll come around, but that's two important people in my life who didn't react to the news as I hoped."

"What about your mom?"

She sighed. "I haven't told her yet."

"Why not?"

"I'm feeling a tad fragile and need to be in a stronger frame of mind to tell her."

"If it makes it any easier, I can marry you."

She barked out a laugh. "Thanks for the offer, but that's not going to happen. I can do this on my own."

"I know you can." He cleared his throat, and she sensed a shift in mood from teasing to serious. "Just thought I'd put it out there."

She assumed he meant it as a joke, but a small part of her knew there was more behind his offer. Chivalry? Something more? Whatever his rationale, she imagined what it would be like to have his support through the pregnancy and beyond. Being a single parent could be tough. Having someone to share the load with had its attraction. But she'd already entered a marriage with doubts once before; she couldn't marry for the sake of a child when she could do a fine job of parenting on her own.

"And what do you get out of this platonic marriage apart from raising some other guy's kid?"

He chuckled at her sarcasm. "I don't want kids, never have, so this takes the pressure off with my gran. As for the platonic bit, we can work on that."

She smiled. "You're persistent, I'll give you that."

"No, I'm being a good friend." He hesitated. "Seriously, Samira,

I'm here for you. And while I'm confident you'll work everything out, know that you can off-load to me whenever."

"Thanks," she murmured, touched by his support. "Means a lot."

"Okay, I've got to go pick out wallpaper for the nursery and book Lamaze classes."

She laughed as he'd intended, and it struck her how much lighter she felt by telling him everything.

"And don't forget, you still owe me that lunch I didn't get when I left you and Kushi to sort things out."

"I'll be in touch, okay? Because if Mom didn't like the news about Rory, I have a feeling that learning she's going to be a grandma may require a lot more 'sorting out.'"

He chuckled. "Good luck. And take care."

"Thanks, you too."

She disconnected and placed the cell back on the bedside table. She would never enter another marriage not based on true love, but for a scant second, when she envisioned doing all this on her own versus having a supportive guy like Manny by her side, she'd been tempted.

Thirty-One

Fatherhood.

How could Rory contemplate being a dad when he didn't know how?

Garth had been a lousy role model. All he'd learned from his father was how to be a harsh disciplinarian, not spend much time with your kid, and throw money at the problem. Way to go, Dad.

Not that Rory didn't like kids. He did. After all, wasn't he putting himself out there in the most terrifying way possible by hosting *Renegades* to help kids?

He liked hanging out with them at the housing commission flats. Kids had an inherent honesty, a bluntness he appreciated. He could relate because he had a low tolerance for bullshit. But spending time with other people's kids and raising one of his own were worlds apart.

He'd been reeling when he left Samira's apartment last night to the extent he hadn't realized until an hour later he may not even be around for his kid. Samira would head back to LA at the end of her six-month stint at Pia's health center, taking his child with her.

It was in that moment of realization he felt something akin to regret.

He may not want to father a child for fear of passing on his speech impediment, but now it had happened, being a dad could grow on him.

Considering the way he'd handled the news, he wouldn't blame Samira for not wanting him anywhere near their child. He'd been an idiot, his insecurities manifesting at the worst possible time. She didn't know about his stutter or his fears of passing it on to a child, so she'd see him as a douche rather than a guy dealing with a bone-deep fear of giving his kid an impediment that dogged him to this day and he wouldn't wish on anybody.

He should tell her the truth. But would it be fair, giving her one more thing to worry about? Their kid could be fine and speak fluently, so why burden her with his fears?

Once he got this obligatory visit with his dad out of the way, he'd call her. He needed to apologize and show his support.

As he trudged up the path, glancing at the well-kept garden, the trimmed hedges, the blossoming flowers, he had the same dread in his gut as every time he'd dragged his feet up this path after school each day.

His father's mansion may appear immaculate on the outside, but it was all for show and, just like his dad, cold on the inside. He'd known kids at his snobby private school deigned to acknowledge his existence only because Garth Radcliffe was a highly regarded barrister in Melbourne and they knew he lived in an elite part of Brighton.

Though it didn't stop them teasing him mercilessly, mocking his speech, even though he'd mastered a lot of techniques to control his stutter by the time he finished high school. The only place he'd shone was onstage, encouraged into acting by Amelia as a way to master his fears of speaking in front of others, but then the bullies had teased him for a different reason, labeling him effeminate and worse.

He hadn't told his dad any of it. What would be the point, when Garth already saw him as a failure anyway? Not by his grades; the only time his dad vaguely looked at him with pride was twice a year, when the end of semester brought reports. Rory had always killed it with straight As because he had half a brain in his head, particularly for figures, and spent more time studying than most because he didn't have any friends. His dad had been mighty impressed when he'd chosen to major in economics; less so when he turned his back on a lucrative career in business to tumble around a movie set instead.

As he rang the doorbell, Rory wondered what his dad would make of his impending fatherhood. Not that he'd tell him now, but he knew Garth would view it as yet another disappointment.

A housekeeper he didn't recognize opened the door, a woman of about sixty wearing a plain black dress and her blond-turning-silver hair pulled back in a severe ponytail. "You must be Rory. I'm Bertha."

"Nice to meet you. I'm here to see my dad."

"He's been called away on business, but he asked you to wait for him." She opened the door wide. "Come in. Can I get you anything?"

"I'm fine," he said, clamping down on a flash of indignation. Why hadn't dear old dad sent a text or called him to let him know about the change of plans? They could've canceled this catch-up today and rescheduled. He hated having to wait around like his time wasn't as important as his dad's.

"I'm in the kitchen doing an online grocery order if you need anything," she said, closing the door. "You know your way around."

She left him standing in the marble-tiled hallway, feeling like a stranger in what had once been his home. Not that it felt like one. Too many pristine glass surfaces and shiny floors. He'd hated having to take his shoes off at the front door before he came in, in case a speck of mud dotted the floor. And that had been just one of the many rules he'd had to live by.

Always sit at the table for dinner, even if his dad never spoke to him. No screens after nine p.m., including TV, computer, cell, and laptop. No mixing with the scholarship kids. No social media profiles that could reflect badly on him. Lights out at ten, unless he had tests and had to study. No going out on school nights, which was ironic, as he'd have to have friends to do that. On and on, a long list he'd hated almost as much as the fraught silences whenever he was with his dad.

He often wondered why Garth didn't ship him off to boarding school. Would've made their lives a hell of a lot easier. Instead, they'd coexisted in this mausoleum of a house, tolerating each other with frosty silences.

He paced the hallway a few times, tempted to slip away. He could text his dad with the same excuse Garth had used, "called away on business." Glancing at his watch, he decided to give him another fifteen minutes before heading off.

He strolled into the library, a large room where his dad did the bulk of his work behind a monstrous mahogany desk, surrounded by floor-to-ceiling matching shelves filled with law texts and classics. No commercial fiction for Dad.

As always, whenever he entered this room, his gaze landed on the single framed photo on the wall near the door, the only space not covered by a bookshelf. It must've been taken when he was about one. His mom held him, and his parents were both resting their heads against his, wearing matching doting smiles.

After his mom left, this photo had given him hope: that she'd come back, that she still loved him despite her absence, that his dad actually cared. But as the years went by, she never returned and his father grew more taciturn, leaving him to resent the faux image of a happy family.

However, seeing the photo now made a tiny bud of hope unfurl in his chest. Maybe he could be a good dad, one who looked at his kid like that until he was old?

Buoyed by an uncharacteristic surge of nostalgia, he headed for the one place he might find some of his baby things: the attic.

He'd loved exploring it as a kid. Not that it was an attic per se, more a small room tucked into the front of the house on the second story, with a pitched roof and creaky floorboards. It had been his go-to place to hide away and shut out the world, where he'd immerse himself in a book to escape.

All his mom's stuff was in there, in boxes. Clothes and trinkets mostly, stuff he always wondered why his dad never got rid of. Then again, all his childhood stuff was up there too, so perhaps Garth compartmentalized belongings like he did his family, and once they'd left, he stored everything in boxes and tucked it away. Out of sight, out of mind.

Rory took the stairs two at a time like he always did. He doubted Samira would want any of his old baby stuff, but it would be nice to give her something of his by way of an apology.

When he reached the attic, he jiggled the door handle and

leaned his weight against the door. It always stuck a little, and after two good heaves it opened. The place was surprising clean, meaning one of the staff came up here to dust occasionally.

Ignoring the boxes of his mom's stuff like he used to—seeing them stacked in the far corner always made him forlorn—he headed for the opposite wall, where his stuff was neatly categorized: toys, clothes, miscellaneous, baby.

He reached for the baby box and unfolded the flaps. He'd never looked in this box because it had been irrelevant when he'd been older; the box labeled TOYS held more appeal. The box itself was surprisingly light, so he didn't expect it to contain much.

As he pushed the flaps back and glanced inside, he didn't know whether to be relieved or disappointed. No first tooth or first lock of hair, thank goodness—that kind of stuff creeped him out—but a few random items. A bib that appeared to be hand stitched with a giraffe on the front, a strand of colorful plastic circles interlinked, an ornate tarnished silver rattle, and a baby book from a health center.

The rattle could be polished and would make a nice gift for his own kid, so he slipped it into his pocket. Out of curiosity, he picked up the book and flipped it open, expecting to see the usual dates for vaccinations and milestones. However, as he flicked the first few pages, his glance landed on MEDICAL HISTORY and what he discovered blew his mind.

Under RELEVANT PARENTAL HISTORY, he saw "speech impediment: stutter" next to his mom's name.

He stared at that one word, "stutter," for a long time, not knowing what to feel. He could never resent his mom—for leaving him with a tyrant, maybe, but not for this. Medical researchers probably hadn't known back then that stuttering could be hereditary, so he couldn't blame her.

But learning the truth vindicated his decision in not wanting a child. He knew the odds of passing it on, so why would he inflict his stammer on a child of his?

He couldn't fathom why his father had never told him. Then again, Garth never mentioned her. It was as if Rory's mom had never existed, apart from that one photo in his den, the only one in the entire house.

Slamming the book shut, he shoved it back in the box and refolded the flaps to secure it. The rattle bumped his hip as he replaced the box, and for one second, he contemplated putting it back.

He was torn between wanting to support Samira and tell her the truth about why the thought of bringing a child into the world terrified him.

The thing was, their child could be completely fine. So why would he spoil this special time for her because of his fears?

He shouldn't. He wouldn't. He'd clean the rattle and present it to her as a show of support. He'd apologize, and he'd be there for her.

She deserved nothing less.

Thirty-Two

Pia didn't come into work for two days, and she hadn't answered any of Samira's calls. If Samira hadn't already been battling the occasional wave of nausea, she'd be feeling sick to her stomach anyway. But she wouldn't hound Pia. She'd give her another day or two, and if she still ignored her, she'd enlist the help of her mom. Which meant she had to tell Kushi the big news.

Samira had contemplated taking her mom out for dinner—less chance of an overreaction—but it wasn't fair. Of course Kushi would be shocked, and with her mom prone to theatrics—she'd practically fainted when she'd heard the news of Avi's infidelity and their resultant separation—she'd want to do it in the privacy of her home, not visible to curious eyes.

As Samira let herself in, the tantalizing aroma of *rasam* and fried okra filled her nose. It had been her favorite comfort meal as a kid, the simplicity of spice-flavored boiled water poured over steamed rice with a side of okra. Fitting, that her mom was cooking it tonight. She had a feeling she'd need all the comfort she could get after the big reveal.

"Hi, Mom," she said, entering the kitchen and inhaling. "That smells so good."

Kushi glanced up from the stove, tilting her head to receive a kiss on the cheek. "You sounded stressed on the phone, so I made your favorite."

"Everything you cook is my favorite." Samira wrapped her arms around her mom from behind and gave her a brief hug. "I've missed your cooking."

"You should come home more often."

Samira accepted the chastisement and grabbed cutlery to set the table. "How's Sindhu?"

She felt a little guilty for using a roundabout way to pry, but she couldn't ask how Pia was, considering they worked together and her mom would instantly know something was wrong.

"She's almost as bad as you. I never see her." Kushi turned off the stove and removed the lids. "But I understand. She leads a very hectic life, a lot more social than me. She's on this committee and that, always buzzing around like a busy bee."

It shamed Samira she didn't know this. She'd envisaged the two sisters being very close, considering both their husbands had died years earlier and they had no other family apart from their daughters. At least Sindhu had Pia living in the same city and Samira knew she played the dutiful daughter.

It made her feel guiltier for abandoning her mom and only returning home once in over a decade to visit.

"Are you lonely, Mom?"

Considering the news she had to impart, it wasn't the best time to probe into her mom's emotional state, but she felt bad hearing how busy Sindhu was.

Kushi's eyebrows shot heavenward. "I've always been a home-body who values my peace. You know that."

Samira did know. In primary school, while other mothers would congregate at the gate to gossip after their kids had entered, Kushi would give her a wave and walk briskly up the street toward home. The local school she'd attended had been like a gathering of the United Nations, with families from Sudan, Lebanon, Sri Lanka, India, Vietnam, China, and Kenya. The mothers would trade recipes while keeping an eagle eye on their younger children, who were often swinging precariously from the monkey bars just inside the school gate.

But Kushi had never been a part of the school community. It hadn't bothered Samira at the time, because she'd had Pia a few year levels below her, and Sindhu had been on the Parents and Friends social committee. Later, in high school, none of the parents were involved, and they certainly didn't walk their kids to school, so Samira hadn't given it much thought. Had her mom been lonely even when her dad was around?

She'd given up her job as an architect in a small local firm when Samira had been born, and her dad had kept long hours at the university. When he wasn't in town at work, he'd live the academic life at home, with his nose buried in books well past midnight.

Her parents had always seemed happy. Until her marriage debacle, that is. Her dad had been against it from the start, but he'd given in to Kushi because he loved her and saw how important it was to her. But he'd never liked Avi, and her dad was a good judge of character. Once her dad saw how she'd fallen for Avi, he shelved his concerns and supported her like he always did. But when her marriage fell apart, she saw the toll it took on her parents' relationship. Her dad blamed her mom, just like she had, and even though they'd never discussed it as such, she sensed the distance in her parents' marriage.

It had been a relief to flee Melbourne for a number of reasons when her divorce came through, and the guilt over the part she'd inadvertently played in her parents' marriage problems had been one of them. Kushi and Ronald had seemed happy enough after she'd left during their many video conferences, and she could see they loved each other, but it made her feel bad that her disastrous marriage had affected them almost as much as it had her.

She'd been lucky growing up with parents who adored each other, and she'd reveled in their love, but it irked that she'd never really thought of how her mom coped without having her husband and daughter around for the last five years.

She'd been selfish, blaming her mom for her failed marriage, when she should've been reestablishing a relationship rather than punishing her. And now that she'd be bringing her own child into this world, and probably raising him or her alone in LA, it made her want to cherish her mom even more.

"What's got into you, *betee*? Why are you asking these questions about loneliness?"

Samira inhaled and blew out a breath to steady her nerves. "I have something to tell you."

Kushi had been spooning okra onto a plate, and the ladle paused midair. "Let me guess. You're leaving earlier than expected."

Considering Samira couldn't wait to flee Melbourne five years earlier after her dad's funeral, it wasn't such a stretch for her mom to jump to that conclusion.

"No." She eased the ladle out of her grasp and placed it back in the pot, and took the plate from her mom's hand and set it on the table, before gesturing at the seat next to her. "Come sit."

"This sounds serious." Worry creased Kushi's brow. "It's not your health, is it? Sushma's sister-in-law's cousin had a recent scare with ovarian cancer—"

"I'm pregnant, Mom."

Samira had planned on easing into it, but with her mom likely to go off on many dire tangents like she usually did, she had to tell her.

Kushi's mouth dropped open, and her eyes widened to saucer proportions. "What?"

"I'm having a baby." Samira placed a protective hand over her belly. "It's early days, but I've had a blood test, and the doctor at work confirmed it."

"But . . . but . . . how . . ." Kushi shook her head, still slack-jawed as she stared at her in bewilderment. "I don't know what to say."

"Say that you're happy for me, that you'll support me, that you'll love this baby as much as I will."

Samira heard the pleading in her tone, and it must've got through to her mom, because Kushi leaned forward and pulled her into her arms.

"Of course I will, *betee*. I love you, and I will love my first grandchild with every fiber of my being."

Tears pooled in Samira's eyes, and she blinked them away. She couldn't afford to cry, because she had a feeling if she started, it would be difficult to stop and she might blurt out the whole sorry mess with Pia and Rory.

When they eased apart, Samira glimpsed the sheen in her mom's eyes too.

"That Aussie you're seeing is the father?"

Samira nodded. "Rory."

"So you said." Kushi made it sound like a curse. "Have you told him?"

"Yes."

"Is he going to marry you?"

Right now, Samira didn't know if Rory even wanted to be involved in his child's life, let alone anything else. Besides, she would never marry for convention. Never again.

"We don't need to be married to raise a child."

"Oh dear." Kushi pressed her knuckles against her temples in a familiar gesture of disapproval. "This is not good."

"This is very good. A grandchild, Mom. How exciting." She reached out and clasped Kushi's hands in hers. "I know you will have a million questions and want me to do this the traditional way. But I'm thirty-seven. I'd given up hope of ever meeting someone I'd love enough to want to marry, let alone procreate with, so this baby is a miracle, considering I have three periods a year and the condom broke once."

Embarrassment flushed Kushi's cheeks, before she slowly nodded. "You are right. This baby is a miracle." She pressed a hand to her heart. "A grandchild . . ."

A beatific smile spread across her face. "I'm going to be a grandmother."

This time when they embraced, Samira felt safe, cocooned in her mom's love, knowing that no matter what happened, she had her mom in her corner.

Thirty-Three

Rory took it as a good sign that Samira agreed to see him. He'd tried calling her after leaving his dad's two days ago, but it had gone through to voice mail, so he'd left a message, and while she hadn't called him back, she'd sent a text asking him to meet her at work on her lunch break today.

Lucky he'd been called in to meet with his agent yesterday for a rundown on his upcoming trip to north Queensland to scout out the *Renegades* location, because it took most of the day and kept his mind off dwelling on how much he'd screwed up when she'd told him about the baby.

Now, as he waited for her in the foyer so they could stroll to a nearby café, with the rattle in his jacket pocket, he hoped to make amends. While he still couldn't see himself as a father and all that entailed, he needed to do right by her. Starting now.

The receptionist had left the front desk unattended. Then again, the place was quiet at this time of day. With its sleek ambience and excellent position in town, he expected the center to be busier. But technically, it was a start-up, so it would take time to build clientele. He'd happily sing its praises, considering Pia's expertise had helped him land the biggest role of his career.

As if thinking about her conjured her up, he saw Pia slip into the corridor via a side door and glance furtively around. Guess that meant she hadn't made up with Samira yet, because it looked like she was scanning her surroundings to avoid someone.

She caught sight of him, and he waved. She hesitated, but it would be rude to avoid him, so she strode down the corridor toward him.

"Hi, Rory, how are you?"

"Great, you?"

As she drew nearer, he had his answer before she spoke. Pia had looked like a supermodel during their sessions, with flawless makeup, glossy hair, and stylish Indian pants and loose flowing top combos. Today, no amount of concealer could hide the dark smudges under her eyes, her hair was pulled back in a messy bun, and her skin looked dull rather than glowing.

"I'm okay." She managed a tight smile that didn't reach her eyes.

"Thanks again for all the work you did with me. I'll make sure to spread the word among colleagues who need dialect coaching."

"Thanks."

Rory heard a door open behind him, and by Pia's startled look, it had to be Samira.

"I have to get back to work, Rory. Nice seeing you," she said, turning away and all but breaking into a sprint to escape.

Man, Samira must really feel like crap if Pia was still avoiding her. He turned, not surprised to see Samira staring at Pia's rapidly retreating back, sadness clouding her eyes.

"Hey," he said, bundling her into his arms before she had a

chance to say anything. She looked like she needed a hug, and he still felt shitty about the way he'd reacted to the baby news.

She melded to him, resting her head on his shoulder and sliding her arms around his waist. He liked the way they fit. It felt . . . right. He'd never felt this comfortable around a woman before. Maybe it had something to do with her maturity, but she didn't play games like other women he'd dated. Though one or two dates didn't equate with what he'd shared with Samira. They may not have spent a lot of time together, but it was the quality not quantity that counted.

And now a baby bound them. Interesting, that every time the thought pinged around his brain, he didn't feel so stressed anymore.

He could do this.

He had no idea how long he held her, and when she finally eased away to blink up at him with wide eyes filled with uncertainty, he wished he could hold her some more.

"You okay?"

She nodded. "You give the best hugs."

He smiled, placed his finger under her chin, and tipped it up. "And the best kisses."

He grazed his lips across hers, once, twice, clamping down on the urge to devour her when what she needed right now was tenderness.

She sighed against his mouth before snuggling into him again, holding on tight.

"You feel good," he murmured, pressing his lips to her hair. "How is it possible that we haven't known each other long yet it feels like a lifetime?"

She stiffened for a moment, before straightening to look him in the eye. "Not only are your hugs and kisses pretty damn good, but you know the right thing to say exactly when I need to hear it."

"Not always," he said, with a slight wince. "I'm sorry about how I reacted to the baby news. I was a jerk."

She placed a finger against his lips to silence him. "No, you were stunned, and I don't blame you for asking what I planned on doing." She bit down on her bottom lip. "Considering the brevity of our relationship, I should've expected it. We barely know each other, we live on different continents, I guess it's only natural."

She was letting him off lightly, and they both knew it. "Shall we go have lunch and talk about our baby?"

Her eyes sparked when he said "our baby," and he smiled. "I may have been an idiot when I first heard the news, but I'd like to make amends if you'll let me."

"Let's go," she said, slipping her hand into his. But as she fell into step beside him, he saw her cast a longing glance down the corridor toward Pia's office.

That was one problem he couldn't fix, but he hoped these two amazing women resolved their differences soon.

It didn't surprise him that neither of them were hungry and ordered coffees instead.

They had a lot to talk about.

"I've got something for you." He reached into his pocket and pulled out the rattle, which he'd polished to gleaming. "It used to be mine."

He placed it on the table between them, where it shone in the café's muted downlights. "It's an apology of sorts, because I'm not proud of the way I reacted when I first heard the news." He nudged it toward her. "I don't know the history behind the rattle, but it looks ancient, and it'll be nice for the baby to have something of mine."

He wondered if she'd understand the questions he was hedging around: Would she return to Melbourne permanently? Would he have a chance to parent his child?

Her eyes sparked with understanding. Smart woman. "I haven't made any decisions regarding where I'll live after the baby is born."

She picked up the rattle and shook it, eliciting a soft tinkle. "And this is beautiful. Thank you." Heat suffused her cheeks. "It means a lot to have your support."

"Not that I'll be any good for the next few weeks. I'm on location in north Queensland, scouting things out for when filming commences."

"That's fine. I don't have any tests or anything scheduled, just my first appointment with an ob-gyn." She hesitated, and he glimpsed uncertainty in her eyes. "Exactly how involved do you want to be? Do you want to come to appointments like that? To ultrasounds? And because of my age I'll probably need to have an amnio. Then there's pre-natal classes . . ."

She huffed out a breath. "I'm exhausted already."

He chuckled and reached out to snag her hand. "I'll be as involved as you want me to be. No pressure. Whatever you want."

She nodded, her lips curved in gratitude. "Let's just play it by ear, okay?"

Whatever that meant. The enormity of the situation, that he'd be helping support a child with little money and no clue, meant he should be glad she wasn't pressuring him. But he'd always liked clear-cut guidelines: for refining his speech, for dealing with his father, for everything.

So he blurted what he'd been contemplating the last few hours before their meeting.

"We should get married."

Her eyebrows rose above wide eyes before she laughed. "Well, that's just about the most romantic proposal I've ever heard."

Rueful, he swiped a hand over his face. "We should. It's the right thing to do for the baby."

She leaned over and tapped the side of his head with her finger. "Hey, you in there. This isn't the fifties. It's no big deal to have a baby without the parents being married."

He grinned and swatted away her finger. "I know, but I grew up without a mom. Wouldn't it be nice for our kid to have us together?"

The amusement in her eyes faded, and she slid her hand out from his. "I'm sorry, I shouldn't have made light of your proposal. That must've been hard growing up without her."

She didn't know the half of it. But now wasn't the time to tell her about his dysfunctional upbringing.

"It was, but that's not the only reason I proposed."

"Yeah?"

He nodded. "I like you. We're good together. Our kid will be lucky to have parents like us."

The corners of her mouth curved into the smile that kicked him in the chest every time. "Again, not the most romantic proposal."

When he opened his mouth to respond, she held up her hand. "You're a great guy, but I've already got one marriage under my belt. I'm not going to enter into another for the wrong reasons."

It made sense, and relief filtered through him. He didn't want to get hitched, not really. But among the relief, a small sliver of disappointment pierced him.

Under different circumstances, even if they were madly in love, would someone like her say yes to him?

The closer they got, the more his flaws would be revealed. His inherent insecurity couldn't be denied.

He wasn't good enough for her.

"Hey, you okay?" She touched his arm, and he nodded.

"Yeah. My bruised ego will heal." He winked. "And I know just the way to soothe it."

She laughed, not responding when the waitress deposited their coffees on the table, waiting until she'd walked away.

"As much as I'd love to spend the afternoon in bed with you, I have to get back to work."

She tipped a sugar into her coffee and stirred it, staring at the swirling spoon as if hypnotized, but not before he saw the concern return to her eyes. She was thinking about Pia.

"So you haven't sorted things out with your cousin yet?"

She shook her head as she raised her gaze to his. "I'm going to catch up with her after work tonight."

"Does she know this?"

"No, but it's been long enough. We need to get past this, and I'm taking over the management next week while she's away, so we have to at least talk before then."

"If there's anything I can do . . ." He sipped at his coffee, wishing he didn't feel so out of his depth around her.

Samira never brought up the age difference between them, and it didn't register with him, but at times like this, he wished he had more experience with women so he knew what to do to make things easier for her.

He cared about her. Seriously. And even if there wasn't a baby involved, he knew that the longer they dated and the closer her time came to return to LA, the harder it would've been to say goodbye.

"Thanks, but this is something I have to do," she said, placing the spoon on the saucer but making no move to pick up her coffee. "Want to catch up at my place tonight?" She grimaced. "Though if things go badly with Pia, I can't promise I'll be good company."

"Maybe I can cheer you up?" He trailed a fingertip down her bare forearm. "I've been told I'm very good at it."

"You are," she murmured, eyeballing him. "Just for the record, pregnant women have very high libidos."

"Is that a fact?"

"It is, one I can prove to you tonight."

He grinned, loving how they could switch from earnest to lighthearted so easily. He'd never had a serious relationship, and he'd never imagined it could be like this. Being with Samira was . . . easy. Maybe that was an age thing too; she was mature and self-confident and didn't feel the need to play games.

She would be a good mom.

"Hey, I've just realized something," he said.

"What?"

"We've never been on a real date."

"Sure we have. That day we spent together in Dandenong." She pressed a hand to her heart and pretended to swoon. "Our first date. How could I forget?"

He chuckled at her theatrics. "I was thinking along the lines of something classier, more elegant."

She smiled. "I don't need all the bells and whistles. I just like spending time with you."

"Yeah, but I'm going away for a few weeks. I think it would be nice for us to go out tonight."

Joy sparked her eyes. "You're a romantic. How quaint."

Embarrassment heated his cheeks. "I'm about the least romantic guy ever, but you're special, and I want to do this."

A soft smile curved her lips. "It's a date."

Thirty-Four

Having coffee with Rory at lunchtime had left Samira feeling warm and fuzzy all afternoon. Ironic, that she'd never date a guy ten years younger, usually, but Rory far surpassed her expectations in the maturity stakes.

His proposal had been cute and reeked of old-fashioned chivalry, and while she'd never seriously take him up on it, it had been nice for him to ask. He wanted to be a part of this baby's life, and that meant a lot.

When she'd fled Melbourne over a decade ago, she never contemplated moving back. She'd established a great life in LA and loved living there. But the moment she'd discovered she was pregnant, she'd known she'd be facing some tough decisions about her living situation. And now with Rory wanting to be a part of their child's life if she wanted him to be . . . and with her mom here . . . it made sense that she seriously consider moving back home.

Hopefully, she'd have Pia's support too, and she was about to take the first steps to mending their fractured relationship.

Pia couldn't resist rocky road, so Samira had ducked out to

Haigh's to purchase their delicious chocolate/marshmallow/nutty combo. They'd rarely argued as kids, but if they had a disagreement, Samira always softened up her cousin with chocolate.

With the last patient gone and the receptionist locking the front door after exiting, Samira headed for Pia's office, rocky road in hand. Pia had been avoiding her, coming in late, leaving early, and booked solid with patients when she was here. The fact she hadn't left yet—Samira had checked with the receptionist—gave her hope that she may be ready to talk.

She stood outside Pia's door, steeling herself, when it opened and she came face-to-face with her startled cousin.

"Thought you might be hungry after a busy day," she said, holding out the rocky road.

Pia's eyes lit up as she spied her favorite chocolate, but the light soon faded when she glanced at Samira's stomach.

"You can't avoid me forever, Cuz," Samira said, hating this awkwardness between them. "We need to talk."

Pia hesitated, her hand on the door, and for one second Samira thought she might slam it in her face. But Pia sighed and opened it wider, beckoning her in. When she made no move to take the chocolates, Samira placed them on her desk, unsure whether to sit when Pia remained standing.

"Pia—"

"Don't." Pia held up her hand. "I'm so ashamed I can barely look at you. The way I reacted the other day when you told me about the baby . . ." She shook her head, a swath of glossy black hair half hiding her face. "I'm mortified."

"It was a shock. I get it."

"No, you don't." Pia swiped her hair away and finally eyeballed her, her eyes filled with regret and embarrassment and sadness. "I've been consumed with having a baby for the last few years. It's debilitating, and it's ruining my marriage . . ."

A sob escaped Pia's lips despite her doing her utmost to compress them, and Samira stepped forward to bundle her cousin into her arms.

"I'm sorry, sweetie," she said, unsure what she was apologizing for but wanting to offer whatever comfort she could.

She'd asked Pia when she'd first got back how Dev was dealing with the fertility problems, and Pia had said he was coping. She'd taken her at her word. Then again, if anyone had asked her fourteen years ago, she would've said the same, not wanting to articulate how increasingly distant her husband became when she didn't fall pregnant. In Dev's case it could be harder, considering he was the cause of the infertility and so much of a male's macho was caught up in reproduction.

Pia clung to her, crying softly like she used to as a kid, making snuffling noises rather than full-on sobs. When she quieted, she backed away and Samira released her, but guided her to the nearest chair before pulling up one next to her.

"You okay?"

"Not really," Pia said, her eyes puffy and her nose red. "I've behaved appallingly, and I'm really sorry."

Samira waved away her apology. "I knew you would take it hard, finding out about my pregnancy. I remember what it was like, being surrounded by fertile women proudly showing off their baby bumps while I tried everything to get pregnant."

"All the more reason I should've been happier for you," Pia said, her expression downcast, guilt twisting her mouth. "I hate to admit it, but when you told me, I was totally consumed by jealousy, and all I could think was how unfair it was, why you and not me."

"I get it." Samira took hold of Pia's hands and squeezed in re-assurance. "I hated not being able to talk to you about all this, especially when I knew how hard it must've been for you."

"I'll be okay." Pia sniffed, several times, before continuing. "And our marriage is okay, I think, but Dev's losing patience with the whole process. He's withdrawing from me. I can feel it." She blinked rapidly. "Our sex life is rote bordering on nonexistent, he's not interested in date nights anymore . . ." She shook her head. "He's not keen on this alternative-therapies retreat, but I booked it as a way for us to reconnect and to show him that conceiving doesn't have to be all about procedures and hospitals."

Pia gnawed on her bottom lip before giving her head another shake. "The retreat also discusses other options, like adoption, something Dev hasn't been too keen on."

"Why not? There are many ways to have a child."

"I know, but I think the infertility thing is wearing him down. He's never said it, but I know he feels guilty . . ." Pia trailed off, her voice barely above a whisper and filled with so much sadness. "He said to me once that this entire process is emasculating, having to use donor sperm to father a child. I reassured him, but there's a pal-pable distance between us now, and it feels like nothing I say or do can reach him."

Samira was the last person qualified to give advice, considering her own marriage had imploded under the weight of infertility, but she wanted to do whatever she could to support Pia. She'd thought it strange that in all the time she'd been back in Melbourne, she hadn't seen Dev once. She knew he'd been traveling for work, but the fact Pia hadn't tried to arrange a get-together meant they were probably struggling and Dev wanted to avoid her family.

"Pia, I'm going to ask you something, and know it's coming

from the right place." Samira pressed a hand over her heart. "If IVF doesn't work and Dev doesn't want to adopt, would you be happy with just him? The two of you together for the rest of your lives?"

Samira's stomach went into free fall, because she saw the answer written all over Pia's face before she answered.

"I used to think it would be okay, just him and me, but lately I'm not so sure." Tears filled her eyes. "I know he wouldn't cheat on me like Avi did with you, he's not that kind of guy, but . . ." She shook her head, sadness evident in her posture, shoulders slumped in defeat. "I love him, but our marriage is suffering because I want a baby so damn badly and I'm not sure he does anymore."

Crap. Samira's heart ached for her beautiful cousin. She knew all too well what it felt like to feel helpless in a marriage, unsure what to do to save it. For her, she doubted she'd ever really loved Avi. She'd loved being in love, and once that had worn off and he'd started to show his true narcissistic side, she'd grown indifferent.

In that moment, she realized something. All these years she'd been blaming him for ruining their marriage. He'd cheated. He'd got some teenager pregnant. He'd left her and divorced her and made her a laughingstock within the close-knit Indian community. And while there was no excuse for him straying rather than trying to work on their marriage, she had to admit she might have contributed to the distance that had opened up between them the longer it took for her to fall pregnant.

They'd had sex to procreate, but there'd been no intimacy in their marriage, not from the start. She'd played the role of the dutiful young wife, establishing her physical therapy career, attending many family functions, parading her suave Indian husband with pride. But behind closed doors, their marriage had been shallow.

All gloss and no substance. She hoped Pia's marriage could survive the battle with infertility in a way hers couldn't.

"This retreat is a last-ditch effort to see if we can relax and have some fun with this baby stuff rather than it being a chore all the time."

Samira read between the lines. "Last-ditch effort for your marriage, you mean?"

Pia bit her bottom lip and nodded. "We're in trouble, Sam, and the kicker is, I don't know what to do. I want to fight for us because we love each other, but I need Dev to make an effort too. It seems like he's filled with self-recrimination, even though we worked through the initial shock when we discovered he's sterile, and I think it's consuming him."

"Oh, sweetie." She clasped Pia's hand and squeezed. "Is that why I haven't seen him since I got back? Because you two aren't in a good place?"

"Yeah. He hasn't been around to Mom's or any family dos, because he says he can't pretend."

"I get it. Avi started avoiding my folks at least two months before he broke the news about his affair." She snorted. "I should've known there was something wrong, but I was too busy playing the perfect bride to worry about it."

"Avi was an asshole, end of story."

Samira paused. The last thing she wanted to do was bring up more baby talk around her cousin, but she couldn't very well ask her mom what had been bugging her.

"Hey, I heard through the grapevine his wife's expecting their second child. That's a massive gap between kids. Do you know what that's about?"

Pia's eyes widened in surprise. "It's not like you to ask about the asshole."

"Just curious."

Pia shrugged. "People don't talk around me when it has anything to do with him because they know we're close, so no, I have no idea." A cheeky glint lit her eyes for the first time in a long time. "Maybe his dick shriveled and he couldn't get it up."

Samira laughed, and thankfully, Pia joined in. It wasn't that funny, but with the pent-up tension between them draining away, they laughed long and loud, until tears seeped from their eyes.

When their laughter petered out, Pia's expression turned serious again. "I'm sorry for overreacting to your baby news, but I'll be honest, Sam: it's going to take me a while to process, and until then, I'm not going to be the best support person for you."

"That's okay."

Though it wasn't. Pia was her best friend, and without her to bounce ideas off or share her fears, Samira knew she'd be lost.

"How did Rory take the news . . ." Pia's hand flew to her mouth. "Have you told Kushi yet? Man, she's going to freak."

"Actually, Mom was pretty good about it, a lot better than expected. And Rory's come around."

"I bet he didn't freak as badly as I did."

"Not quite, but it was a shock."

"For us all." Pia managed a wry smile. "I know I don't have to say this, but please don't mention anything to your mom about me and Dev having problems."

Samira made a zipping motion over her lips. "I hope the retreat helps clarify things for you."

"Me too."

"I'm here for you," Samira said, pulling her in for a quick hug. "Anytime."

"Thanks."

Pia didn't say the same, and Samira couldn't help but feel disappointed. Then again, at least they were talking again and Pia had been honest about needing time to process. She couldn't expect miracles.

"Shall we do handover tomorrow?"

Pia nodded. "Let's meet at three in the conference room."

"Deal. And Pia?"

"Yeah?"

"For what it's worth, I like Dev, always have, but it takes two to make a marriage work. If he's struggling with everything, maybe he should seek professional help?"

If her bluntness surprised Pia, she didn't show it. It may have sounded harsh, but Samira wished someone had given her honest advice about marriage when she'd felt alone in hers.

"We had fertility counseling before starting IVF, but the way he's spiraling, I think he needs more." Pia raised stricken eyes to hers. "I've mentioned it a few times, but he gets defensive or shuts down."

"If you two are in this for the long haul, perhaps give him a gentle shove and make the appointment?"

Pia didn't respond, but Samira almost saw the thoughts pinging around her head. "Can I ask you something?"

"Anything."

"I know Avi was a lying, cheating asshole, but did you blame yourself just a tad for your marriage breakdown when you couldn't conceive?"

Remembering the guilt and sorrow at the time, Samira nodded.

"It didn't make sense, because he broke us, not me, but I always wondered if I'd been able to have a baby, would he not have strayed. Why do you ask?"

"Because I know Dev blames himself for our predicament. I've never made him feel that way, but I'm afraid the more insular Dev becomes, the more he withdraws from me, I won't know what to do to drag him back to me, if that makes sense."

Samira nodded. "Perfect sense. I felt incredibly guilty, which is irrational, because medical problems happen, but I also felt worthless and helpless and a big fat failure."

"I'm so sorry you felt that way." Tears shimmered in Pia's eyes. "I can imagine how my big, brave husband, who's been a high achiever since he started school, might be feeling the same way, and I don't want him to be self-flagellating."

"I really think he needs to see a professional. You too, sweetie."

"Yeah, you're right," Pia said, reaching out to touch her arm before heading for the door. "Thanks for the great advice as usual. See you tomorrow."

Samira wished she could ease her cousin's pain, but she had a feeling things would get worse before they got better. She liked Dev, he was a good guy, and he adored Pia. They were a great couple, and she really hoped they could work through their issues. It saddened her. Just as her life was looking up, her cousin's was falling apart. But she couldn't think about that now. She had a date to look forward to with her baby's daddy, and while she hadn't made any long-term decisions yet, she intended to enjoy herself for now and live in the moment.

Thirty-Five

T hough Rory had signed the *Renegades* contract, he hadn't seen the first payment yet, and that meant his date with Samira would be low-key. But that didn't mean it wouldn't be romantic. He wanted to show her how important she was to him. Every time they'd met up before this had resulted in them being in bed sooner rather than later, and while he had no complaints, he wanted to do this right.

The security guard who'd taken him up to her place several times now gave him the side-eye as he paced the foyer. She'd texted him that she'd meet him down here. He'd wanted to ask how things went with Pia, but he'd see soon enough by her expression.

The elevator doors slid open at that moment, and as he glimpsed her genuine smile, the breath he'd been unaware he'd been holding whooshed out. She looked relaxed, happy, and heart-stoppingly beautiful in a clingy black dress that highlighted her body and skimmed her curves. His gaze flicked to her belly for a moment; silly, because she was only a few weeks pregnant, but he imagined her belly swollen with his child, and he could've sworn his chest expanded with pride. He may be terrified of passing on his stutter to his child, but there was no turning back now. She was keeping the baby. They would be parents. He had to stop catastrophizing and focus on the positives: this woman, in his life, for however long he was lucky enough to have her.

He strode across the foyer, his heart pounding. He wanted tonight to be perfect, because three weeks away from her would be too long.

"Hey, beautiful." He slanted a kiss across her lips, savoring the way she melded into him.

"Hey, gorgeous," she murmured against the corner of his mouth, and he grinned as he eased away.

"You look pretty happy, so I'm guessing things went well with Pia?"

She nodded, but some of the joy in her eyes faded. "We had a good chat about the baby, but she's going through some tough stuff with her hubby, and I'm worried."

"You're close, so it's natural to worry," he said, smoothing the tiny frown line between her brows. "But she has you in her corner; she can't lose."

"There you go again, knowing the right thing to say." She caught hold of his hand. "I thought you were super quiet when we first got together, but I like that when you speak, it's worth listening to."

"I am quiet," he said, as realization dawned. Usually, when he felt comfortable around someone, his chance of stuttering increased, but with Samira that hadn't happened. In fact, in their last few interactions, he hadn't even worried about it.

Had landing the *Renegades* gig given him a much-needed confidence boost? Or was there something else at play here? Had he moved beyond "comfortable" with Samira and had genuine feelings for her?

"Quiet or verbose, I like you just the same," she said, resting her head on his shoulder. "At the risk of scaring you off, I haven't felt so connected with a guy in forever. It's just so easy between us."

"Yeah, I know what you mean."

She must've heard something in his voice, because she lifted her head to look at him. "I know tonight's about having fun, but maybe after you get back from Queensland, we can discuss the future."

"Uh-oh, the F word." He pretended to wince. "You already said no to my marriage proposal, which wounded me deeply, for the record, so I'm assuming you mean we'll discuss where you'll have the baby, if you'll stay in Melbourne, that kind of thing?"

"Yeah." She slugged him on the arm. "And I said no because you asked out of chivalry, not undying love."

"Can't it be both?" He clutched at his chest. "You have no idea what you do to me."

"That's lust, not love." She rolled her eyes. "And if we don't go on this date right now, we'll have to wait even longer to get to the lust part."

He'd never been so tempted to say screw the date and just screw her. But he wanted to do this right, no matter how much he wanted her.

"Let's go."

He liked the feel of her hand in his as they strolled out of her building and into a balmy Melbourne evening. The Yarra River, visible between a nearby hotel and an office skyscraper, shimmered with the city's reflected lights. He loved Melbourne but was looking forward to the challenge of living in a small community on set in the outback.

"You've reverted to quiet," she said, swinging their arms a little.

"Just thinking about the next few weeks on set."

"You haven't told me much about the show."

"I don't know a lot, to be honest. That's what the next three weeks are about."

"When do you actually start filming?"

"In roughly eight weeks."

He paused, wondering if he should tell her the rest. When he'd accepted this amazing opportunity, he hadn't envisaged being a father or having to support her through this. With filming promising to go on for months, he wouldn't be around much and would miss the important stuff like scans, prepping the nursery, that kind of thing. Though nothing or nobody could keep him away from the birth.

Then again, would she even want him there if he wasn't around for the rest?

"And you're quiet again." She swung their arms a little higher.

"I could be away for several months," he said. "I hate that you'll have to go through a lot of this pregnancy on your own."

She stopped walking and tugged on his hand so that he faced her. "I won't be on my own. I've got Mom and Pia." A blush stained her cheeks. "And if I'm going back to LA, I'll be on my own anyway, so don't worry about it."

His heart sank at the thought of her leaving, but he didn't want to get into this now. Time enough for the big discussion when he got back in a few weeks.

"Okay, I won't worry." He raised her hand to his lips and pressed a lingering kiss on her palm before curling her fingers over it. "Now, are you ready to be wooed properly?"

A coy smile curved her crimson-glossed lips. "Bring it on, handsome."

Thirty-Six

Samira had never cruised on the Yarra River. Growing up an only child meant she spent a lot of time with her parents on the weekends. On the occasions when the three of them would spend time with her dad's friends, she'd have her nose buried in a book while her dad waxed lyrical with his fellow academics and her mom hung out with the wives, holding her own with talk of her architectural dreams.

She'd never realized how much Kushi had given up when she'd decided to be a stay-at-home mom or wondered why she hadn't returned to her career once Samira had gone to school. It wasn't something they'd discussed, and bringing it up now might make her mom sad.

In her teens she'd become self-absorbed, caught up in school dramas and crushes and getting good marks to get into uni for her physical therapy degree. Being time poor, she'd mostly hung out in Dandenong and its surrounds, venturing as far as Glen Waverley with friends. Besides, cruising on the Yarra seemed like a couple thing to do, and even when she'd started dating Avi, he hadn't been overtly romantic.

Rory, on the other hand . . . He'd surprised her tonight. After initially freaking out at the baby news, he seemed to be throwing himself into this relationship wholeheartedly, though she couldn't dismiss a niggle of worry that he was still holding back about something. Then again, she hadn't told him all her deep, dark secrets. They weren't that kind of couple. In fact, the realization he wouldn't be around for most of her pregnancy rammed home that if she decided to return to LA, it wouldn't be such a big deal.

Kushi would be devastated, but why couldn't her mom come and stay with her in LA for as long as she liked? She didn't have anything tying her to Melbourne. Samira had always wondered why her mom had never come to visit but hadn't pushed the issue. How could she, when she avoided Melbourne?

But a baby would change things, and she knew if she asked Kushi to come stay with her in the first few months after the birth, her mom would agree.

She had a lot to think about.

"While I love our mutually comfortable silences, you've been quiet for an awfully long time." Rory dropped a kiss on the top of her head, where she snuggled into the crook of his arm, tucked under his shoulder as their gondola drifted along, the gondolier behind them humming an eighties pop song.

"Just thinking," she said. "And savoring the most romantic date I've ever had."

She glanced up at him and batted her eyelashes, and he laughed. "I'm surprised fish-and-chips on the banks of the Yarra followed by a short cruise impresses you so much."

"Why?"

"You live in LA. I imagine you've been wooed by pricey dinners on Rodeo Drive or strolls along Santa Monica Pier or hitting the hottest Beverly Hills nightspots."

She made a *pfft* sound. "I don't need flashy."

He stared at her with clear intent in his gaze. "What do you need?"

Heat shot through her, setting her alight. How did he do that with a single glance?

"You," she murmured, reaching up to draw his head toward her. "I need you."

His lips grazed hers in an all-too-brief kiss, a kiss of promise, a kiss of what was to come.

A subtle clearing of the gondolier's throat had them easing apart with regret.

"I've loved every minute of tonight, but are you ready to head back to my place?"

His wicked grin was all the answer she needed.

He glanced over his shoulder at the gondolier. "Can we head back now please?"

"Sure thing, mate."

Samira smiled. She'd never been to Venice, but she imagined the gondoliers on the Grand Canal didn't call anyone "mate." Thankfully, the guy had powerful arms, and he dropped them off at their pick-up spot in seven minutes; seven long minutes of being all too aware of Rory's subtle citrus scent, the press of his thigh against hers, his fingertips tracing lazy circles on the top of her arm. She snuggled into the nook of his arm tighter, craving contact, barely able to contain how badly she wanted him. She could blame her horniness on pregnancy hormones, but she'd been this hot for him since their first night together.

Sensing her urgency as he helped her from the boat, he leaned down to murmur in her ear, "You're driving me crazy too, sweetheart."

"Let's go," she said, taking his hand and all but breaking into a jog.

He laughed and picked up the pace. Once again, neither of them spoke as they reached her building, and she didn't mind. Anticipation thrummed between them, making her blood fizz and heating her from the inside out.

As they stepped into the elevator and the doors slid shut, she muttered, "Wish this stupid thing didn't have cameras."

"What would you do if it didn't?"

He pulled her in front of him and slid his arms around her waist, pressing his rigid erection into her, making her mouth go dry.

"I'd push you up against the wall, unzip you, and go down on you."

He made an odd choking sound a second before the elevator stopped and the doors slid open.

"You're killing me," he said, matching her brisk steps as they reached her apartment and she slid the card through the slot with an unsteady hand.

"Yeah, but what a way to go."

As the door closed, she pushed him up against it and slammed her mouth onto his. Their teeth bumped a little, and their noses squished, but she didn't care, and by his low, appreciative groan, he didn't either.

He had this way of using his tongue that made kissing him the most sensual experience in the world, and as he slid his hands under her skirt and tugged her panties down, she never wanted this to end.

He gripped her ass and hoisted her high, spinning around so he had her pinned to the door. She wriggled, craving closer contact, and he obliged by unzipping. Wrapping her legs around his waist, she gasped as he slid into her with one smooth thrust. Filling her. Completing her.

"So good," she whispered against the side of his mouth, and he responded by withdrawing slowly, inch by infinitesimal inch, before plunging back in. Repeating it over and over until she was mindless and clinging to him and clawing at the edges of an orgasm to end all orgasms.

"Rory . . . oh . . . yeah . . ." Every muscle in her body tensed as he drove into her, hard and fast, so freaking hot.

His mouth claimed hers again a moment before she climaxed on a loud cry, the pleasure so intense it brought tears to her eyes.

They'd had some phenomenal sex in their time together, but nothing like this, and as he lowered her slightly and she unwrapped her legs from around his waist, the tears in her eyes threatened to spill out.

"Fuck, are you crying?"

He cupped her face between his hands and brushed under her eyes with his thumbs. "Did I hurt you, baby?"

The urge to cry intensified, and she bit down on her bottom lip and shook her head.

"Sam, tell me what's going on."

He looked so concerned, she had to tell him.

"That was the best sex of my life," she said, and his eyes lit up with typical male pride.

"And you're crying?"

"From happiness, you dufus." She whacked him on the chest and sniffled. "Now take me to the shower so we can clean up and do it all over again."

"I like the way you think." He grinned and dropped his hands to her shoulders. "You're amazing. You know that, right?"

"You can keep telling me in the shower." She sagged against him, suddenly boneless.

"Hey." He tipped up her chin and brushed a kiss across her lips. "We were so hot for each other I didn't use a rubber."

She'd been so mindless with want she'd barely noticed. "It's not like getting pregnant is an issue, and we already established when the condom broke that we're clean?"

"Yeah." The faintest blush stained his cheeks. "I get a yearly physical, and my last was six months ago, and I haven't slept with anyone but you since."

Ridiculously, the thought pleased her. He could've slept with a hundred women and it shouldn't bother her, but for now, she was glad they were monogamous and happy.

"As clean as we are," she said, threading her hand through his hair, "we could get cleaner . . ."

She tugged his head down for another hot, openmouthed kiss that had her wanting him more than ever.

He broke away, his breathing ragged. "Shower. Now."

His gaze locked with hers. "But just so you know, three weeks away from you is going to be pure torture, babe, so I intend on making up for lost time all night long."

Samira could hardly wait.

Thirty-Seven

After the night he'd spent with Samira, the last thing Rory felt like doing was visiting his dad. But he wanted to tell him about the baby, and they hadn't had a chance to talk since he'd discovered the truth about his mom. Getting his head around fatherhood and the incessant fear he might pass on his affliction to his child was hard enough without the million-dollar question pinging around his head.

Why had Garth never said anything about his mom's stutter?

Then again, he'd hated any kind of verbal interaction with his dad growing up, so after asking Garth about his mom a few times, and the resultant foul moods, he hadn't broached the subject again.

He'd lived in a mansion his whole life, had the best of everything, but the one thing he craved the most.

Family.

He doubted Garth would want to talk about his mom now, but he'd be damned if he let this go, not with what he'd discovered in the attic.

Bertha, the housekeeper he'd met last time, let him in and asked him to wait in the library. Crazy, being told where to wait in the house he'd grown up in, but he was used to the games his dad liked to play. Meeting in the library was a chastisement for the way he'd left last time without waiting as instructed for Garth to come home.

Garth had always used the library as a punishment for him growing up, thinking he hated books. The joke had been on his dad, because those hours he'd been told to stay in the library and not come out had been bliss, uninterrupted time where he'd be lost in the pages of a book and not having to interact with his stern, poor excuse for a father.

He strolled the perimeter, checking out the spines for anything new, but predictably, Garth Radcliffe didn't waste time reading current fiction. Rory knew his dad still worked long hours—being a renowned barrister in Melbourne meant he was in demand—but how did his dad spend his downtime? The fact he had no idea saddened him.

He'd sat around on set many times over the last few years, listening to other guys talking about golfing or fishing or going to the footy with their dads on the weekend, and he'd wonder anew what was wrong with him that Garth treated him like an inconvenience to be tolerated rather than a son?

The door opened, and his father strode in. "Rory, what's this all about? I've got a meeting I can't miss in an hour, so—"

"This won't take long."

A disapproving frown slashed Garth's brow. In all their years, Rory had never interrupted him.

"You're going to be a grandfather."

Rory took pleasure in delivering the news with bluntness, as his father gaped in openmouthed shock.

"When . . . I mean who . . . How . . ." Garth swiped a hand over his face and started again. "I didn't even know you were dating anyone."

Rory snorted. "Why would you? We never discuss our personal lives." He snapped his fingers. "In fact, we don't discuss much of anything, which leads me to ask, why didn't you tell me Mom stuttered?"

Garth's frown deepened. "Why is this relevant now?"

"Cut the crap, Dad. When you blew me off last time I was here, I went into the attic looking for my baby stuff, because I'm going to have a kid, and I found my records with Mom's medical history."

Garth fixed him with a steely stare before he pulled up the nearest chair and sat, pointing at the chair opposite.

"I didn't blow you off. I asked you to wait for me."

Rory barked out a harsh laugh. "Out of everything I just said, that's what you go with?"

To Rory's surprise, his father appeared suitably ashamed. "I'm processing."

Rory rolled his eyes. "I've got somewhere to be too, Dad. I landed the role as host for Australia's next biggest reality show. I'm on set in Queensland for the next three weeks, and I'm leaving shortly."

Garth's eyebrows rose. "You're full of surprises today."

Rory hadn't expected his father to congratulate him, but a small part of him still hoped that one day Garth would actually acknowledge his successes.

"What's all this about you becoming a father?"

"The woman I'm seeing, Samira, is pregnant."

A frown furrowed Garth's brow. "Is this what you want?"

"Like how you didn't want me, you mean?"

Garth's gaze shifted away, and the old, familiar hurt of being unwanted tightened Rory's chest.

"What makes you say that?"

Rory shook his head. "Where should I start, Dad? The fact you barely tolerated me when I was a kid. How you got this pained look on your face every time I had to talk to you. How your impatience made you finish every sentence I ever uttered. How you never spent time with me." He held his hands out. "Should I continue?"

Pain contorted his father's face before he finally raised his eyes to meet his. "I always wanted you," he said. "But I harbored a lot of guilt, and it manifested in a way I couldn't control."

Confusion made Rory chuckle when it was the last thing he felt like doing. "You're a control freak, so I'm pretty damn sure you could get a handle on this so-called guilt."

If his dad wanted him to ask what he felt guilty for, he'd be waiting a long time. Rory didn't want to hear his excuses. He wanted to learn more about his mother.

Folding his arms, Rory sat back and raised an eyebrow in a silent challenge. Finally, Garth gave a small nod, as if coming to a decision.

"Your mother had a minor stutter, hardly noticeable at all. But she was very self-conscious, and when my career started to take off, we had to attend a lot of legal functions. She made an effort, but she hated them because of her irrational fear of slipping up and making me look bad."

Rory knew that fear of slipping up, and it sucked. He felt for his mom and wished she'd been around so he'd had someone who understood what he'd gone through growing up.

"I did everything to reassure her that she could never make me look bad, that I loved her wholeheartedly, but the more successful I became, the more she withdrew . . ."

Sorrow darkened his dad's eyes. "We grew apart, and I had no idea how to fix it, so I focused on my work. She was busy with you, and we muddled along, until the day I came home after a major criminal case wrapped up to celebrate with her and she'd left. Left a note saying she didn't want to hold me back any longer, I deserved someone I could proudly parade at functions, that she was failing as a mother because you were copying her speech and stuttering . . ."

Rory didn't know what shocked him more, his dad opening up like this or the sheen of tears in his eyes.

"I was devastated initially, but then the anger set in. Even if she didn't love me, how could she abandon you?" Gruffness deepened Garth's tone, and he cleared his throat. "I couldn't forgive her for that. I wanted to. I could've found her if I wanted to, but I let my anger consume me, and by the time I'd calmed down enough, it was too late." Garth blew out a long, slow breath. "She died in a car accident about two months after she left."

Pain, swift and unrelenting, stabbed at Rory's chest. "And you never told me?"

Garth shrugged, regret evident in the slump of his shoulders. "What would've been the point? She'd left, regardless, and you were struggling enough. I didn't want to add to your burden."

"Dad, I'm twenty-seven. Did it ever enter your head to tell me this at some point when I grew up?"

Garth shrugged again, and it infuriated him.

"You stopped asking about her after a while, so I figured you didn't care . . . You were so young when she left, you wouldn't have remembered her."

Damn his father for being right. He could've pushed for answers when he was older, but he'd settled for nursing his resentment toward his father.

"You should've told me."

He'd never seen his father look so grave as he nodded. "You're probably right, but it's yet another mistake in a long list of mistakes I've made with you."

Rory resisted the urge to glance at the floor. Had hell just frozen over?

"I've been a crap father." His mouth turned down. "After your mother died, I spent a lot of time second-guessing myself. Had I done enough? Had I pushed her away unwittingly? Should I have seen the signs of her wanting to leave earlier? Should I have gone after her sooner? Would she have come back if I'd gone to her and begged? I neglected you, and when I tried to rectify that, it was too late; you stared at me like I was a stranger." He shook his head. "And when you spoke, you reminded me so much of her it killed me."

When his father eyeballed him, Rory could hardly believe the depth of pain he glimpsed.

"So I stupidly treated you the same way I had her. I missed her so much, and you were a constant reminder of how I'd screwed up, so I withdrew from you too, and let you down in the same way I did your mother."

Regret clogged Rory's throat for all the wasted years. Why hadn't his father opened up to him about all this in the past?

"I—I don't know what to say."

Not that he wanted to speak, because whenever he was over-emotional, he stuttered, and this was one of those times.

"It's a lot to take in, Son, but I want you to know I'm sorry for being a lousy dad. I hope you'll do a better job than me."

They stared at each other for what seemed like an eternity, but for the first time in forever, Rory didn't feel bitter or angry or resentful. His father may have screwed up in so many ways, but the past couldn't be undone. The best he could hope for was a better relationship moving forward. And he had to admit, a huge part of him was relieved his father hadn't looked down on him because of his stutter but had withdrawn from him out of love for his mother.

"I appreciate you telling me the truth," Rory finally said to break the silence.

"Long overdue." Garth cleared his throat again. "Anyway, let's leave all this sentimentality alone and tell me about your new job. Landing a hosting role is a big step up for you. Uh . . . it would involve a lot of speaking?"

Pleased that his father had the insight to recognize what a big deal it was for him to speak in front of a camera, Rory nodded. "I've been receiving dialect coaching to land the role. It's helped a lot. Most of it will be reading off a cue, with minimal ad-libbing, so I should be all right."

Admiration glinted in his father's eyes. "You've never let anything stop you. Now tell me about this Samira."

Rory didn't want to tell his father anything, because he was too used to him tearing down his dreams, so he settled for a pared-down version of his relationship.

"She's Melbourne-born but lives in LA, has for the last decade. Runs a thriving physical therapy practice, is working here for six months in a state-of-the-art facility her cousin runs in South Wharf. Her mom's Indian, her dad's American, and she's beautiful."

Rory glimpsed respect in his father's steady stare. "I hope I get to meet her sometime soon."

Try never, but Rory kept that gem to himself. He didn't want anything tainting his fledgling relationship with Samira, let alone a cynical father who didn't have a paternal bone in his body. But his father's revelations today had given him hope that maybe they stood a chance at some kind of father-son relationship after all.

"I have to go, Dad." Rory stood and held out his hand. "I'm glad we had this chat, but I don't think either of us expects a miracle to happen overnight. We're not close, but who knows, with time and effort, things may change?"

His father rose and shook his hand. "I think we should make that effort, if not for our sakes, for the sake of my grandchild."

A flicker of disappointment had him releasing his father's hand quickly. Of course Garth Radcliffe would be interested in his grandchild; yet another pawn to mold and conform into his version of the ideal progeny. Rory would do anything to curtail his father's influence in his child's life, no matter how much Garth seemed to have opened up in the last ten minutes.

"I'll be in touch, Dad."

Rory had made it to the door when his father cleared his throat and said, "I truly am sorry for everything, Son."

Emotion tightened Rory's chest as he glanced over his shoulder and gave his father a terse nod. He would forgive him eventually, because hanging on to grudges wasn't his style.

But for now, he had a job to focus on and a woman he would miss terribly while he did it.

Thirty-Eight

"M om, you are killing me with kindness," Samira said, as she sat at her dining table at the end of another long day while Kushi served her a plate piled high with mutton biryani and a side serving of raita. "And I love you for it."

"You are eating for two," Kushi said, sitting next to her. "I must look after my girls."

Samira smiled at her mom's conviction she was having a girl. She'd performed some silly old wives' trick involving a gold wedding ring on a chain held over her belly, and the direction it swayed convinced Kushi her baby was female. Samira would rather rely on science at her twenty-week scan.

It seemed a lifetime away, considering she hadn't had her twelve-week scan yet, but with each passing day she felt more "pregnant." The nausea persisted, and her ankles ached at the end of a workday. Her heart ached too, considering this was the end of Rory's fifth week away and he'd just had his time extended in the outback for another three weeks.

She'd told herself it was for the best. Getting used to being apart, especially if she divided her time between LA and Melbourne. But considering she'd been spending almost every evening being fussed over by her mom, either in Dandenong at her childhood home or here in her Southbank apartment, Samira knew the chances of returning to LA to live were slim.

She enjoyed bonding with her mom, making up for the years of lost time. And by the smile perpetually on Kushi's face, the feeling was mutual.

Her unmarried status was still a sticking point between them, but every time Kushi hinted at the proof children were happier with two parents under the same roof, Samira would change the subject: any baby talk was guaranteed to send Kushi into a grandmotherly swoon, and Samira played it up to her full advantage.

"Shall we watch a Bollywood movie after dinner?" Kushi poured water into a glass and placed it in front of Samira. "The latest Shah Rukh Khan blockbuster has just started streaming."

"Sounds good, Mom . . ." Samira bit back a cry as a sharp pain jagged low in her belly.

She stilled, trying to clamp down on the irrational fear making her palms sweat. It could be nothing, a momentary cramping of her uterus, but she laid down her spoon just the same and eased her chair back from the table.

"I need the ladies, Mom. Back in a sec."

How she managed to walk to the toilet at a sedate pace, she'd never know, because the moment she stood, another pain, harsher than the first, ripped through her and she bit back a cry.

Fear, strong and potent, gripped her as she closed the bathroom door and tugged her panties down to sit on the toilet.

The spots of blood on her underwear had terror coursing through her.

Tears filled her eyes, but she gritted her teeth. She shouldn't jump to the worst conclusion, but it was pretty hard not to, considering her age.

She had to get to the hospital.

Now.

The last thing she wanted to do was send her mom into a panic—Kushi was an expert at immediately jumping to the worst conclusion. But as she changed her underwear and added a sanitary napkin, something she hadn't needed in many months, she'd never been more grateful to have Kushi around.

When she opened the bedroom door, she found her mom on the other side, worry accentuating the lines creasing her face.

"What is wrong, *betee?*"

Samira managed a wan smile. "How do you do that?"

"You are my child." Kushi laid a comforting hand on her cheek. "I know you better than I know myself."

Samira burst into tears, and Kushi bundled her into her arms. If she could be half the mother Kushi was, she'd be doing okay.

If she had a baby to mother.

The thought instantly sobered her, and she eased away, dashing the tears from her eyes with the back of her hand.

"Mom, I need to get to the hospital."

The color drained from Kushi's face, but to her credit, she didn't fly into a panic as Samira had expected.

"Do you need an ambulance?"

Samira shook her head. "The cramping has stopped, but I'm spotting."

"Let's go." Kushi slid an arm around her waist, and Samira had never been more grateful to lean against her mom even though she could walk perfectly well.

Growing up, her dad had often teased Kushi for traveling at a snail's pace in the car. Back then her mom had rarely driven beyond Dandenong, mainly to the market and school. But she'd obviously honed her road skills, because she made it to the hospital in under fifteen minutes, running a yellow light or two.

Kushi pulled up outside the ER. "Will you be okay to go in on your own while I park?"

"Thanks, Mom, I'll be fine."

Though she knew the lack of pain after the first two episodes meant nothing; the spotting was a possible indicator to something not being quite right.

"I'll be back soon," Kushi said, reaching across the console to squeeze her hand. "Be strong, my girl."

Emotion clogged Samira's throat as she forced a half smile before getting out of the car and walking slowly into the ER.

The next two hours flew by in a blur of questions and tests while she waited for the resident ob-gyn to arrive to perform the ultrasound that would provide conclusive evidence of her baby's condition.

Having her mom bedside, holding her hand, offering soft words of encouragement, should've provided comfort. It didn't, because she couldn't shake the numbness, a purely defensive mechanism, her body's way of shutting down her emotions so she wouldn't sob her heart out if the news wasn't good.

Finally, after what seemed like an eternity, a youngish woman entered the cubicle, wheeling an ultrasound machine beside her.

"Hi, Samira, I'm Dr. Englehart, and I'll be performing your ultrasound today."

The doc made it sound like a routine scan when they knew nothing could be further from the truth.

"Thanks," Samira said, shooting a quick glance at her mom to find her staring at the doctor with wide, fearful eyes.

Samira believed in God, but she rarely attended church, yet in that moment, as the doctor lifted her robe, squeezed gel on her abdomen, and pressed the ultrasound head onto her, she sent yet another prayer heavenward, one of many in the last few hours.

"Your tests looked good, so let's see what's happening in here."

The doctor moved the probe around, and Samira held her breath, her gaze riveted to the screen, searching for the small pulsing on the screen that would indicate her baby's heartbeat.

She couldn't see it, and her throat tightened with sorrow. Kushi clutched her hand so tight her grip bordered on painful, but it was nothing to the pain squeezing her heart at the thought of losing her baby.

"Ah . . . there we are." The doctor pointed at the screen, and Samira exhaled in relief. "A strong heartbeat, exactly what we want to see."

Samira's gaze locked on her mom's; tears leaked from their eyes simultaneously as the enormity of the ultrasound sunk in.

"Right, everything looks good here." The doctor removed the ultrasound probe and handed her paper toweling to wipe the gel off her stomach. "But the spotting can be a concern, so please keep a close eye on it, and if you have any doubts, come back in straightaway." She picked up Samira's chart and flicked through it again. "After a scare like this, it's pertinent to point out that because of your age there's an increased risk for gestational diabetes and preeclampsia, so I'd like to keep a closer eye on your blood pressure, blood glucose levels, and urine for protein and sugar."

Samira nodded, having already read up on "geriatric pregnancy" over the age of thirty-five. While the risk factors terrified her—stillbirth, chromosomal defects, low birth weight, prematurity, labor complications, as well as the diabetes and preeclampsia the doctor had mentioned—all she could feel right now was bone-deep relief that her precious baby was okay.

The doctor glanced at her watch. "I'd like to keep you in overnight, because as much as I don't want to scare you, the risk of miscarrying after an incident like tonight's is higher. So rest up, and I'll check in with you in the morning."

"Thanks," Samira said, while Kushi added, "Thank you, Doctor."

When Dr. Englehart left, Samira turned to her mother. "Mom, I don't know what I would've done if you hadn't been with me tonight, so I think now's as good a time as any to tell you I'm moving back to Melbourne."

A smile of pure joy spread across Kushi's face. "That's wonderful, *betee*. I'm so happy."

"This little one needs his or her grandmother." Samira placed a hand over her belly. "And I need my mom."

This time, they shed tears of joy, and Samira knew she'd made the right decision, for all of them. Almost miscarrying clarified her plans like nothing else. She been terrified of losing this baby, and she couldn't do this on her own.

Now, she had to break the news to Rory.

That was when it hit her. She hadn't thought about him until now. For the last few hours, she'd been so focused on her baby, she hadn't given a thought to the baby's father and how he would feel if they lost their baby.

She had to call him. Tomorrow.

For now, she'd try to relax and get through the next twenty-four hours, focusing all her positive energy on ensuring this baby stayed put.

Thirty-Nine

"Y ou have to stop stalking me like this."

The deep, familiar voice roused Samira from her doze, and she opened her eyes to find Manish grinning at her, looking dapper in his white coat and stethoscope draped around his neck.

"What are you doing here?"

She struggled into a sitting position and glanced around the room, looking for Kushi.

"I sent your mom to the cafeteria for something to eat. She looked pale and tired."

"It's been a long night." She winced. "I had a miscarriage scare."

His smile vanished as he nodded, grave. "I saw your notes. You came through the ER, and I always go through last night's cases for handover."

"Ah, right," she said, feeling oddly comforted that she'd chosen the hospital where he worked to check in last night.

It hadn't really registered at the time, but it had the best reputation in Melbourne, and it had seemed like the natural choice. In a way, she was glad he hadn't been on duty in the ER last night, because that would've been too weird. Friendship and medical emergencies didn't mix.

"You're feeling okay?"

"Yeah, but only slightly less terrified than last night."

He nodded. "We're going to discharge you shortly, but come back if you're worried at all."

He laid a hand on her lower leg. "Or better yet, call me."

She smiled her gratitude, and of course that was the moment her mom chose to enter the room. Her astute gaze zeroed in on Manish's hand touching her, and she positively beamed.

Samira wriggled a little, and he removed his hand, but not before shooting her a cheeky wink that said he knew exactly what Kushi was thinking: she should book the reception venue immediately.

"Have you eaten, Auntie?"

Kushi visibly melted under the onslaught of Manish's concern. "Yes, Manish, thank you." She turned to Samira and sent her a pointed look. "He's such a nice boy."

Samira bit back a groan. Only her mother could turn a horrid hospital visit into a matchmaking opportunity.

"He is, Mom. Manny's a good friend."

Kushi's scoffing *pfft* made Manish smile.

"He could be so much more if you had half a brain in your head," Kushi said, waggling her ring finger, while Samira felt heat scorch her cheeks.

"Mom, he's right there."

"I know, and that's why I'm speaking my mind." Kushi waved her hand between them. "Samira is moving back home to Melbourne. She's having a baby. She needs a good man to be her husband, and I think that is you, Manish."

Manny's grin widened, and Samira shot him a death glare. "You are right, Auntie. I am a good man. But alas, I have offered to marry your daughter, and she has refused me. She is very stubborn."

"Yes, she always has been." Kushi's loud, theatrical sigh made Samira want to giggle.

Manny had a killer sense of humor, and he was playing up to her mom at her expense. She'd make him pay for it another time.

"On that note, I have rounds to do." Manish gave a mock bow. "Ladies, if you need anything at all, don't hesitate to contact me."

He glanced at Samira, and this time, his gaze held concern rather than teasing. "Seriously, if you need anything, call me."

"Thanks, Manny." Samira waved while her mom rushed after him. She couldn't hear what they said at the door, but she guessed it had something to do with inviting Manny to a family dinner for three, where Kushi would proceed to find something to do, leaving the two of them alone.

When the door closed, Samira held up her hand before Kushi could say a word. "He was joking when he asked me to marry him. He has a good sense of humor, and we're friends, that's it, as I've told you countless times before."

"But, *betee*, he is so wonderful. What man would offer to raise another man's child?"

"Exactly." Samira snapped her fingers. "Don't you think it's strange we hardly know each other yet he'd offer to do that? He must have an ulterior motive."

Kushi rolled her eyes, where the kohl had smudged from their shared tears of relief last night. "Why can't you take him at face value?"

"Because I'm older and wiser, Mom, and not the naive, stars-in-her-eyes girl I was years ago."

Kushi made a disapproving clucking noise in the back of her throat. "I think you are still being naive if you think it's easy to raise a child on your own. This man is being noble and chivalrous. Why can't you take a chance on him? Love may grow—"

"We've discussed this, and I'm not going down the traditional route again."

Though a small part of her knew her mom was right. Love had grown with Avi once she'd opened herself up to the possibility.

And look how that had turned out.

But Manish wasn't like Avi, and while he may have offered to marry her in jest, and she wondered at his motivation for doing so, she allowed herself to daydream for a moment what it would be like to be married to him.

Culturally, she'd be accepted back into the fold of the extended Indian community. She wouldn't be judged or gossiped about, which was exactly what would happen when they discovered she was pregnant. Her child would grow up with a stable, respectable father figure. She would have help and support and many laughs.

But her baby already had a father, and she didn't love Manish. Which meant she had to introduce Rory into her mom's network to soften the blow of her pregnancy news and let the aunties do their worst.

"Mom, I'd like you to meet Rory."

Kushi rolled her eyes again. "This Ro-ry. Where was he last night when you needed him, huh?" She threw her arms wide. "Not here. What kind of father will he make? What kind of partner to you if he can't be here when you need him the most?"

Samira glimpsed fear in her mom's eyes, and she knew her concern came from the right place. But she wouldn't let her malign Rory, not when he didn't deserve it.

"He's away for work, Mom, in far north Queensland, so please don't cast aspersions on him when you don't know him."

Affronted, Kushi tilted her nose in the air. "Fine, you tell me when he's back and I will arrange a party."

That's what Samira had been afraid of, but there was no easy way to do this: Rory would be thrown into the deep end of endless speculation because of his age and nationality, and once the aunties learned of her pregnancy, he'd be scrutinized even more.

Besides, she wanted to see how he handled himself with her extended family network, because with her moving back to Melbourne, she'd be reabsorbed into her culture whether she liked it or not.

"Thanks, Mom, but keep it low-key, okay?"

"Of course," Kushi said, nodding, but Samira didn't trust the calculated gleam in her mom's eyes, not one bit.

Forty

Rory wasn't a fan of flying, but he'd never been so glad to see the small Cessna at the end of the makeshift runway not far from the set.

The plane had made countless trips, flying in crew and supplies over the last eight weeks, getting everything prepared for filming. But today, it would be flying him to Brisbane, where he'd catch a commercial flight back to Melbourne.

Back to Samira.

He didn't like the distance between them, and he wasn't just referring to the physical. He'd always preferred texting over talking via the phone. His thumbs could articulate words a lot faster and clearer than his mouth. But he'd wanted to hear her voice, so he'd rung a few times, had videoconferenced once, but each time she'd sounded . . . aloof. Withdrawn.

She said all the right things and forced a laugh or two at his anecdotes about living in the bush with a bunch of strangers, but in his gut, he knew something was wrong. He'd wondered if the baby was okay, but she'd assured him everything was fine. He didn't believe her, and he hoped she wasn't hiding some devastating truth from him because of the distance between them.

He'd missed the twelve-week scan, but she'd sent him a pic to his cell. It had been a godsend, keeping him sane at the end of a long day when the effort of trying not to stutter had taken its toll, leaving him exhausted and grumpy. He'd lie on his makeshift cot, staring at that pic of his kid, knowing he had to do right by him or her.

The fear hadn't left him that his kid could face the same difficulties he had growing up if he passed on his stutter, but he had to stop letting it taint the way he viewed this pregnancy. He should be celebrating it with Samira, not dreading something that may never eventuate.

"Safe travels, Rory." Sherman Rix, one of the directors who he'd auditioned for, clapped him on the back. "You've done well acclimatizing the last eight weeks, exactly why Allan and I chose you for this job."

He managed a sedate "Thanks," as this man intimidated him as much today as he did at the audition over two months ago. While he'd done his best to fit in on the set, he knew most of the crew viewed him as a recluse who preferred his own company than hanging around a campfire at night chugging beers and swapping bullshit. It didn't bother him, because the less time he spent talking to people beyond the scope of reading off a cue, the easier it would be not to slip up.

But the tension had taken its toll, and he couldn't wait to escape to his grungy Middle Park flat, no matter how tiny or illequipped. As well as seeing Samira, he was looking forward to dropping by the rec hall at the housing commission flats and seeing

Amelia's program in action. His first payment had gone into his bank account two weeks ago, and he'd forwarded the lot to her, keen to get the program started sooner rather than later. She'd responded by sending him pics of the hall with kids at tables around the room, working with therapists. It had warmed his heart and vindicated the sixteen-hour days he was pulling to ensure he did a great job as host of *Renegades*.

"See you back in Melbourne." Sherman held out his hand, and Rory shook it. "Take a break. Rest up. Because we start shooting in a month, and we need you on top of your game."

"No worries, I'll be ready." He gave a brusque nod, hiked his duffel over his shoulder, and headed for the plane.

Once ensconced in a small seat, he stared out at the barren landscape, admiring its rugged, red-dusted beauty but glad to see the back of it for now.

*E*ight hours later, after dumping his stuff in the wash at home and showering, he headed for Samira's. The security guard still gave him the side-eye as he stood outside her door, but he didn't care. In a moment, he'd be seeing the woman he'd fallen for, and he could hardly wait.

His heart pounded and his palms grew clammy. Crazy, considering they'd moved past the early dating stage, but his nerves had everything to do with seeing her again and hoping their connection hadn't waned.

The door opened, and he released the breath he'd been holding. She smiled at him, wide and genuine, before gesturing him in.

"Hey there, cowboy, long time no see." She nodded at the guard. "Thanks, Ru."

He waited until the door closed before sweeping her into his arms and seeking her mouth.

"I've missed you," he murmured, a second before claiming her lips in a searing kiss that proved actions spoke louder than any corny words he could say.

She clung to him, her tongue sweeping into his mouth, taunting, teasing, driving him crazy with want. Lust slammed through him. His hands skimmed her curves, plucking at her dress, craving more.

But they had to talk. He wanted to make sure everything was okay with her and the baby. "I brought you something."

She pressed her hips against his and winked. "I bet you did."

He laughed. "Nice to know those pregnancy hormones are still running riot, but I want to give you this."

He slid the smallish flat box from his back pocket and held it out to her. "I thought this might be a nice way to celebrate our impending p-parenthood."

Thankfully, she didn't notice his slipup, with her eyes focused on the blue velvet box balancing on his palm.

"You're sweet." She took the box and opened it, her soft sigh and curve of her lips indicating he'd done well. "It's beautiful," she murmured, slipping the silver charm bracelet out of the box and handing it to him. "Help me put it on?"

As he fiddled with the clasp, she stared at him with so much warmth his chest tightened with emotion. If he could, he'd give this woman the world. She'd breezed into his life and turned it upside down when he least expected it, and while the thought of being a father still scared the crap out of him, he felt like he could do anything with her by his side.

"There." He lifted her hand to his mouth and pressed a kiss to the back of it. "The first charm is a pacifier, and I thought I could add a new one for the baby's milestones, like first tooth, first step, that kind of thing."

"You're too much," she said, tears shimmering in her eyes, before she buried her face against his chest and he wrapped his arms around her.

He cradled her close, breathing in the fragrance of her, the faintest scent of cinnamon and cloves she used to make masala chai and a deeper, more alluring scent of her, all her.

He'd never been in love and had feared for a long time he wasn't capable of it. It wasn't like he knew much about it, considering his upbringing. But he'd done a lot of thinking while he'd been away and had a sneaking suspicion that with thoughts of Samira consuming his every waking moment, and this feeling of completeness now he had her in his arms again, he was in danger of falling headlong into an emotion he knew little about.

His arms tightened around her, and he rested his cheek on the top of her head. He had no idea how long they stood there, locked in an embrace that helped eradicate every painful moment of being apart, but when his eyes stung, he knew he had to aim for levity before he started sniffling too.

"Will it push you over the edge and really make you bawl if I tell you I've been reading a digital book on pregnancy while I've been away and can practically deliver our baby myself?"

She chuckled against his chest before easing away and whacking him playfully. "You can tell me all about your newfound knowledge over dinner, but first . . ."

He saw the exact moment the tenderness in her eyes gave way to desire, as if she too needed a distraction before blurting her innermost feelings.

With a coy smile, she grabbed his shoulders and guided him to the nearest chair, pushed him down on it, and clambered on top of him.

When he opened his mouth, she pressed a finger to it, silencing him, before unzipping him and taking his rigid cock in her hand and guiding it toward her.

Only then did he realize: she was going commando.

She slid onto him, lush, wet heat, and he groaned. He'd missed her, missed this, this intimacy that he'd never experienced with anyone but her.

Blood thundered in his ears as she rode him, bracing her hands on his shoulders, clenching his cock with her inner muscles, driving him to the brink all too quickly.

But he didn't hold back. She didn't want him to if her muttered urgings were any indication, and when his balls tensed and he surged upward, she thrust down at the same time, her neck arched, her head thrown back in wild abandon, crying out his name.

He came in a blinding rush that made his head ache, but as the pleasure subsided and he held her close, he knew without a doubt he'd come home.

Forty-One

That was some homecoming," Rory said, handing Samira a cup of peppermint tea. "Makes me wonder what kind of welcome I'll get when I'm away for over three months with the actual filming."

She smiled her thanks, but he saw the disappointment in her eyes. "That long?"

"Yeah, it's a killer schedule, but once it's done I'll be back for good." He sat next to her on the sofa and placed her feet in his lap. "And I'll definitely be back for the birth."

"Uh-huh."

She didn't say anything else, preferring to sip her tea rather than elaborate. But he could sense her disapproval, and it made him bristle.

"You knew I'd be away for most of this pregnancy when I got the *Renegades* job. And as much as I don't like it, it's something I have to do."

"I get it, I do, it's just . . ." She trailed off, an odd mix of guilt and regret clouding her gaze. "I had a scare not long after you left. Cramping and spotting, so I went to the hospital."

He stiffened, his blood chilling in his veins. "You almost miscarried?"

She bit her bottom lip and nodded. "It was terrifying. I had my mom with me, and she was great, but it really rammed home how much I can't do this alone, so I'm moving back to Melbourne for good."

Annoyance tempered his elation. She should've told him about the hospitalization; he should've been here for her. But to hear she'd be in Melbourne permanently offset his anger. They could have a real relationship, and he could be a dad to his kid.

"I'm not happy that you didn't tell me about the scare, but I'm rapt you're moving home," he said, picking up one of her feet and massaging it.

"So am I if you do that every night."

"Count on it," he said, pressing his thumbs into the sole, eliciting a low moan that turned his thoughts naughty in an instant.

"With me moving home, it also got me thinking it's time you met my mom and her cronies."

"Of course," he said, thrilled she wanted to move their relationship forward. "Anytime."

"Be careful what you wish for," she said with a grimace. "You have no idea what you're in for."

"How bad can it be?"

Her eyebrows shot up. "Are you serious? My mom is still bound up in tradition so would love to see me married to Manish before the baby is born, and the aunties, a bunch of scary women who pass judgment on every Indian living within a thirty-mile radius of Dandenong, are even more traditional than her." She shuddered. "They'll eat you alive."

He laughed and kneaded her other foot. "I'm a big boy. I can take care of myself."

He reached out and laid a hand on her belly. "And I intend on taking care of you and the little one too."

Her expression softened as her hand covered his. "A small part of me hated that your three weeks away was extended to eight, and I wondered if that long apart would dim my infatuation for you, but I have to admit I'm still smitten."

"Smitten kitten, how cute." He picked up her foot and gently raised her leg so he could press a kiss to the inside of her ankle. "And I intend on making you purr all night."

"You did not just say that," she said with a chuckle. "A guy intent on charming the aunties should leave the lame puns alone."

He lowered her foot before clutching at his chest. "You think I'm lame?"

Her gaze softened. "I think you're spectacular."

"That's better," he said. "Now let me show you exactly how spectacular I am . . ."

Forty-Two

A re you sure you want to do this?"

Pia snagged Samira's arm before they entered Kushi's house.

"He has to meet everybody sometime," Samira said, with a diffident shrug, when in fact a hothouse of butterflies was slam dancing against her rib cage. She'd liked having Rory to herself for the last three weeks since he'd returned, but the time had come for him to meet the jury; the aunties would definitely judge and announce a verdict.

"Yeah, but he should've met your mom first, not the whole crazy crew at once."

"Throwing him in the deep end is better," Samira said, glancing over Pia's shoulder to the car where Rory was getting a giant bouquet of gerberas, her mom's favorite flower, out of the trunk. "Sink or swim."

"For your sake, I hope he's good at freestyle," Pia said, casting a concerned glance his way. "He's a great guy, but you know they're a tough crowd."

"Yeah, I know." Samira sighed, hoping she had enough false

bravado for the both of them. Rory had been exceptionally quiet on the drive over, his folded arms and rigid posture telling her exactly how nervous he was.

"Speaking of tough crowds, does anyone know about you and Dev?"

Pia shushed her, casting a frantic glance around. "No, and I intend to keep it that way."

Samira touched her arm. "Cuz, you've been separated for three weeks now. Word is going to get around."

"I'm handling it." Pia gritted her teeth, her jaw clenching as she jerked her thumb toward Rory, who was approaching them with the bouquet. "Besides, one crisis at a time, and right now, this guy doesn't know what's about to hit him."

Since Pia had returned to work after the aborted week away with Dev at the alternative-therapies fertility getaway, she hadn't wanted to talk about her marriage. Samira had stumbled on the truth—that her cousin had actually separated from Dev—by pure chance when she'd tried calling her house recently and Dev had answered, saying he'd leave Pia a message and was sorry they hadn't seen each other but it was easier this way, with the two of them separated.

Samira had been shocked and called Pia on her cell straightaway. But Pia had been screening calls, and when they saw each other at work the next day, Pia had been brusque, all business. She'd confirmed the separation, saying it had been her way of jolting Dev into seeking professional help, but she didn't want to talk about it.

Samira had respected her wishes, but it had been a long twenty-one days, and she intended on broaching the subject again at a better time.

"Ladies, ready to go in?"

"Are you?" Pia gave an exaggerated shudder before winking at Rory. "Because seriously, you have no idea what you're up against in there."

"I can handle it," he said, but Samira heard an edge beneath his defiance. "Lead the way."

"Don't let them railroad you." Samira squeezed his arm. "I've been facing this crowd since birth, and they still terrify me."

"Not helping," he muttered, shooting her an affectionate glance. "Besides, I charmed you easily enough, didn't I? The rest of them should be putty in my hands."

If only it were that easy. Not that anyone would be overtly rude, but she'd been privy to the sniggers and innuendos and gossip in the past, and she knew this time wouldn't be any easier.

She'd bear the brunt of it, because she knew what to look for: the nuances in behavior, the subtle snubbing. Hopefully, Rory would be oblivious and she could tick this off her to-do list: "Introduce boyfriend and baby daddy to Indian community without him being publicly labeled a boy toy and her a cougar."

Interestingly, the age difference didn't matter to her anymore. The moment he'd committed to being a father, he'd instantly grown in her estimation. Considering his transient job and lifestyle, a young guy in his twenties could've pretended to care without wanting any involvement. But Rory wasn't like that, and she hoped the crowd today saw what she saw: a kind, caring guy invested in them for the long haul.

Samira turned the doorknob. Unlocked, of course. Even a stranger would be admitted to an Indian party and welcomed unreservedly. Hospitality ranked up there with arranged marriages as par for the course.

Bhangra music blasted her eardrums as the pungent aroma of fenugreek assailed her nostrils and she cast a quick glance at Rory. Rather than appearing stunned, he sniffed appreciatively and grinned.

"It's like stepping into a real Bollywood movie," he said, gesturing her forward. "Lead the way, gorgeous."

Pia made mock barfing sounds and strode ahead of them, leaving her to lean into Rory and murmur, "Thanks for doing this."

"Hey, we're a couple, right?"

She nodded. "Yeah, but I could've eased you into this by meeting Mom first."

"This will be fun." He did a little jive, complete with gyrating hips. "I watched a Bollywood flick last night. I'm going to wow them."

She smiled and kissed his cheek. "You've wowed me, and I'm the toughest crowd there is."

His tender gaze told her more than words ever could. Neither of them had remotely mentioned the L word—it was too early for that—but his support and willingness to meet everybody went a long way to cementing what she already knew: she was more than halfway to falling for him.

"Samira, is that you? Why are you hiding in the dark?" Kushi stood at the end of the hallway, silhouetted by the kitchen light. She wore a festive emerald green sari shot through with gold silk, an old favorite Samira knew she only wore on special occasions; like meeting prospective sons-in-law, if she had her way.

Samira sighed. "Come meet my mom. And remember, ignore any talk of our wedding, which she would've already planned to the nth degree in her head."

Rory laughed. "Got it."

When they reached the end of the corridor, Samira said, "Mom, this is Rory."

"P-pleasure to meet you, Mrs. Broderick." He held out the gerberas, and Samira watched for her mom's tell of disapproval: a tiny pulse beating at the base of her ear.

But there was nothing but a reserved smile from Kushi as she accepted the flowers. "Thank you. These are beautiful. Now, don't be nervous, young man, come and meet everyone."

A blush stained Rory's cheeks. Samira had picked up on the slight nervous stutter too, and she found it endearing. She knew Kushi could be lulling him into a false sense of security, but her mom had eased up on the Manish talk the last few weeks and seemed resigned to accepting her baby's father. Only time would tell if the rest of the aunties were as accommodating.

"Are you hungry, Rory?" Kushi laid the gerberas on the kitchen bench before gesturing at the table in the corner, laden with *pakoras* and *vada*.

Samira knew this was a test. If Rory didn't consume his body weight in spicy snacks and ghee-laden sweets, Kushi would hate him forever. Samira had warned him about the Indian propensity to force-feed their guests, and to her relief, he shot her a wink before smiling at Kushi.

"I'm ravenous, and your cooking smells divine."

Kushi gave a nod of approval. "Help yourself while I put these flowers in water."

"Take three of everything," Samira murmured under her breath, and he grinned.

"I love tasty Indian morsels," he said softly, leaning in to whisper in her ear. "But I thought you already knew that, considering how I feasted on you last night . . ."

Heat surged to Samira's cheeks, and she elbowed him away, but not before her mom had witnessed their exchange. To her surprise, Kushi looked at them with benign acceptance rather than disapproval as she filled a vase from the kitchen tap, unwrapped the flowers, and placed them in the water.

"These are my favorite flowers, young man, so what else did my daughter tell you about me?"

"She said you're an excellent cook, a wonderful mother, and a big fan of Bollywood movies." He gave Samira the plate he'd piled with snacks, before helping himself to another; a huge tick in Kushi's eyes by the approving glint. "Did she tell you I'm in the TV industry?"

Kushi nodded and bustled over to them. "Yes, I'd be very interested to hear all the behind-the-scenes gossip."

And to Samira's shock, Kushi threaded her arm through Rory's elbow and led him to the door. "But we can talk later. For now, let me introduce you to everyone and then you can eat."

Samira gaped as she followed them, bracing for the wave of noise to hit as Kushi opened the back door leading to the garden.

But as the three of them stepped out, the chatter and laughter stopped, as about thirty pairs of curious eyes fixed on Rory. Thankfully, the music filled what would've otherwise been an awkward silence, and she fixed a smile on her face.

"Everyone, I'd like you to meet Rory. My boyfriend," she added, not that there'd be any doubt. She'd only ever brought one guy to a gathering like this in her childhood home, and she'd ended up marrying him.

A chorus of hellos rang out before the cacophony of voices rose again, and she could've sworn Kushi breathed as loud a sigh of relief as she did.

"That wasn't so bad," Rory said.

"The night is young." Samira elbowed him, and Kushi nudged her away from his other side.

"Leave him be, Samira. He has to meet everyone at some stage, and no time like the present." Kushi pointed to his plate. "But first, you eat."

"Because once the aunties start their interrogation, you won't have a chance to."

Rory picked up a *pakora* and bit into it, his eyes widening with pleasure. "These are amazing."

Kushi flushed. "Try the *vada*. They're my specialty."

He obliged, and this time a little groan escaped his lips. Overkill, Samira thought, but then again at the rate he demolished it, he wasn't faking.

"You are an amazing cook." Rory touched her mom's arm. "Thank you."

"And you are a sweet boy," Kushi said, clearing her throat. "Rory, let me take you around, but first I want to have a quick word with Samira. Why don't you refill your plate and meet us back here?"

Rory shot her a glance like he'd done something wrong, and Samira gave an approving nod. After he'd stepped back into the kitchen, her mom pulled her close.

"Samira, I will be honest. I was prepared to dislike this Australian man who has fathered your child out of wedlock. I intended to make life difficult for him here tonight." She glanced away, shamefaced. "But I was wrong. He is a lovely young man. He has manners and he is respectful and I see the way he looks at you . . ."

When Kushi met her gaze again, there were tears in her mom's eyes. "I still think Manish would make a good husband for you, but if this Rory makes you happy, I will try to support you as best I can."

"Thanks, Mom."

Not a stamp of approval, exactly, but enough of an admission that Kushi would let up on the matrimonial machinations—hopefully.

However, as Samira accompanied Rory while her mom performed introductions to the aunties and a plethora of hangers-on who'd obviously come out of curiosity, the hour dragged. She didn't blame Rory for becoming increasingly quiet, considering he'd fielded questions from "Are you related to Chris Hemsworth, because you look alike?" to "You're very young. Do you know how old Samira is?"

Rory seemed amused by it all. Hell, if this was painful, what would they say when she announced her pregnancy? It wouldn't be long now. She'd worn a loose dress tonight to hide her small baby bump. She'd considered passing it off as a rice belly, but she knew astute eyes would put two and two together and come up with ten. Wild assumptions were a daily ritual with the aunties.

They'd made the rounds of the garden when they came to Sushma, Samira's least-liked auntie. Shrewd and calculating, she'd been one of the ringleaders in her lynch mob back in the day when she'd left Avi. And their first meeting again months ago hadn't endeared her to the annoying woman.

"Auntie, I'd like you to meet Rory," Samira said, forcing a smile.

Sushma's beady eyes glittered, shrewd and appraising, as she looked Rory up and down. "Hello, Rory. You seem awfully young for our Samira. Let's hope she won't tire of you." Her exaggerated wink held more spite than amusement. "She's been around the block a time or two already, you know. Married and divorced. And barren, so if you're wanting children—"

"That's where you're wrong—"

"Rory, it's okay." The last thing she wanted was for him to blab her pregnancy now. She didn't want his introduction to be hijacked. This crowd was tough; one shock at a time. "Auntie, Rory and I have no secrets between us. We're happy, and it would be nice if others could be happy for us too."

Sushma's eyes narrowed at the direct jibe. "Your mother had a mixed marriage, and look how that turned out."

Anger wasn't good for the baby, but Samira couldn't help the wave of rage that washed over her. How dare this cow belittle what her parents had shared? And worse, ostracize her mother for so many years because of it.

"My father died after many happy years with my mother. Aren't you a widow too, Auntie? Your husband may have been Indian, but he died just the same."

Samira had been taught from a young age to never talk back to the aunties. Respect first and foremost. But Sushma had gone too far, and she couldn't help but retaliate.

"Living in America has made you rude." Sushma tut-tutted, waggling her finger. "Maybe if you had an Indian husband you would learn some manners—"

"I think your mom's calling us," Rory said, slipping his hand into hers and squeezing. His touch instantly infused her with a calm she desperately needed.

"Excuse us," Rory said, with a brief nod to Sushma, before guiding Samira toward the back door leading to the kitchen.

"That vile cow—"

"Hey, don't let her get to you." He opened the door and guided her into a thankfully empty kitchen.

"They're all so bloody judgmental," she said, shaking her head. "It's one of the reasons I fled Melbourne after my divorce. I couldn't get away fast enough."

He hesitated before saying, "Now that you're moving back, won't you cop the same shit again, especially when they discover you're pregnant?"

She jabbed at him. "Thanks for almost blurting the news, by the way."

He grimaced. "I wanted to shut her up."

"It was a close call . . ." She trailed off, wondering why she really cared whether they announced their news now or not.

Initially, it had been out of deference for her mom. This crew had finally accepted her mother at a time Kushi had needed it most; they were her friends, and while Samira wouldn't have to see them often even when she moved home permanently, her mom would. They'd been Kushi's support network for years when she hadn't been around, and she owed it to her mom to be circumspect. But she'd like nothing better than to barge outside again and announce to everyone she was expecting Rory's baby.

"You were awfully quiet out there," she said. "Overwhelmed, huh?"

He glanced away, his expression shuttered. "Something like that."

Before she could quiz him further, she heard a clearing of a throat and glanced up to see Manish in the doorway leading to the hallway.

"Sorry to interrupt, but the front door was open and I let myself in."

"Come in," Samira said, torn between wanting to throttle her mom for inviting Manish tonight and doing a happy dance because he could meet Rory. "Manish, I'd like you to meet my boyfriend, Rory."

Rory tensed and stepped forward as if poised for battle. "Nice to meet you."

"Likewise." Manish shook Rory's hand, his smile guileless, but Samira couldn't get a proper read on the flicker of unease in his eyes. "You're a brave man."

Rory's eyebrows rose as he released Manish's hand. "How so?"

Manish pointed toward the backyard. "Meeting that crowd for the first time is like walking into a lion's den holding ten pounds of sirloin steak."

To her relief, Rory laughed. "Man, you have no idea."

"Actually, I do. I'm Anglo-Indian, I'm forty, and I'm single. Whenever I'm around those aunties, I'm the sirloin, a piece of meat ready to be bartered."

Rory laughed again. "Want a drink?"

"Yeah, that'd be great."

Samira's head swiveled between the two of them; she was relieved they were getting on. Moving back to Melbourne meant she'd like to keep Manny as a friend, and she didn't need her boyfriend getting jealous over it.

"There's lassi or nonalcoholic fruit punch?" Rory asked.

"Punch is fine." Manish turned to her. "How are you feeling?"

"Good." Her hand automatically drifted to her belly like it always did whenever she thought of that night eight weeks ago and how close she'd come to losing her much-loved baby.

"You haven't been back to the hospital, and I haven't heard from you, so I assumed everything's okay."

Rory's quizzical gaze darted between them as he handed Manish a glass of punch. "You know about the miscarriage scare?"

Manish nodded, hesitant, as if he knew he'd just stepped on a land mine. "I work in the ER at the hospital where Samira was admitted. I saw her the next morning."

A tense silence stretched between them before Rory finally said, "I'm glad she had a friend around for her. Thanks, man."

"No problem," Manny said, raising his punch in a cheers.

But by Rory's rigid body language and the mutinous clenching of his lips, Samira knew there were problems.

And she wasn't in the mood for dealing with them.

Forty-Three

After Rory survived the inquisition at Kushi's house, Samira dropped Pia off at the health center to catch up on some admin before heading to his place. He'd been grateful for Pia's presence in the car, because she kept up a steady stream of conversation, from amusing anecdotes of the various people he'd met at Kushi's, to accurate imitations of the aunties that had him laughing when nothing about the evening had been remotely funny.

He'd been out of his depth from the moment he'd walked into that cozy family home in Dandenong. Samira's mom had been lovely, and they'd got on well, but as for the rest . . . he'd wanted to charm them, but he'd clammed up like he'd done many times before when floundering. He'd probably come across as moody and recalcitrant, but Samira hadn't seemed to mind.

Then Marvelous Manish with his piercing gray eyes and movie-star smile had strutted in and really turned the evening on its head.

Why hadn't Samira told him Manish had been there for her at the time of the miscarriage scare?

He wasn't jealous per se, more annoyed that some guy who her mom would rather see her married to had been around to support his girlfriend when it should've been him.

The moment he'd stepped off the plane at Tullamarine, he'd almost kissed the ground. He was a city boy through and through, and being stuck in the outback for eight weeks, faking it in front of a bunch of tossers, had made him crave home.

Now that he was back and re-bonding with Samira, he knew it would be damn near impossible to leave her again; this time for much longer.

He would miss the entire pregnancy: the five-month scan where they'd discover the sex if they wanted to, the fitting out of a nursery, the Lamaze classes.

It sucked.

He didn't like being an absentee boyfriend, and he sure as hell didn't like the thought of Manish hanging around Samira to pick up the slack. He'd be gone for a long time . . . unless . . .

"Do you mind if I don't come in?" Samira kept the engine running. "I'm beat."

"You've never been inside my place. Aren't you the slightest bit curious?"

She recoiled at his abrupt tone, and he dragged a hand over his face. "Sorry. I guess I'm beat too."

"Then let's catch up tomorrow—"

"I'm thinking of quitting *Renegades*," he blurted, knowing it sounded ludicrous but strangely relieved.

He knew it wouldn't be easy getting out of the contract he'd signed, and the money would help support the baby beyond the ten grand he'd given Amelia, which they couldn't take back thanks to careful wording in his contract courtesy of Chris's astute wrangling, but he wanted to gauge Samira's reaction. Did she want him around for this pregnancy as much as he wanted to be?

"Where's this coming from?" She switched off the engine and swiveled to face him, her expression inscrutable in the dim lighting. "It's your dream job. You said so."

"I want to be here for you and the baby." He reached across and placed his palm flush against the curve of her belly. "I don't want to be stuck in the outback at the other end of the country if something goes wrong."

She stiffened slightly. "Is this about you being jealous of Manny? Because I already told you, we're friends, that's it, and he happened to be working in the ER the morning after the miscarriage scare."

"Why did you choose that hospital?"

"Excuse me?" Her eyebrows shot up, disapproval radiating off her. "It happens to be the best in Melbourne, and in case you were wondering, I'm booked in there to have the baby too. Got a problem with that?"

He'd riled her. Her eyes flashed with anger as she shoved his hand off her belly.

"It's not about being j-jealous," he said, hoping he could get the rest of what he had to say out without stumbling. "It's the thought of some other guy being around for you when you need support most, and that guy isn't me when it should be."

He held his hands out, hiding nothing. "I can get other jobs. But I won't have this time with you again, and I want to be here for you and our child."

If she heard his genuine intent behind his impassioned declaration, she didn't show it. Instead, she scuttled back in her seat until her back pressed against the car door. She glared at him with wide eyes, as if seeing him for the first time; and she didn't like what she saw.

"You should honor your commitment to *Renegades*," she said, her tone oddly devoid of emotion. "Go. You can be involved with your child when you come back."

His blood chilled. What did she mean "involved with your child"? It sounded like she didn't want any part of him.

"What are you saying?"

She sucked in a breath and wrapped her arms around her middle, shrinking back from him farther, if that were possible.

"You were there tonight. You saw what it's like for my mom and me. She's old, and this pregnancy will bring a lot of judgment and shame on her, from her closest allies who've been around for her when I wasn't. So I should do the right thing. Embrace tradition rather than run from it."

Icy trepidation washed over him. She couldn't be saying what he thought she was saying . . .

"Manish has offered to marry me, and I should accept."

She sounded like she'd rather have a root canal, and he knew in his gut she was lying.

"Look me in the eye and tell me you want to marry him."

She couldn't, and his gut instinct intensified. Did she feel guilty for abandoning her mom all these years and that was why she was doing this? But if so, why not raise the baby alone? Were the cultural implications of being a single mother in this day so dire? Was tradition so important to her that she'd give up what they shared in favor of marrying a man she didn't love? Unless she did . . .

"Do you have feelings for him?"

When her lips thinned and she still couldn't meet his eyes, a bark of harsh laughter burst from his lips. "You're fucking kidding me. You can't marry that guy. You don't love him. You . . ."

He trailed off as realization hit. She didn't love him either. She'd never said the words. She didn't depend on him or need him. Hell, she wanted him gone for the next umpteenth months and it wouldn't bother her.

He'd been about to say "you love me," but nothing could be further from the truth. Considering he'd just realized he loved her when she'd announced her intentions to marry some other guy, his timing sucked.

He couldn't tell her. Not now. It would sound desperate, a last-ditch effort from a guy who'd just had his ass dumped.

"You don't understand tradition and cultural obligations," she said, her tone tight with emotion as she placed a hand over her belly. "My mom was ostracized because of her mixed marriage, and in turn, I suffered, because we didn't have a lot of friends growing up. Pia was my best friend, and I always felt like an outsider at every Indian function I attended. I want this baby to be loved and adored and accepted, and he or she will have all that being raised in a close-knit community."

"With two married parents who don't love each other?"

She flinched at his sarcasm. "I loved my first husband, and look how that turned out. Manny's a lot nicer than him."

Stunned at her callous about-face, he opened the car door. He had to get out of here before he said something he'd regret.

"You'll always be a part of this baby's life, Rory, so I'll keep you updated while you're away, and I hope you make it back in time for the birth—"

"How fucking magnanimous of you," he muttered, slamming the door shut on the rest of her bullshit.

Maybe this was for the best. If she didn't love him, they never would've worked out. This way, he'd get to work his ass off and earn enough to set up a trust fund for his kid and be as involved as he wanted.

Yeah, that would be his new plan.

So why did it hurt so fucking much?

Forty-Four

Since Samira had deliberately driven Rory away by telling him that monstrous lie about marrying Manny, it had been the worst month of her life. She missed him more than she could've imagined and spent an inordinate amount of time listening to soppy songs on a playlist designed for heartbreak and having the occasional crying jag she blamed on hormones.

Elsewhere, when she wasn't blubbering at home, things were okay. Work was good, Pia and Dev were talking again despite still living apart, and the nausea that had plagued Samira during the early months of her pregnancy had vanished, leaving her ravenous most of the time. She'd been craving *idlis* and *sambhar* rather than pickles and ice cream, her yearning for the steamed rice cakes and spicy vegetable-laden soup almost making her reconsider her living arrangements and move back home.

But having Kushi whip up her favorite meals and having her in her face twenty-four seven were worlds apart, and she'd stayed put in Southbank. She'd instigated proceedings to sell her physical therapy practice in LA and had arranged for her apartment to be sublet. She'd even started browsing baby furniture online. Being busy should've helped ease her heartache. It didn't, because every night when she lay in bed alone, with too much time to think, she remembered Rory's stricken expression the night she'd lied to him.

She would never marry Manish, but Rory didn't need to know that. Her heart had leaped when Rory had offered to leave his precious job to be with her throughout the pregnancy. She could think of nothing better than having him by her side to share in every new experience, every joyful wonder.

Until she realized what it would mean long-term.

He'd already told her how much the job meant to him. He could help those underprivileged kids and set himself up professionally for bigger roles. He'd been so damn keen to score the role, he'd flipped out when he'd discovered her coaching his rival. And she knew he needed the money from snippets of what he'd said.

So to walk away from that because of her and the baby? Ultimately, it would never work. He'd grow to resent her, and the baby, and she could never have that. She cared for him enough to never make him choose between her and his career.

She'd sent him two short texts over the last few weeks, updates about the glucose test she'd done and the later results. He'd responded with a short, sharp "thanks." That's what it would be like for the next few months until the birth, and she had to get used to it. Didn't mean she had to like it.

Stepping into the Punjab sweetshop, she inhaled deeply, the heady aromas of ghee, milk, sugar, and cardamom never failing to soothe her. Smells of her childhood. Smells to comfort. She knew a lot of sugar wasn't good for the baby, but she was feeling particularly morose today, nothing a few pieces of cashew *barfi* and carrot *halwa* couldn't fix.

She placed her order, pointing at the brightly colored morsels in the display window. *Gulab jamuns*, plump, bronze balls soaked in sugar syrup, bright orange swirly *jalebis*, creamy *rasmalai*, cottage cheese dumplings soaking in cardamom-infused milk, and yellow *peda*, Indian milk fudge. Her stomach rumbled, and she imagined her mom's expression when she walked in the door with her goodies. Kushi would feign disapproval, but she had a wicked sweet tooth and would enjoy devouring these tasty morsels as much as Samira.

A few hours in her mom's company would distract her from the inevitable loneliness when she got home, and the constant question whirring through her head: *Did I do the right thing in driving Rory away?*

Leaving the shop, she had to sidestep a guy walking too quickly. He didn't apologize, and she cast him a scathing glare, at the same time he stared at her.

Oh no. No freaking way.

"Hello, Samira."

Avi had this way of looking at a woman, part leer, part proprietorial, that made her skin crawl. She hadn't noticed it at the start of their courtship—she'd been too smitten with her real-life Bollywood hero at the time—but later, when the cracks began to appear in their marriage, she noticed the way he looked at other women. Now, like then, it made her want to douse herself in antiseptic.

"Avi." She managed a brisk nod and tried to sidestep again, but he blocked her path.

"Why the hurry?"

She could play polite, make meaningless small talk, but he'd given up the right to any of her graciousness the moment he told her he'd got a teenager pregnant and was leaving her.

"I've got better things to do than stand around talking to you," she said, staring him down in defiance.

Mistake. Big mistake. Avi loved a challenge, and taking her down for her feisty response would be something he wouldn't walk away from.

"Better things? Like what?" He glared at her belly and quirked an eyebrow. "Incubating a bastard?"

"That's rich, coming from you, considering your first child was born out of wedlock." She snapped her fingers. "Because you were a cheating scumbag still married to me and had to wait a year for our divorce to come through before you could marry your mistress."

Avi preferred subservient women, women who deferred to him, women like the starry-eyed sucker she'd once been, so she knew her smart-ass response would get to him. The eyes she'd once imagined staring into for the rest of her life glittered with malice, and his upper lip curled in a sneer. "Let's not rehash the past. We've both come a long way."

He leaned in closer, and she edged back, inadvertently holding her breath as the familiar aftershave washed over her, an overpowering musk blend she'd never liked. "You're looking more beautiful than ever, babe." His bold gaze raked over her, possessive, and she subdued a shudder. "Pregnancy becomes you."

"I'm not your babe," she muttered, taking a step back, hating that he'd invaded her personal space like he used to.

"You were once, and you loved it."

Samira bit back a laugh. Was he coming on to her? She could say so much, most of it nasty and derisive, but as he stared at her with a gleam in his eye she didn't like, most of her animosity drained away.

What was the point of trading insults? He meant nothing to her anymore. Interesting, that he hadn't changed much beyond a few wrinkles around his eyes. Still the same slicked-back black hair, big brown eyes, and smooth skin. It would've been better if he'd sprouted nose hairs and had a wart or two on his nose. But once again, she was giving him more thought than he deserved.

"Goodbye, Avi."

His eyebrows arched in surprise, and as she sidestepped him, this time he let her go.

"Samira?"

She sighed and gritted her teeth against the urge to flip him her middle finger. "What?"

"I behaved deplorably when we were married, and for what it's worth, I'm sorry."

She accepted his long-overdue apology with a gracious nod and kept walking.

Forty-Five

*I*f Rory's first eight weeks in the outback had dragged, it had nothing on the next sixteen. Four long months where he spent endless days in front of the camera, reading off cues, trying to appear enthusiastic about a bunch of wannabe models and B-grade celebrities following clues toward the ultimate prize.

Not that the *Renegades* concept was bad; it wasn't. It was his attitude that stank. Faking it all day every day for the cameras was tough, so when he reached the confines of his tent at night, he dropped the pretense and crawled into bed with his cell for company.

He'd grown damn attached to the thing, considering it was the only way he stayed connected to his kid. Samira sent him regular updates, texts with test results or growth charts. He liked the one comparing his kid to various fruit and his or her corresponding size. From pea to lemon to avocado and beyond. It made him smile, when little did these days.

He hated how hope blossomed every time his cell pinged with

a message from Samira. What did he expect, that she'd say, *Surprise, I've changed my mind, I want you, I love you, come back?*

Thankfully, the updates were only about the baby, and she didn't mention anything to do with her. Then again, he could imagine exactly what she was up to, in excruciating detail: she'd be planning a wedding, something low-key, being embraced by one big, happy Indian family, while his child grew in her belly. Wrong on so many levels. Not the part about her being surrounded by a support network that would care for her, but the marriage part to M.D. Manish. What made the guy better than him? A few degrees on a wall and a plethora of initials after his name?

Though that was petty. Samira wasn't impressed by that kind of stuff. She'd made it more than clear how into him she'd been, even when he was nothing more than a stuntman.

No, his own insecurities blamed Manish and fate and whatever else he could come up with for ruining the best thing to ever happen to him. Though that was the kicker; he didn't really know what he'd done wrong. One minute she'd introduced him to her mom and the aunties; the next she'd told him she'd be marrying Manish.

He hadn't seen any spark between them at her mom's house. He'd looked for it too, especially when Manish mentioned being there for her during the miscarriage scare. But there'd been nothing more than friendship between them, and Rory could almost like the guy given half a chance. Manish had a sense of humor, and in any other circumstance Rory could see the two of them sharing a beer and a laugh. Ironic, considering that may well happen if Samira married the guy and he'd be forced to see him every time he went to pick up his kid during access visits.

The thought made him grab his cell. He needed to get grounded, fast, and seeing a pic of his kid would do that better than any-thing. His favorite picture was the snapshot of the five-month scan, where he could actually see the baby's fingers raised toward its mouth. It looked like a wave, and he loved tracing the outline of his child, wondering what he or she would look like. They didn't know the sex; they wanted a surprise. But he could imagine a gor-geous little girl with hazel eyes like her mom or a cheeky boy with her smile.

"Hey, Radcliffe, you in there?"

"Yeah," he called out, sitting up in bed and shoving his cell back in his pocket as Sherman Rix stuck his head through the tent opening. "There's a call for you."

Fear gripped him. The few people he knew would call him on his cell, which meant this call came from official channels.

"Do you know who it is?"

Sherman hesitated before saying, "Some hospital in Mel-bourne. I didn't catch the name."

Fear morphed into full-blown panic as Rory scrambled off the bed and ducked through the flap, breaking into a run toward the main truck that housed the cameras, IT equipment, and satellite phones.

If something had happened to Samira or the baby and he was stuck all the way out here, he'd never forgive himself. He shouldn't have listened to her. He should've fought for her. What a dickhead.

As he bounded up the steps into the truck, he sent a silent prayer heavenward for the safety of a baby he never knew he wanted so badly until faced with the threat of losing him or her.

Snatching up the satellite phone, he willed himself to calm the hell down so he could formulate the words needed to ascertain ex-actly how serious this was.

"Rory Radcliffe speaking," he said, clenching the phone so tight it made an odd crackling sound.

"Hi, Son."

Relief filtered through him, and his muscles relaxed, but only momentarily, as he realized his dad was calling him from a hospital.

"Are you okay, Dad?"

"Uh, yes. I had a minor stroke, but I'm okay."

Shock rendered him speechless for a moment. "You sure? What happened? How long will you be in hospital for?"

He might not have been close to his father growing up, but he hated the thought of him lying helpless in a hospital bed.

"I had a little turn at work. Couldn't make sense of the documents I was reading, and my PA said my mouth was drooping on one side, so she overreacted and called an ambulance. I got here this morning. They've run tests, said it's very minor, no major damage. I'm on blood thinners for potential clots, but I should be home over the next few days."

His dad wasn't telling him everything. If the stroke was so minor, why would they keep him in hospital?

"I'm actually wrapping up filming tomorrow, Dad, then I'll be on the first flight home. Is that okay?"

"I'll look forward to seeing you, Son."

Rory clutched the phone to his ear. He'd never heard the great Garth Radcliffe sound so uncertain. While it would take them a long time to repair the yawning gap in their relationship, his father wouldn't have called unless he was feeling particularly vulnerable. Rory wouldn't wish him ill, but this could be a turning point for them, a way to start making inroads toward some kind of bond.

"Take care, Dad, and call me if you need anything."

"I will," Garth said, sounding particularly gruff, before hanging up.

Rory stood in the truck for a long time, listening to the dial tone. He'd never felt so helpless, and he couldn't wait to wrap up this damn show tomorrow and get home to the people he loved.

And this time, he'd make sure Samira knew it.

Forty-Six

Samira hadn't wanted a baby shower. She didn't want the fuss, not when most of the aunties barely looked at her at the last gathering she'd attended, a Diwali celebration at the Dandenong Town Hall. The festival of lights was supposed to promote peace by celebrating the triumph of good over evil, light over dark, and blessings of freedom and enlightenment.

Some of those judgmental aunties could do with a hefty dose of enlightenment.

After Rory had left Melbourne, she hadn't wanted to face them, so she'd chickened out and got her mom to break the pregnancy news to her cronies. Kushi had been circumspect when Samira had asked about their reactions, but she knew her mom was protecting her. The aunties, especially Sushma, would've had plentiful advice to remedy her unwed state and the scandal of having a child without a husband at her age or otherwise.

To take some of the heat off her mom, which she knew Kushi would be copping with, Samira had attended the Diwali celebration. But whether she'd been admiring the *rangoli*, the intricate floral design made of colored rice and flowers at the entrance to the town hall, or helping light the lanterns surrounding the main room's perimeter, or watching the fireworks, she'd felt the aunties' stares boring into her. Cynical. Harsh. Judgmental. They'd spoiled her appetite so she couldn't even enjoy the Indian feast laid out for attendees.

So why would she want a baby shower with these women in attendance?

But Pia had insisted, saying they could be found lacking together, a way of giving the aunties the finger, that they were happy in their life choices and wouldn't be criticized for it.

So Samira had gone along with it, but now, as she sat in the middle of her mom's family room, surrounded by cakes made out of diapers and baskets filled with lotion and baby clothes, all she wished for was the sanctity of her apartment.

She'd been having Braxton-Hicks contractions all morning while the ache in her lower back intensified. If it persisted, she'd get it checked out, but at thirty-two weeks, this baby was a long way off from being born.

Besides, she may not want a relationship with Rory, but he deserved to be at the birth if he wanted, and she had no idea when he'd be getting back. He hadn't responded to any of her texts beyond the same "thanks" to every one. He didn't ask how she was feeling or whether she'd been attending prenatal classes. Then again, she'd made sure he wouldn't when she'd told him she'd be marrying another man.

As for Manny, she'd distanced herself from him too. She felt bad using him as a tool to drive Rory away, even if he didn't know it. So they'd chatted a few times on the phone, but there had been no more coffee dates, and she'd made Kushi promise on her grandchild's life not to invite him around anymore.

Thankfully, her mom was resigned to the fact she'd be a single mother. The one and only time Kushi had asked about Rory, Samira had snapped that they weren't together and she didn't want to discuss it. Again, her mom had surprised her by giving her the space she wanted. But today, surrounded by baby paraphernalia and listening to tales of water births and hypnosis to experience a painless labor, a small part of her wished she had Rory by her side.

She thought she'd loved Avi once; she'd been wrong. Because ending her marriage hadn't hurt half as much as watching Rory walk away from her car that night several months ago.

She'd been a fool. A fool who hadn't thought this through much beyond that night, because what would happen when he came back and discovered she hadn't married Manish after all? Could she keep holding him, and her feelings, at bay when he wanted to be involved in raising the baby? More importantly, did she want to?

"Samira, there's one more gift," Pia said, touching her arm before leaning in and murmuring, "Are you okay? You seem really out of it."

"False labor pains." She forced a smile that ended on a hiss at a particularly vicious stab low in her abdomen.

Pia's gaze clouded with worry. "You sure it's false? Because it's too early—"

"I know," she snapped, instantly regretting it when Pia's expression closed off. "Sorry, Cuz, I know how hard this must be for you, throwing me a shower, and I can't thank you enough. But this pain is making me crabby, and I really want to get out of here."

Pia nodded as she started gathering up wads of torn gift wrapping and stuffing them into a trash bag. "Consider it done. Open this last gift, and I'll start ushering them out on the pretext of a half-price sale at that new sari shop at the end of the block."

When Samira was younger, she'd almost been caught in a stampede when the aunties had heard about one of those sales, so she knew it would do the trick.

"You're a lifesaver . . ." Samira couldn't speak as a slash of pain from her abdomen ripped through to her back. She stiffened, bracing for another, exhaling slowly when it didn't come, but fear making every muscle in her body tense.

"You're not okay," Pia said, helping her to her feet. "Come with me. You rest in the bedroom. I'll get rid of this crew."

Samira managed a grateful smile and mumbled a collective thanks to the aunties before Pia led her to her old bedroom. Kushi had been in the kitchen, and when she entered the family room and took one look at her, her mom rushed over to help too.

"Don't panic, you two, but I think I need to go to the hospital," Samira said, as they led her to the bed and she sank onto it. "The pain is pretty intense, so I'm starting to wonder if it's more than Braxton-Hicks."

Pia blanched. "Fuck," she muttered, and the fact Kushi didn't even blink told Samira exactly how worried her mom was.

"I'll send everyone home," Kushi said, "and you ring for an ambulance."

When Samira didn't protest, her mom's and cousin's worry lines deepened. A worry that didn't let up when the paramedics arrived, examined her, and pronounced her three centimeters dilated.

"Your baby is on its way." The older paramedic, a woman with BARB on her name tag, took her blood pressure. "Nothing can stop these little blighters when they want to come."

Samira waited until the cuff pressure eased before murmuring, "But it's too early. I'm only thirty-two weeks."

She glimpsed a flicker of something in Barb's eyes before the paramedic said, "We'll take good care of you. You can give us your ob-gyn's details in the ambulance, but I'll be honest, love, you're not going to the hospital you probably booked into. We're taking you to the closest one."

Samira bit back a cry as another blinding cramp, which she now knew to be a contraction, tore through her. Sweat broke out over her skin, and her palms grew clammy.

"Take me anywhere you goddamn want," she said through gritted teeth.

"Done." Barb squeezed her hand. "You'll get the best possible care. Now, can you walk out to the stretcher?"

Samira nodded, though it was more a hobble as it felt like her baby had descended and was clawing its way out of her. She may be a physical therapist who knew about strengthening the pelvic floor and strong core and abdominals to help with labor, but she knew next to nothing about the possible complications of a premature birth.

She'd been lulled into a false sense of security, feeling invincible she could do this on her own. She thought she'd done everything right by this baby, but what if the stress of pining for Rory had brought this early labor on?

A wild supposition, maybe, but as they strapped her into the back of the ambulance, then she clung onto the metal railings as it seemed to travel at breakneck speed to the nearest hospital, she hated the ongoing doubt that she'd done the wrong thing in making herself unhappy and thus affecting her cortisol levels.

Her mom and Pia were driving behind the ambulance, and one of them would have her cell. Amid the terror and the fear and the pain, she knew what she had to do.

She had to contact Rory and tell him their baby was on the way.

Forty-Seven

*R*elieved his dad would be okay, Rory headed toward his car parked out front of the hospital. He'd wanted to make sure his dad wasn't underplaying his stroke before he made an all-important phone call to Samira. He had his plan all worked out, and this time he wouldn't take no for an answer.

As he slid behind the steering wheel, his cell beeped and he glanced at the screen. Fantastic. Just the woman he wanted to contact. However, as he read the message, fear gripped his heart and squeezed tight.

She was in labor at a hospital in Dandenong. She'd let him know as soon as the baby was born. The message was short and didn't tell him much, but for a genius who had aced his economics degree, he could do the math.

This baby was being born eight weeks early.

Rory wasn't a worrier as a rule. He let fate run its course. But after firing off a quick response, **I'M HERE FOR YOU, WILL BE THERE AS FAST AS I CAN,** he broke the land speed record between Prahran and Dandenong, reaching the hospital in twenty-five minutes.

She wouldn't be expecting him. She'd think he was still in the outback, and while he didn't wish his dad ill, he was glad he'd come back a few days early to visit Garth. Otherwise, he would've missed the birth of his child, and considering the complications of a premature birth . . . He didn't know the specifics, but he knew enough to figure this could be dicey.

It took him five minutes to find the maternity ward and another five to convince the nursing staff his girlfriend was about to give birth. It wasn't until Pia caught sight of him and told the nurses he was indeed the father that they let him in.

He didn't know what to expect as he knocked on the door of Samira's birthing suite. Loud screeching, moaning, maybe an expletive or two directed his way when she caught sight of him. However, as he eased the door open and saw her lying propped up in bed, her pallor matching the sheets, something in his chest twisted and he couldn't breathe.

She looked absolutely terrified.

When she caught sight of him, she tried a tentative smile that ended in a crumple as she broke down, and he flew to her side, bundling her in his arms.

"It's going to be okay," he said, hoping to God it was true.

"It's too early," she murmured, ending on a sob, and he tightened his grip, infusing her with strength for what they were about to face, before easing away to look her in the eye.

"Whatever happens, we're in this together."

She bit down on her bottom lip and nodded, but the shimmer of tears in her expressive eyes gutted him.

"They've given me an epidural, and I'm heading off to surgery soon, because the baby is showing signs of distress . . ." She swallowed, several times, before continuing. "I'm so glad you're here. I don't know how or why you are, but I'm glad."

"We can talk later," he said, as a team of midwives bustled into the room.

"Is this Dad?" the oldest one asked, a fierce sixty-something woman who looked like no baby would dare do the wrong thing as they came into the world.

"I am," he said. "Rory Radcliffe."

"Well, Rory Radcliffe, you can gown up at the OR and watch your baby being born," the nurse said, taking Samira's pulse. He didn't like the small frown that appeared between her brows. "Let's get this show on the road."

Rory had jumped out of moving cars and taken tumbles off bridges, but the fear of injury performing stunts had nothing on the terror dogging his every step as he followed the nursing entourage to the operating room. He walked beside Samira's bed as the orderly wheeled it, clutching her hand like a lifeline he needed.

After traversing endless corridors, they reached their destination and a nurse stopped him. "I'll take you to get gowned up now."

"Okay." He bent down to press a kiss to Samira's lips. "I'm here for you and our baby. Today and forever."

Either she didn't register the implications of what he'd just said or she was too withdrawn into her fear, but she offered a brief nod before they wheeled her through the swinging doors.

Leaving him bereft.

If he'd had any doubt about his feelings for Samira before now, this moment, today, had solidified his love.

He loved her.

Whatever may come.

Hopefully, she'd give him a chance to prove it to her for the rest of their lives.

"Come on, Dad, let's get you gowned up."

As he entered an area where medical staff scrubbed down and a nurse handed him a gown, cap, and mask, a surprisingly young doctor approached. With her black hair in a ponytail and her face free of makeup, she looked about eighteen.

"You're the dad of the baby being born in this upcoming C-section?"

"Yeah, I'm Rory."

"Okay, Rory, I'm going to give you a heads-up before we get started." She hesitated, as if she didn't want to say more, and he held his breath. "At thirty-two weeks, your baby is what we class as very preterm. So it will be small, about three pounds."

Rory's stomach went into free fall. Three pounds. How could a baby that small survive?

"There's also the possibility of respiratory distress due to immature lung formation, and feeding difficulties, due to lack of sucking and swallowing reflexes. Heart and gastrointestinal problems are also common."

Fuck, this just got better and better.

Some of his terror must've shown, because she offered a reassuring smile. "But rest assured, we have a fantastic team in the neonatal intensive care unit, where your baby will spend the first few weeks of its life until it can breathe and feed on its own, and we'll do our best to ensure you take home a healthy baby."

He managed a mumbled "thank you," as he followed her into the OR. The sight of a pale Samira lying on a gurney, her lower half shielded by a blue sheet, clutching at the side of the bed tight, made his heart flip.

They would get through this. He had to be strong, for both of them. And their baby.

He sat by her head, clutching her hand, maintaining eye contact the entire time. He saw her flinch slightly when the doctor made the first incision, he saw her grit her teeth as the doctor tried to pry their baby free of her uterus, and he saw the relief mingled with joy as the doctor held up their baby and they heard a feeble cry.

"A boy," she murmured, tears leaking from the corners of her eyes. "We have a son."

Rory couldn't remember the last time he cried, but in that moment, he rested his forehead against the woman he loved and let the tears fall.

Forty-Eight

Over the next seven days, Samira's world constricted. Nothing else existed but her room at the hospital and the short walk from the maternity ward to the neonatal intensive care unit. She'd always hated acronyms, but NICU became her focus day in, day out. She spent every waking hour beside her son's incubator, watching him, willing him to grow and be strong and survive.

She ignored the tubes helping him breathe and the ones feeding him. She ignored his tiny size. She ignored the bone-deep dread that took hold when she allowed the doubts to flood in, doubts that centered on whether he would live or die.

She didn't care about the doctor's dire warnings revolving around long-term damage, vision and hearing problems, learning difficulties, chronic health issues, recurrent infections, and all kinds of bad stuff.

All she cared about was survival.

And through it all, Rory was by her side.

He held her hand, he cradled her in his arms, he wiped away her tears. She'd never known anyone so stoic, so strong.

Pia and her mom were as bad as Samira, their expressions equal parts frightened and sad when they peered through the glass into the NICU. Not that they weren't supportive—they'd been great—but she had enough to deal with, with her fear, to manage theirs too.

Through it all, Rory had protected her. He hadn't spoken much, and that was one of the things she liked the most. He didn't offer trite platitudes. He didn't fill fraught silences with false humor. He didn't expect anything from her. He was just there, and she loved him for it.

A fine time to discover she loved him, when they clung to each other beside their son's crib, willing him to start breathing on his own.

There would be time enough to tell him. For now, they had more important things to discuss.

"We should name him," she whispered, hating to disrupt the peace of the NICU. Despite the infernal beeping of various machines keeping premature babies alive, the place exuded a calmness she needed. "Do you have any ideas?"

Rory flashed the lopsided grin she loved so much. "Rocky, because he's a fighter."

"Uh, no." She cleared her throat, surprised how emotional she was by her choice and hoping he'd go for it. "I was thinking Ronald Garth. After his grandfathers."

His eyebrows rose. "Wow, you are a traditionalist."

"Not really." She managed a soft laugh. "I've spent a lifetime trying to buck tradition. Hell, I fled to another country to escape it."

She reached out to touch his hand. "But I've quit running, and I think it's nice that our son embodies the best of both our families."

"I-I don't know what to say." He blinked and turned his hand over to capture hers. "Ronnie sounds close enough to Rocky, so let's do it."

She smiled as he lifted her hand to his mouth and pressed a kiss on the back.

"We can leave the discussion of his surname until another day," he said, with a meaningful stare.

Samira wasn't a fool. She may be spending most days in a fog of restless sleep and silent praying, but she knew what Rory meant. He may not have actually said the words "I love you," but she'd heard him say he'd be with her forever just before she'd been wheeled into surgery. And by his actions the past week, nothing had changed. Now that she loved him, what would she say if he wanted to make their relationship official? He'd once proposed out of obligation. What would she do if he did it for real?

But she didn't want to preempt anything or pressure him into making a declaration he didn't want, so she said, "Ron Radcliffe sounds good to me."

He blinked again, several times, and the tenderness in his eyes almost undid her. "Thank you."

"No, Rory, thank you. For being here the last week. For everything."

He wanted to ask questions, she saw it in his gaze, so she buried her face in his chest and let him hold her tight. They would talk. Eventually.

But for now, they needed their beautiful baby boy to live.

Forty-Nine

Rory hadn't asked Samira the hard questions yet.

Are you engaged to Dr. Dickhead?

Do you only want me around because of Ronnie?

Is our closeness an illusion born of mutual fear of losing the one thing that binds us?

He couldn't ask her any of that, not when only fourteen days had passed and their son still lay in that crib hooked up to machines helping him live.

The pediatricians were cautiously optimistic. Ronnie had gained over one pound, and while his suck-swallow reflex still wasn't well coordinated, the weight gain was a good sign.

But seeing his son lying in that crib behind hardened plastic still stabbed him in the chest every time he saw him. He hated everything about the NICU. The faux perky nurses, the doctors speaking in hushed tones, the antiseptic smell. There were other babies there, smaller than Ronnie, and parents who wore the same terrified yet stoically optimistic expressions he did.

Samira appreciated his strength. She clung to him whenever they entered that sterile room, a room emanating false cheer with orange giraffes and purple elephants splashed across the walls. But he wasn't buying it, because bad things happened in that room. Babies lost their lives; parents lost their kids. He wouldn't breathe properly again until they got the all clear from the medicos and could take Ronnie home.

That wouldn't be for a while yet. The next two weeks would be critical. If Ronnie reached thirty-six weeks and started breathing and feeding on his own, they'd be okay. As for the doctors' predictions of possible doom in the future with learning disabilities and the rest, he'd deal with that when he faced it.

Though one good thing came out of sitting by his son's crib day in, day out over the last fourteen days. The enormity of what his child might face in the future put his stutter into perspective.

He'd been an idiot. He'd spent his entire life feeling inadequate because of it, feeling self-conscious and less than others. He'd become increasingly insecure, and it had affected his relationships with women.

Not anymore.

If the worst thing his kid had to suffer was a stammer, Ronnie would be doing okay. And it was time he came clean to Samira about it too.

As he strode toward the NICU, he spied a tall figure coming the opposite way. The closer he got, Rory recognized him, and his steps slowed. The last thing he needed was a run-in with Samira's supposed fiancé. But he couldn't avoid him, considering they were about to cross paths, and Rory gritted his teeth against the urge to slug the too-perfect doctor.

"Congrats on your son, Rory." Manish stuck out his hand, and he had to take it rather than appear churlish.

"Thanks, he's amazing."

"He is."

Manish released his hand, and Rory glanced over his shoulder, eager to get back to Ronnie's bedside. But this was an opportunity to ask Manish the hard questions he couldn't ask Samira, not right now with their child battling for every breath he took.

"So you're engaged to Samira despite not loving her?"

Manish's jaw dropped for a moment, before he recovered. "I'm not sure where that came from, but I wouldn't believe everything you hear on the Indian grapevine. You'll get used to it eventually, but they take that old cliché of making mountains out of molehills to extremes."

Confused, Rory shook his head slightly. "Is that a yes or no?"

"It's a hell no," Manish said, looking faintly amused. "We're not engaged. Samira's great, but we're friends." He smirked. "Besides, even if I went in for all that arranged marriage stuff, it wouldn't happen, because she's in love with you."

Something stilled inside Rory, like the entire world had gone quiet and every one of his senses was heightened. He could see the stubble along the doctor's jaw where he'd missed a spot shaving, he could hear the faintest siren of an ambulance miles away, he could smell a pungent ammonia mixed with a hint of lemon.

Samira loved him?

She hadn't given him the slightest indication. In fact, saying she wanted to marry this guy was pretty much the opposite of being in love with him. So what the hell was going on, and how did this guy know about it before he did?

"Mate, you look shell-shocked." Manish chuckled. "Look, I don't know what's happened between you two, but I haven't seen Samira in months. Not since the last time we ran into each other at her mom's place. We've texted a few times—that's it."

"But she told me she was marrying you . . ."

Manish held up his hands like he had nothing to hide. "Like I said, I don't know what went down between you, but it sounds like she used me as an excuse to push you away. I have no idea why, but she's probably terrified, considering she's been married before, the cultural implications, the age difference—"

"Thanks, I get the idea."

Manish laughed at his dry response. "Take it from a perpetual bachelor: if you love her, go for it. Prove to her how much she means to you."

Rory had every intention to do exactly that, and he certainly didn't need relationship advice from this dude, but something Manish had said snagged his attention.

"What did you mean by 'cultural implications'?"

"I know she was born here, but unless you've lived within the Indian culture, you have no idea what it's like."

"It shouldn't matter if we love each other." He sounded like a romantic idiot. He knew relationships were hard work. It was why he'd avoided them until now.

"I didn't say it mattered; I'm just putting forward possible reasons why she used me as an excuse to push you away."

Manish slapped him on the back. "Good luck, mate. There are reasons I stay single, and this kind of convoluted drama is one of them."

"Thanks."

"And enjoy fatherhood, another thing I never want to experience." Manish gave a mock shudder. "See you round."

Okay, so the guy wasn't so bad. Rory had been a jealous jerk and taken a disliking to the doc because of it.

But if Samira hadn't been engaged to Manish all these months he'd been away filming *Renegades*, why hadn't she told him? Or better yet, why had she said she'd be marrying him in the first place?

Rory hoped Ronnie kept improving, because he had a lot of questions for Samira, and this time he wouldn't walk away if he didn't like the answers.

Fifty

Samira had never envisaged sleeping in her old bedroom at home in Dandenong when she'd left so many years ago, but it felt right bringing her child here for the first few weeks of Ronnie's life outside hospital walls.

For the simple fact being a mother petrified her and having Kushi around would be a godsend. Her mom had been amazing in the fraught weeks after Ronnie's birth; she'd never seen her so calm, when Kushi usually saw the worst in every scenario.

Rory had been pretty darn amazing too, and she had every intention of telling him once she tucked Ronnie into his bassinet.

A soft knock sounded at the door, and it eased open. "He's such a precious boy," Kushi whispered, entering the bedroom. "My darling boy."

"He is a darling," Samira said, staring down at her angelic son, sleeping now he had a tummy full of milk. She would never get tired of this. Watching him sleep. The shift of his eyeballs beneath paper-thin skin. The quirk of his lips in the corners. The smoothness of his peachy cheeks. "I'm so lucky, Mom."

Kushi slid an arm around her waist, and she leaned into her mom. "These things are meant to be, *betee*. Your Rory came into your life for a reason, and despite my best efforts to push you elsewhere, your choices resulted in my beautiful grandson."

Her mom glanced up at her. "So I am done, Samira. No more interference in your love life from me. You do what makes you happy."

Samira smiled. "Did you feel that?"

"What?"

"That rumbling under our feet?" Samira made a grand show of shuffling across the fluffy crimson rug she'd picked out as a thirteen-year-old. "I think hell just froze over."

"Cheeky girl." Kushi pinched her cheek, chuckling softly. "Now go. Your young man is waiting for you outside." Her fond glance fell on Ronnie. "Let me have some alone time with my beautiful boy."

"Okay."

Samira leaned down to place a butterfly-soft kiss on Ronnie's forehead, before letting herself out of the room she'd spent so many hours in growing up, dreaming of Bollywood princes and marriage and babies. Her life may not have turned out quite the way she'd envisioned back then, but having Ronnie completed her in a way she'd never imagined.

She'd resigned herself to not having kids, and she'd been okay with that. But now that he was here, and the long weeks she'd sat by his bedside willing him to get stronger, she couldn't imagine her life without him.

And speaking of males who'd become ingrained in her life . . . she owed Rory an explanation and an apology. She'd underestimated him, using his age as an excuse to push him away when he'd proved his maturity above and beyond while by her side the last six weeks.

He'd rarely left the hospital and had been a silent support when she'd needed it most. He hadn't bombarded her with questions. Heck, he hadn't even asked about Manny once. But she knew he deserved an explanation, and with their son home and out of hospital for the first day, the time had come.

Kushi had made a big pot of mutton biryani for her homecoming, and her stomach rumbled appreciatively at the tempting aromas of spicy meat and rice laden with turmeric as she passed through the kitchen. But she would eat later. She had to talk to Rory. Now.

She found him in the backyard, standing by the curry leaf tree. He wore a pensive expression, but his eyes were clear and showed nothing like the perpetual worry that had clouded their aquamarine brilliance the last month and a half.

"Hey," she said.

He turned toward her, and his lopsided grin made her heart flip-flop the way it had the first time he'd come to her rescue in that bar. "Is he settled?"

"Sleeping like a baby."

He chuckled. "Aren't you the least bit terrified of what's going to happen when he's not sleeping and he's yelling the house down?"

"Absolutely petrified, but that's why I've moved back with Mom. She raised me, and look how I turned out."

"Good point." He hesitated. "While I think it's a great idea you're living here at the moment, I want to start looking for a place. F-for us."

His nervousness made her heart melt. He didn't need to be. She knew what he was saying, and she welcomed the suggestion. Now she had to tell him.

"I think us living together for Ronnie's sake is great, so that's a good idea."

His eyebrows rose. "You think this is all about Ronnie?"

"Isn't it?"

"For fuck's sake, Sam." He dragged a hand over his face. "I know you're not marrying Manish. He told me. And I think it's time you tell me what the hell is going on and why you told such a p-preposterous lie."

She sighed and nodded. "You don't have to be nervous—"

"I'm not nervous!" he yelled, before appearing shamefaced. "I've got a stutter. Had it since I was a kid. Really bad back then, but through endless speech therapy and the acting stuff, I can control it most of the time."

Shock rendered her mute. Damn it, she'd worked with health professionals, including speech pathologists, for years. Her interest in dialect coaching had stemmed from Pia's proficiency in speech therapy. She may not be an expert, but she should've figured it out.

"It can be inherited," he said, sounding tortured. "That's why I freaked out when you first told me about the pregnancy. I never wanted kids because I didn't want to risk passing it on, because I hated how fucking insecure and inadequate it made me feel growing up."

His expression softened. "But then Ronnie was born, and nothing else mattered but him growing to be a strong, healthy, happy kid." He shrugged, adorably bashful. "I love him. And I love you. More than I could've ever thought possible."

That shock rendering her speechless wasn't easing up anytime soon. He loved her. This incredibly strong, supportive man loved her. And she'd done nothing to show him she felt the same way.

Stepping forward, she cradled his face in her hands and kissed him.

A gentle, soul-searching kiss of affirmation and hope, of promise and future. A future for the two of them and their beautiful baby boy.

When she eased away and lowered her hands, she glimpsed wonder in his eyes.

"I love you, too. That's why I told that monstrous lie about marrying Manny, because I didn't want you to give up your dream of hosting your first major TV show for me."

"But it was never all important to me—"

"Shh. Let me finish." She pressed a finger to his lips. "I thought if you chose me over your career, you'd end up resenting me for it, or worse, resenting the baby, so I couldn't take that chance. Besides, I've been independent for a long time and didn't think I needed you to help me raise our child."

"And now?"

"Now I know what I want, and that's you." She blinked away the sting of tears. "You and me in this for the long haul, raising our amazing son together."

Her strong, silent type didn't respond. He didn't have to. He opened his arms, and she stepped into them, peace enveloping her as he tightened his grip on her. She rested her cheek against his chest, comforted by the solid pounding of his heart, and slid her arms around his waist.

They clung to each other, the heat of his body, the hardness of it, reminding her to ask at her first ob-gyn visit when she could resume relations post-birth.

"Rory?"

"Hmm?"

"The aunties were right about one thing."

"What's that?"

"Dating a younger man would lead me down a wicked path." She leaned back to meet his eyes and winked. "I am so ready to get wicked with you for a long time to come."

Epilogue

Samira didn't mind the pomp and ceremony of Indian weddings: hundreds of guests in their finest silks, the expensive jewelry, generous gifts, elaborate decorations, copious amounts of delicious food, and joyful dancing well into the night.

But all that hoopla wasn't for her.

Not this time around.

"What's going on?" Pia grabbed Samira's arm as she tried to sneak past her bedroom door.

Samira wanted this wedding to be a surprise for everyone. It had been eight weeks since they'd brought Ronnie home from the hospital and she'd managed to keep tight-lipped about her plans, swearing Rory and Kushi to secrecy too. But she should've known she couldn't hide much from Pia. They'd been close for a long time, and her cousin could read her better than anybody. "Nothing." She feigned wide-eyed nonchalance. "Just checking on Ronnie to see if he's still asleep."

"You're up to something." Pia's eyes narrowed with suspicion.

"If this party is to introduce Ronnie to the aunties and their crew, why has he spent most of the time in your room?"

"Because he's a baby and he sleeps a lot." Samira rolled her eyes, hoping Pia would buy her act. "Let's go back outside and join everybody."

"You're giving me the brush-off." Pia poked her in the arm. "Don't worry, I'll ask your mom."

"Go ahead," Samira said, knowing Kushi would keep her secret. Her mom couldn't be happier that her wayward, divorced, single-mother daughter had finally succumbed to her matrimonial machinations, even if the groom wasn't her first choice. But Kushi had fallen for Rory as much as she had, though if he kept eating the Indian food her mom force-fed him, he'd need to up his hours in the gym.

"Come on, Cuz, tell me." Pia slipped her arm through Samira's elbow as they headed for the backyard, where a crowd of about fifty had gathered, comprising the aunties and the rest of Kushi's local Indian community. "I need a little fun in my life."

"Did someone say fun?"

Samira laughed as Manish bounded up the back steps to hold the door open for them.

"It's rude to eavesdrop," Pia muttered, shooting him a mock glare, when Samira knew his exuberance amused her cousin as much as it did her.

"Maybe you were talking too loud?"

Samira bit back another laugh. She'd seen Manish's faux innocence before; he channeled a naughty boy playing good very well.

"What are you doing here, Manish?" Pia shooed him away like a bothersome fly. "Or didn't you hear, Samira's already spoken for?"

His mouth eased into a confident grin as he eyeballed Pia. "Maybe I've set my sights elsewhere?"

Pia rolled her eyes at Manny's usual over-the-top antics. "Don't look at me."

"Why not?"

Manny shot Samira a playful wink, enjoying playing up to her cousin, who seemed to be enjoying it less so, if her compressed lips were any indication.

"Because you know I'm married and my husband will kick your ass."

With a smug smirk, Pia pushed past him and stomped away, managing to look incredibly graceful in her silver stilettos and powder blue *salwar kameez* while doing so.

"You shouldn't tease her like that. She's going through a rough time," Samira said, pleased that her cousin still proudly referred to Dev as her husband. It looked like Pia's plan to jolt Dev into considering counseling had worked and he'd booked an appointment. They had a long road ahead of them, but Dev had taken the first step to dealing with his insecurities regarding his sterility, and she knew Pia would fight hard for the reunion she so desperately wanted.

"I thought you said she's communicating with Dev and things are looking up?"

"They are, and I'm hopeful, but she seems fragile to me, and your incessant teasing of every woman within a five-foot radius isn't helping."

"Okay, I'll tone it down," he said, suitably chastened for a moment, before flashing her his signature cocky grin. "Anyway, that favor you asked me for has just arrived."

"Great." Samira rubbed her hands together, more to quell her nerves than anything else. "Let's do this."

"You sure you want Rory? Because I'm still available—"

"Shut up, you idiot, and go tell your friend we'll be ready to start in a minute."

Manny gave her a rakish salute. "Yes, ma'am."

As he strode away, she stood on the back step of her childhood home and glanced around the garden. It had never looked so beautiful, with orange and magenta lanterns threaded through the trees, and matching chiffon draped from branch to branch. Fairy lights were strung along the veranda and the fence line, while monstrous bouquets of crimson, fuchsia, and sienna gerberas stood atop tall pedestals.

It looked like a Bollywood dream, complete with the gossiping crowd and shrewd eyes. Samira had wanted them all here. What better way to embrace tradition yet show them a cultural assimilation by marrying Rory in a surprise ceremony?

"Ready, *betee*?" Kushi appeared by her side, looking resplendent in a peacock blue sari, her hair slicked into a tight bun perched high on her head.

"Ready, Mom."

Samira bent down to kiss her mom's cheek. "I love you, Mom. Thank you for everything."

Tears shimmered in Kushi's eyes as she brushed her fingertips along her cheek. "I'm proud of you, *betee*, and I'm so glad you've come home for good."

The first haunting strains of a sitar had them both glancing toward the far corner of the garden, where Rory stood in front of one of Manny's friends, a marriage celebrant.

Rory wore a navy suit with an ivory shirt open at the collar. Big. Bronze. Broad shouldered. Blue eyes. Casual sexy. All hers. His dad stood beside him, a stern man she'd only met a handful of times, but Garth seemed to adore his grandson as much as Kushi did.

As Samira linked arms with her mom and they strolled toward the celebrant, her heart expanded with happiness, filling her chest to bursting.

When she stood beside the man she adored, professing her love in front of everyone regardless of their judgment, she knew falling for Rory had been unexpected and complicated but oh so right. They had a wonderfully exciting life ahead of them.

She could hardly wait to start living it.

AUTHOR'S NOTE

While I can identify with Samira in many respects (same profession, mixed race, fertility issues, home city), it is Rory I truly connect with in *The Boy Toy*.

Like Rory, I have a speech impediment.

I've stuttered since I was a child and, like Rory, went through many sessions with various speech therapists. I can empathize with his feelings of frustration, embarrassment, and that bone-deep mortification when you stammer in front of a crowd.

Like Rory, I've had to deal with people "helpfully" finishing my sentence for me, providing a word I'm stuck on, and the slightly impatient look they get on their faces when it takes me longer to enunciate. And like Rory, while I try to master my stutter most of the time and put techniques I learned many years ago into practice, having to speak in front of a large group or in an interview always terrifies me.

Being an author is the perfect introverted profession for me. And while I've never done any drama training, I understand Rory's confidence when he mentally rehearses before speaking because I do that too.

I hope you enjoyed *The Boy Toy* and had as much fun with these characters as I did creating them.

Nicola x

ACKNOWLEDGMENTS

Seeing *The Boy Toy* published is a dream come true. I had the glimmer of an idea for it many years ago and wrote three chapters before putting it on the back burner. It wasn't until I connected with my agent, Kim Lionetti, that this idea come to complete fruition. We brainstormed a lot, tweaking the synopsis, swapping characters around, clarifying motivations, until we got it right and thankfully, Cindy Hwang thought so too. So my immense gratitude to the following people:

Cindy Hwang, editor extraordinaire, I'm still pinching myself we get to work together. Thanks for seeing the potential in this story and helping me polish it into a gem. I love working with you. And I'm thrilled Dr. Manny gets his story soon too.

Kim Lionetti, my agent, who is a brilliant brainstormer and always in my corner with sage advice. Shaking things up with this one really hit the mark, Kim. Thanks for the back-and-forth until we nailed it.

Angela Kim, editorial assistant, for being prompt and professional.

Sonali Dev, Spurthi Gowda, and Ritu Bhathal, for their assistance in translating the Hindi words. Any mistakes are mine.

My parents, Olly and Millie, for instilling Anglo-Indian tradition—especially traditions involving food!—in me.

My writing buddies, Natalie Anderson and Soraya Lane, for their ongoing support. Being on the publishing roller coaster with you is fun!

The speech therapist I had over forty years ago. I may not remember your name, but I remember having several before you, and when I walked into your office, you were patient and kind. You're the inspiration behind Amelia in this story.

My hubby, who likes to think he's my boy toy but isn't. Laughs like this are important daily.

My boys, who light up my life every single day. Love you always.

Keep reading for an excerpt from Nicola Marsh's
next contemporary romance . . .

THE MAN BAN

Coming soon from Jove!

H arper didn't believe in karma.

Unlike her best friend, Nishi, the most beautiful bride she'd ever seen, who waxed lyrical at length about how meeting Arun at a Diwali celebration in Melbourne's South East had been fate, how they'd taken one look at each other and fallen madly in love, how a psychic had predicted this when doing her chart at the time of her birth.

Nishi had been her best friend since high school, so Harper didn't disillusion the loved-up bride. Her cynicism could easily explain Nishi's version of "fate": meeting Arun was random, it was lust at first sight considering they ended up shagging the night they met, and the tall, handsome, rich doctor the psychic predicted was a generic promise given to thousands of hopeful Indian parents after the birth of a daughter.

But Harper had to admit, being maid of honor and witnessing Nishi and Arun exchange vows earlier that day, there'd been something almost magical about the couple who'd been so sure of their love they committed to each other in front of five hundred guests.

Five hundred guests who would hopefully take one look at the food she'd styled and gush on every social media app.

Harper needed work. Food styling may be her passion, but it didn't pay the bills half as much as her previous career in catering. She needed a big break, and Nishi had assured her that among the throng of five hundred were many online influencers. All it would take was one photo, one perfect pictorial image of her beautiful *bondas*, precise *pakoras* or vivid *vadas*, and she'd be on her way.

As the guests mingled in the outer foyer of the Springvale Town Hall, she cast a final critical eye over the buffet tables. Two trestles lay end to end along an entire wall of the hall, laden with enough food to feed a thousand. The crimson tablecloths were barely visible beneath gold platters piled high with delicious Indian finger food, with squat ivory candles casting an alluring glow over everything.

She'd never styled a job this big and had balked when Nishi first asked. But her bestie had insisted, and it had been her gift to the happy couple. Everything looked perfect, and she blew out a breath, rolling her shoulders to release some of the tension. The edge of her sari slipped, but before she could pull it up, a hand tugged it back into place.

She turned and locked gazes with one of the groomsman. She couldn't remember his name after being introduced earlier in the day, what felt like a lifetime ago, but she remembered his eyes, a mesmerizing, unique gray that were currently lit with amusement.

"Can't have you unraveling and distracting the guests," he said. "Though personally, I wouldn't mind a little entertainment along with my entree."

Harper bit back her first retort, that his flirting was wasted on her. She had a firm man ban in place, ensuring the last twelve months had been angst-free, leaving her to focus on her career and not a never-ending parade of dating disasters.

"Sorry to disappoint, but the only entertainment you'll be getting tonight is from the ten-piece band playing later."

If he heard the bite in her words, he didn't show it. Instead, he grinned, and something unfamiliar fluttered deep. That was the only downside to her ban: she missed the sex.

"Too bad."

His glance flicked over her, a practiced perusal from a guy who probably flirted with anything in a skirt. At six-two, with thick, wavy black hair, sharp cheekbones, broad shoulders that hinted at gym workouts, a killer smile, and those stunning eyes, this guy would be used to women preening under his attention.

When she frowned and didn't respond, an eyebrow quirked and he thrust out his hand. "We met earlier. Manish Gomes, but my friends call me Manny."

"Harper Ryland." She shook his hand and released it quickly. "Don't you have to go help the groom, *Manish?*"

He laughed at her sarcastic emphasis. "Arun's got everything under control. Besides, we're not exactly best buds. I think the only reason he asked me to be a groomsman was because we pulled two all-nighters in a row around the time he proposed to Nishi and I had biryani leftovers I shared."

Figured. Manish's confidence came from saving lives alongside Arun in the ER.

"Nishi's my best friend."

Her response sounded judgmental, like she couldn't figure why Arun would ask some fellow doctor to be part of his wedding party when they obviously weren't close.

"You work together?"

She shook her head. "High school."

"Right."

They lapsed into a silence that bordered on awkward. She may not be the most extroverted at the best of times but she could hold her own in social settings. But something about this guy had her on edge and she didn't like it. Not his fault he was gorgeous and charming; her latent insecurities made her want to rush to the bathroom and check her hair and makeup.

"Well, if you have any further sari emergencies, you know where to find me," he said, pointing at the head table set just below the stage. "I'm chivalrous that way, in case you were wondering."

"I'm not," she muttered, earning another grin. "Besides, you should be thankful I didn't slap you for fixing my sari when I didn't ask for your help."

His eyebrows arched in surprise at her snark as he held up his hands in apology. "You're right, my bad. I'll see you later."

Harper bit back a sigh as she watched him stride toward the foyer, all long legs and impressive shoulders shifting beneath a perfectly fitted kurta. She'd been envious when Nishi had told her what the guys were wearing; the slim-fitting pants and flowing top combo looked a lot more comfortable than the saris chosen for the women. She'd been in a perpetual state all day for fear of tripping over and causing the unraveling Manish had mentioned. But she had to admit the bridesmaids looked stunning in the cream silk shot through with gold thread, and she'd never felt so glamorous, even if she was one step away from a revealing disaster.

She'd been curt with Manish to the point of rudeness and he hadn't deserved her brusque treatment. She blamed her nerves. This job meant everything to her, but deep down she knew better.

His perfection rattled her, and a man hadn't unnerved her in a long time.

Not that it mattered. Once this wedding was done, she'd probably only see him at the occasional function Nishi and Arun hosted: birth of their first child, baptism, that kind of thing. By then, she'd feign forgetfulness of their first meeting.

What Manny thought of her didn't matter. She had a job to do, and with the revelers soon lining up for the food, that's where her focus should be.

Bold men with unusual slate eyes should be forgotten.

Photo by Jemm Photography

USA Today bestselling and multi-award-winning author Nicola Marsh loves all things romance. With seventy novels to her name, she still pinches herself that she gets to write for a living in her dream job. A physiotherapist for thirteen years, she now adores writing full-time, raising her two dashing young heroes, sharing fine food with family and friends, cheering her beloved Kangaroos footy team, and curling up on the couch to read a great book. She lives in cosmopolitan Melbourne, Australia.

Ready to find
your next great read?

Let us help.

Visit prh.com/nextread

Penguin
Random
House